THE FIFTH MAN

Roy Burgess

Also by Roy M. Burgess

The Fifth Tweet
The Fifth Thunderbolt

Published by Mill Tower Books

First Edition

Paperback ISBN : 978-1-7394807-1-4
Ebook ISBN : 978-1-7394807-0-7

1

I flinched as the door burst open. In came a woman with untamed, greying hair and a phone pressed to her ear. She dropped several bulging folders on the table but didn't even glance at me. The woman raised a finger as if that explained everything and continued talking. Whoever she was speaking to put her on hold. She dragged a folder from the middle of the pile and spoke without looking up.

"My name is Darlene Chandler. The court has appointed me to defend you."

Defend me? What? I tried to explain this was all a big mistake, but the finger came up again and the rapid fire talk continued (as did the pounding in my chest).

"We'll have a longer talk later. I'm due in court in ten minutes, so I'll keep it brief." Turning a page, she sighed. "Jesus. For somebody religious, you sure went to town on them."

Again, I tried to speak. Again, the finger. I feel it's only fair to point out it was the index finger, as in 'hang on a minute', rather than the middle finger as in 'swivel', but still.

Rude.

Darlene Chandler continued, without bothering to take a breath.

"As your lawyer, I'm not interested in whether you are guilty, just in building a defence. Right now, I can't see a world where we call you as a witness. The Fifth Amendment may just come to your rescue. Pleading the fifth is ironic, you being a preacher. Some groups take the Fifth Commandment as 'Honour thy father and thy mother.' Others see the fifth as 'Thou shalt not murder.' Double whammy for you. Parricide is the technical term."

Darlene, pleased with herself, looked at me for the first time, then back at her notes, before back to me.

"Wait. You're not Wendell Bell, are you?" I shook my head. "Well, why didn't you say something? Wasting my time. Can't you see how busy I am? Dumbass-idiot."

Darlene grabbed her folders and phone, shot me an angry stare, and stormed out of the door. The room was back to being silent. Five minutes before, the silence had been threatening. I think I preferred it. Still, whatever was happening to me, at least I wasn't Wendell. He appeared to have been a naughty boy. Me? I was innocent. Well, sort of. Better than Wendell, at any rate.

Maybe it's time to fill in a few gaps. If we haven't met before, I'm Frankie. Don't worry, you'll catch up soon enough. If we have met before, I think I owe you an apology. Last time we met, I kind of withheld a bit of the story. I didn't lie – I have to stress that. Maybe I got a bit carried away with everything that was happening and just forgot. So, I reckon there are two things to get you back up to speed.

First, the conversation with Jen that led to me upping sticks to accept a dream job in New York. It happened on the night of the premiere of our film. Second, how I ended up in a police cell being accused by Darlene of killing my parents. They send their love, by the way — my parents. I wish I was with them now in Bridlington.

2

It was getting late. Technically, it was getting early, but you know what I mean. We were celebrating. Last night, the film premiere at Bernard's tiny cottage cinema had been a tremendous success. For several hours, I'd floated on air. At that moment, I was floating on a sea of red wine. I'd got to the stage that I was lovely and drunk. The wine was lovely. The last sausage roll was lovely. Jen was lovely. It was all…

"Right. I'm off to bed," said Jason. He looked lovely, a little unsteady on his feet. I was fairly confident he'd just gone through the wrong door. There was a crash and muffled swearing before he reemerged. "Wrong door. Night."

Dignity restored, Jason staggered into the night. The two of us waved him off. I stifled a giggle. It looked like our film's co-producer couldn't hold his drink. At least there was something he wasn't good at. Jason had become a minor celebrity on the back of Jen's book about how his gangster father ended up taking his family into witness protection. Maybe the instinct to hide had driven him into the cupboard. Then again — lightweight. I reached out for the bottle and topped up Jen's glass.

"Not for me, I'm a bit… go on then. Just a small one," she giggled.

We were in the pub where we had rooms for the night. We'd stayed here when we were filming *The Hubberholme Syndrome*. Jim, the landlord, had already gone to bed. He trusted us to turn the lights out when we retired. I picked up my glass and stared straight ahead. This was the moment. I had to talk to Jen about the decision I'd made months ago. For various reasons, largely cowardice, I'd put off breaking the news that I was about to start a new life in New York. In the end, we spoke in unison.

"I have to tell you something."

We both burst out laughing. What were the chances of the happening? Jen pointed at my chest.

"You first."

"No. I insist. Ladies first." I was always polite like that. Besides, what she had to say might get me off the hook.

Jen fiddled with her glass before speaking. Her voice was hesitant.

"You know how much you mean to me, don't you, Frankie?"

She reached out a hand. I was just about to take it in mine when she brushed flaky pastry from my posh jacket.

"Mucky pup. I'm proud of what we've achieved. The film looks like it's going to be an enormous success. I love working with you. We have a laugh."

Shit.

There was a 'but' coming. Buts are never good at this stage.

"But?"

"God, this is hard."

"What is it Jen? You can tell me anything."

I did a quick mental check, decided that my hankie was pristine and handed it over without looking. Jen took it and dabbed at her eyes, composing herself.

"It's my dad. I couldn't say anything before now. He's…" a wave of sobbing engulfed Jen. I shuffled closer on the bench and she buried her face under my outstretched arm. As the wave subsided, Jen continued.

"He's been feeling unwell for a while. Wouldn't see a doctor. Mum finally convinced him and he got the results this week. It's stage four, inoperable." Sobs engulfed her again. I held her close and whispered the things you say in these circumstances. I knew none of it would do any good. When push comes to shove, sometimes a good sob is all that helps. My one rule was not to tell her it would be okay, that doctors can do amazing things. She'd see through that lie. She needed a shoulder to cry on.

The sobbing gradually subsided. We sat in silence, our breathing now in sync. I was aware of a damp patch on my shoulder and, more worryingly, what I can only describe as an intestinal twinge. The sausage rolls were battling the champagne. One of the chiller cabinets behind the bar hummed, cutting through the darkened room. Had Jen not just imparted her shocking news, this would've been a romantic moment. That and the ominous pain now threatening my insides.

Jen was still and peaceful. I even wondered if she'd fallen asleep. I hated the idea of breaking the spell, but I had to move to ease the pain. Clenching every muscle, I gently shuffled to the right. Barely an inch, but it was enough. I let out a note that reminded me of the sax solo in *Jungleland*. Strange what can go through your mind. A split second later, Jen punched me lightly in the chest. She laughed, forgetting the tears for a moment.

"I'm so sorry," I said.

She dabbed at the red stain on my shoulder.

"Pig! There I was, all peaceful and feeling protected. Then you let rip like Springsteen on *Jungleland*."

"So it wasn't just me?"

"Course it was just you. I felt it."

"No. That was just me, granted. What I meant was it reminded you of *Jungleland*."

The look she gave me confirmed everything I'd been thinking. I loved the time I spent with this woman. I didn't even point out that it was Clarence Clemons that played the sax solo on *Jungleland*. That would be childish and probably spoil the moment.

"Do you need the loo?"

"No thanks. I feel a lot better now."

"That's a relief. So do I. Thanks for letting me unload like that. This week has been tough." Jen took a sip of wine. "Right, that was my news. What did you need to tell me?"

The moment had arrived. After five months of prevarication and indecision, I had to tell Jen what was worrying me. I took a deep breath and told her everything. I told her how Flic, who'd arranged the financing for our film, had offered me a job on stupid money. How it was in New York and I'd agonised for ages about whether I could accept it. How I'd emailed her on New Year's Eve when I was drunk. I told her how I'd intended to send the draft that turned the job down but clicked on the wrong one. How I'd reasoned that maybe, just maybe, the universe was telling me to take the risk. I'd put my all into making the film a success, but now I would abandon everything and move to New York in a couple of weeks.

"But that's fantastic. What an opportunity. You must be so excited."

"Well, yeah. Suppose I am. It's just… How can I go now?"

"How do you mean?"

"I can't leave you here with all this hanging over you. I'll call Flic in the morning. Explain that I've changed my mind. She'll be okay."

"You'll do no such thing. I've agonised over breaking the news to you about my dad – mainly because I want to take a break from writing. I need to spend time with Dad, support Mum. I was dreading having to break up the partnership, just as we were getting somewhere."

"But what about, you know, us?"

"Distance friendships can work. We'll make it work. There's FaceTime, cheap flights. Three thousand miles is nothing these days."

"Three thousand three hundred and forty-eight. Probably more if you're at your mum's."

"The point is, we can do this. Who knows what things will look like in a year? If you decide it's not for you, come home and we'll find our next project. A year. That's not a long time. You're off to New York, pal, whether you like it or not."

It looked very much like I was off to New York.

3

My shoes and iPad were already on the grey plastic tray as we edged closer to security. I added my belt, watch and loose change. It was only when I checked my jacket pockets for the fifth time that I felt something solid. A cold sweat washed over me. I last wore this jacket on the wild night at the club with Joe and Rupert. Suddenly, the memory was crystal clear. A mate of Joe's had offered me something to 'take the edge off'. I'd politely turned it down as a skinful of beer had pretty much sorted my edges. He'd leaned in close and told me to save them for later, pushing something into my pocket. Now, I was yards from somebody with a machine gun, carrying who knew what drugs.

Oops.

I did what any sensible person would in my position. I panicked. Making sure nobody was looking, I unfolded the tiny package, slipped the two white pills into my mouth, and swallowed. My mouth was dry and I could feel the contraband wedged in my throat. Right on cue, I was called forward to be scanned. Would the scanner pick up the two pills lodged a couple of inches down my throat? An image of ending up in a Turkish prison cell flashed into my mind. My life was over — except I was in Manchester and flying to

New York, so Turkey shouldn't come into it.

What if I had a bad acid trip? I'd read about this. If it was only supposed to take the edge off, maybe it would be pleasant? Just maybe, I would spend the next eight hours blissed-out and I'd surface in the US. Unless the scanner showed two dots, wedged and extremely uncomfortable. I tried swallowing again, but my dry mouth refused to have any part of this. The man waved me through. I held my hands out, ready for the handcuffs to snap on.

"Enjoy your flight, sir."

Was that all he had to say? I looked around for the snatch squad, but I was free to enter the promised land of duty free and stiff drink.

It felt strange to be boarding this flight; even stranger to turn left when I got through the doors. Inner conflict still pecked away at me, to be honest. As I was re-arranging my headphones, iPad, phone, mints and champagne glass on my little table, I thought of the other flight due to take off seven minutes after this one, going to Nice, just down the road from where Jen and Jason were representing the film in Cannes.

Jen had talked about not going. Her mum had saved the day, suggesting the whole family should go. Her dad, Ben, was due to start chemotherapy a week later. This was the last chance to get away for a while. Jen's five-year-old, Charley, was beyond excited when she discovered there was a beach involved. Jason had also made it into a holiday, alongside his wife and two kids.

Pangs of jealousy shot through me when I should be excited. Here I was, on the flight to New York. As of next Monday, I would officially be Vice President of Production (New Markets). I even had a supply of business cards to prove it. The thought of being responsible for the entire division terrified me. Before I could worry again, I noticed a text from Jen.

Enjoy the flight. Go easy on the fizz xx

Ben and Jen, bubbly in hand, grinned at the camera. Loneliness stabbed at my heart because I wasn't there with them. I wanted to enjoy seeing people react to our film. It was just me being silly. The organisers of the festival had agreed to keep us anonymous. Officially, Jen and I were Vince Taylor and they would do all interviews on the understanding that Jen was Vince. It complicated things, but we relished being out of the limelight. The press officer actually liked the idea of building the mystique around an anonymous writer.

Jen had only agreed to go in the first place because I said I would take the job in New York. She could then take a year off, guilt-free, knowing I was playing at being the big studio executive.

With an hour to kill before boarding, I settled in the lounge with a coffee and read through the synopsis I'd been working on. This was my first project in the new job — turning Jen's book about our friend Jason into a TV series.

Burning Down The House took its name from a comment by one of the police team, taking statements from Jason's dad when he turned on the rest of the gang. It also gave me the excuse to play Talking Heads as I worked. The book had been out in hardback for several months and had sold steadily. The author on the cover was Vince Taylor, but really it was Jen. In a fortnight, the paperback and digital versions should boost both sales and the profile of the story. A great time to pitch the TV series. Was it really as easy as handing this over to one of my team and saying — here you go — and heading off for cocktails at some swanky bar? Maybe not.

Flic had offered to help me settle into the new job and act as a sounding board for ideas until I found my feet. I emailed the synopsis to her for feedback before heading to the gate.

I listened to the announcements, feeling smug in my big seat. As instructed, I put my phone into airplane mode and tried to relax. I fiddled with my headphone cable, tapping out the rhythm to *Ant Music*, my foot joining in. Looking around for the fifth time, the steward leapt to my aid. I convinced him I was fine, but accepted the offer of another glass of champagne. I'd never been a nervous flier, but I just couldn't sit still. Was it warm in here or was it me?

So unplug the jukebox and do us all a favour…

In search of a distraction, I opened my iPad. I had planned to spend the flight working on the synopsis. Was there any point? I could just wait for Flic's response. I settled for re-reading Jen's book. It was still difficult to equate the calm, professional Jason with the story of his dad's life as a jewel thief, witness protection, and murder. Jason had then reinvented himself as a successful producer and family man. I suppose that's what makes true stories like his so attractive to us TV executives.

Then I realised that I'd forgotten to switch the iPad to airplane mode. I was about to do it, but I had two new emails. The first, strangely, was from Jason.

Frankie. We had to cancel Jen's press interviews this morning. It seems her dad has picked up an infection and is in hospital. She's upset, but we are all with her. Don't worry. Call me when you land. Jason.

My friend needed me. What the hell was I doing on a flight to New York? I looked around for the steward again. This time, he arrived with the champagne bottle already in his hand. I waved away the offer.

"Look. I know this is unusual, but I need to get off the flight."

I tried to stand up, but the seatbelt pinned me down.

"I'm sorry, sir. Once you are on board, regulations forbid leaving. The doors are closed and we will take off shortly. I'm sure if you try to relax, everything will be just fine."

He forced a smile before turning to leave. Heart pounding,

both feet tapping, I unbuckled the seatbelt. The click was enough to alert the steward, who pivoted and leaned in close.

"Sir. I must insist that you stay in your seat. You're beginning to unsettle the other passengers."

The look he gave me almost buckled the seatbelt by itself. I slumped back — defeated. Muttering to myself, I opened the second email. It was from Flic. That was quick. Then I realised it was from earlier this morning, before I'd sent the synopsis.

Hi Frankie. Just a note to wish you good luck. You are going to smash this!! More exciting news coming soon — sorry can't say more yet. Flic x

My stomach continued to churn. This really was a proper, grown up job. Surely they would work out that I wasn't a proper grown up? Besides, Jen needed me. What the hell was I doing? I should be with Jen. Adam Ant was still having a major impact on my feet. Why couldn't I stop tapping? Why does it have to be so hot in here? I needed to be with Jen. I needed to get off this flight.

"Sir. Please. You need to sit down. We will take off shortly."

"But you don't understand. I have to get off. I'm not meant to be on this flight."

"Sit down now. Asshole!"

That wasn't like the adverts. I had to escape. The steward blocked my path and reached up to the call button above my seat as I reached for my bag from the overhead locker. From this point, my recall of what happened is a little hazy. I only worked out later that the two little pills had moved on from my throat and were now creating havoc in every cell in my body, particularly with their love of early eighties pop dandies.

This is what I sort of remember. There was shouting — not all from me. There was a dark suited giant with a gun strapped neatly under his arm and handcuffs applied to my left arm and the seat arm-rest. Apparently, the giant was an air marshal, and he'd just arrested me for being an arsehole.

I'd protested that Jen needed me and New York could manage without me, but it was no use. Apart from an escorted trip to the toilet, I spent the next eight hours chained to a seat with a surly giant for company and *Ant Music* on repeat in my head. In a nutshell, that's how I ended up in a cell at JFK airport.

4

Like most people of my age, I'd been kicked out of things before. The school play when I was 11 (miscast), a certain dodgy nightclub when I was 22 (led astray) and several relationships (some of them my fault, others less so). But getting kicked out of an entire country was a new one for me. They were polite about it, but firm.

Darlene Chandler had returned a couple of hours later. She was calmer, now with only a handful of files.

"It would seem that somebody around here has taken pity on you. You should be grateful."

"Grateful? I've been here for days, locked up, with no access to a lawyer."

"You've been here six hours and I'm your lawyer. I believe you Brits say — wind your neck in? Is that right?"

I felt a bit of a dick.

"Sorry."

"So you should be." Darlene flicked over a couple of pages from the top folder. "The blood test confirmed traces of an illegal substance in your system. This would account for you behaving like an asshole. Lucky for you, not having any more in your possession has saved you."

I came clean and told Darlene the full story. She cocked her head to one side.

"Like I said — asshole." This time, she couldn't hold back a grin. I think my charm was working. "So, Uncle Sam has decided he can't give a rat's ass and would cordially invite you to disappear back to the UK as soon as possible."

"Could I at least stay for a holiday?"

Darlene looked at me like somebody leaving the bathroom at a party and suggesting you give it ten minutes.

"My guess — a year before Lady Liberty will once more welcome you to the land of the free and the home of the brave."

"But I start a new job here next week."

"I guess that qualifies you as tired and poor. One of the huddled masses. Ain't no way you getting in now!"

Darlene laughed so hard at her own joke she had to wipe the tears away.

"Just supposing I tried to come back next week; what would happen?"

"Well, we'd sling your ass in jail."

"But how would you know they banned me?"

"We got a list — who can come in and who can do a one-eighty. It's a comprehensive list maintained by a wonderful man called Eugene."

"That's impressive knowledge."

"Eugene and me got history. I knew him when he filed all the individual immigration forms by hand. Now, and for the next 192 days until he retires, he goes by some highfalutin title like Director Of Immigration Services. He's also my ride home if I leave now."

"You mean you're—"

"Yep. I've been a Chandler for over forty years. We retire at Thanksgiving. Might just see you in Europe next year. In the meantime, if you decide to appeal the ban, here's my card. Got to scoot if I want a ride. Good luck Frankie Dale —

asshole!"

This time I joined in with the infectious laughter. Within an hour, I was on a plane and heading for home. At least they'd booked my return on my business class ticket.

After my performance earlier, it was a relief to see a different cabin crew. I turned down the champagne this time. It didn't seem like a flight to celebrate. Determined to stay out of trouble, I reclined the seat and prepared to sleep. Trying to filter out the noise in the cabin, I hit shuffle on my phone. I smiled when the first song was Springsteen's *Frankie Fell In Love*. Even my phone knew. In other circumstances, I would have just been excited to be going home, back to Jen. The trouble was, my thoughts kept coming back to how much I'd screwed up. Not that long ago, every day working with Jen was a joy. Now, risking everything to become some big executive, I'd made such a mess.

I would need to call my new boss for a start. How do you broach the fact that you can't come within three thousand miles of your new office for the foreseeable? Let's face it; I was out of a job. At least I'd be able to see Jen again. She was going to need my support as she faced the prospect of losing her dad. Then again, she'd probably kill me for screwing up. This was getting me nowhere. There was nothing to be gained from getting miserable. Besides, I could smell food.

I opened one eye. Sure enough, my fellow passengers were tucking into a hot meal. I was starving. Had I missed my chance of food? I needn't have worried. Beef stroganoff and a glass of merlot soon improved my mood. The wine took me back to those evenings spent at Jen's house. She made me happy. It was as simple as that. We were both getting over relationships when the cosy evenings had started. We agreed that being friends was the limit. Could I be happy like that? Or did I need more?

We both met Jason a couple of years ago when he was

working for the production company, trying to turn *The Woman In The Yellow Raincoat* into a TV series. Last year, he produced our film, *The Hubberholme Syndrome*. After a dodgy start, I now considered Jason to be a good friend. Jason made me jealous when he first came on the scene. I thought he was a rival for Jen. It turned out she was helping to write his life story.

I'd had all kinds of theories last year about Jason's secret life. It was only when he approached Jen to write his biography that the story emerged. What a tale it turned out to be! Jason's dad had been a member of a gang responsible for robbing a series of high-profile jewellers. He'd led a privileged life on the back of the illegal wealth. Things went wrong when one of the gang shot and killed a security guard. Spooked by the violence, Jason's dad had told the gang he wanted out. They disagreed that this was a career option. Fearing for his family, he informed on the rest of the gang. The entire family ended up with new identities and a life of witness protection. When his dad's charred body turned up, it was obvious the gang had found them. They arranged another identity and another life. Years later, with two gang members dead, Jason felt safe enough to tell his story.

Making the series would now appear to have gone up in smoke. Or had it? Even if I got sacked, what was to stop me working on the idea from my cosy little office at home? Maybe Jen would work with me on it? I wanted to support her. It was tough for her at the moment.

No time like the present. I accepted the offer of another glass of wine and retrieved my copy of the book and my laptop. Making Jen proud of me was crucial. I'd soon have feedback on the synopsis from Flic. Positive thinking! The new project was underway.

Half an hour later, the stewardess leaned over my seat.

"Could I get you more wine, sir? Maybe some cheese?"

"That would be lovely, thank you."

She returned with a plate of cheese and crackers, grapes and a bottle of wine.

"I brought you the bottle as the crew are about to get some sleep. Is that okay?"

"That's perfect, thanks."

She smiled, winked, and left me to my work. Several hours later, I finished the last glass just as the cabin lights came on before landing.

So, here I was, back in my home country and back at square one. I had to speak to Flic, but the chances were I had no job. While I was waiting by the luggage carousel, I switched on my phone. An official-looking email from the US government greeted me. It confirmed, in polite but firm language, that I couldn't return to the US for a minimum of one year. They even wished me a safe return flight and best wishes for the future. I can only assume they felt differently about my luggage, as it seems to have gone on a tour of the north-eastern seaboard without me. I trudged away from the carousel to report my loss.

It hit me I had no change of clothes. Once again, I didn't even have a toothbrush, as my luggage thought it was funny to hide away from me. Today was shit. I ignored the expense and jumped into a taxi, heading straight for The Crown. The one bright spot was that the estate agent had been inept at finding a tenant for my house, so it meant I had somewhere to live. Silver linings and all that.

The cab from Manchester would take over an hour to Bradford. Conversation soon petered out. Yes, he'd been working all night. Yes, I was the last job for today. I settled back and scanned my email inbox. There was a reply from Flic. Had she heard? She was going to kill me. Then I realised it was a reply to my email from yesterday. Maybe she hadn't heard; yet.

Is that it?

Odd. I expected polite questions about how things were going. I read on. Flic went straight to the point.

All a bit sparse. The biography was great but has limited sales potential. We'd be looking at trying to get a TV audience of millions. We need more.

I actually spoke out loud — "Like what?"

"Pardon?"

The driver eyed me in the mirror.

"Sorry, mate. I was talking to myself, bad habit."

The eyes went back to the road. I read more.

For starters, Stevens did a deal to expose the gang, but only one of them went to jail. There must have been more. What happened to the rest of them? It would be a lot better story if we tracked down anybody else who was involved. Okay, Jen's notes mention a driver that nobody will identify, but nobody seems to have had a clue who the organiser was. The trail soon went cold.

Imagine the story we'd have if you could work out what happened. The driver that got away? Who killed Gary Stevens? Who was the brain behind the gang? Why was nobody willing or able to identify him? We know three members of the gang: they convicted Gabriel Thompson of murder of the security guard and he died in prison; Danny O'Neill died in a shootout with the police; Gary Stevens — murdered. For me, there are two others.

Who was the driver? Who was the Fifth Man?

Sounds obvious when you put it like that. I had work to do. At least she hadn't ripped me a new one for getting slung out of the country. Something to look forward to.

"Just here will do, thanks."

We pulled up outside The Crown. I tried not to think how much the ride had just cost me as I handed over my credit card. I needed a pint.

"What the chuff are you doing here?"

"Cheers, Rupert. Knew I could rely on you for a friendly welcome."

"Sorry, mate. But aren't you supposed to be playing Billy big-balls in New York at the moment? We had a party and everything."

"Get me a pint, and I'll tell you the full story." Rupert fidgeted when he should've been legging it to the bar. I looked at him, expecting some kind of clue to explain his odd behaviour. When none came, I decided. "Okay, I'll get my own."

"No. Wait," his voice rising to a near squeak. More fidgeting.

"Come on. What's up?"

"It's just… awkward. I'm meeting somebody."

"You've been married a month and you're playing away already?" I was quite angry now.

"No. Nothing like that." Rupert scanned the room. Satisfied that we were the only two customers, he leaned in closer. "I'm meeting my sister's cell mate. At least she was. She's out now."

"I kinda gathered that. Why is that awkward?"

"Well, you and Robbie were engaged. It was you she robbed and ended up inside. Awkward."

"So you said. Why are you meeting her?"

"It was Robbie that asked. She's got things to say and wants to do it through this mate of hers." The expression on Rupert's face changed as he sniffed. "Mate, have you come straight from the airport?"

"Yeah. I thought I needed a pint in a friendly environment. How silly of me."

"When did you last change clothes? Shower, that sort of thing?"

"Cheeky bas—" I stopped myself. He had a point. I was losing track of time. We were well into day three.

"You look knackered," said Rupert. I had to agree, and I was on the ripe side too. "Why don't you get some sleep? We can meet up for a pint tomorrow and you'll have my undivided attention."

The mention of sleep seemed to trigger something in my brain. I'd never felt as tired as this in my whole life.

"Okay. You win. Enjoy your liaison." I put air quotes around the last bit. We bumped fists, and I made my way to the front door. Just then, the back door opened. A woman in her mid-twenties; head shaved at the sides; spiky ash blonde on top; and Doc Martens stepped in and exchanged words with Rupert before sitting with her back to me. The white vest barely covered a huge tattoo that extended down one arm and across her back. Rupert stood and made his way to the bar, making a borderline obscene gesture to me, suggesting that I should leave. I did. Five minutes later I crawled into bed and fell into an exhausted sleep.

It was no good. I was wide awake. According to my watch, it was 4.23. The email from Flic was playing on my mind. She was right. I'd done a half-arsed job on the synopsis. Just one more thing to add to the list of screw ups.

I went downstairs and automatically put the kettle on before remembering the cupboards were bare. No coffee. No tea — nothing.

Bugger.

Even the cafe over the road was a couple of hours away from opening. The kettle rumbled to a boil, then clicked off.

"You can shut up as well," I said.

I settled on a glass of water and plugged in my laptop. No time like the present. This was me turning over a new leaf. I would work hard and produce a brilliant script. At least until the cafe opened and I could go for breakfast.

I grabbed the big notebook that I'd carted to New York

with me and hadn't used and started to make lists. On the left was everything that we knew, as detailed in Jen's book. On the right was a series of questions. This is what I had so far:

1 Danny O'Neill

From Liverpool.

Explosives expert / Ex army.

Shot dead by police — at home and unarmed.

2 Gabriel Thompson

From Derby.

Shot and killed the security guard.

Sent to prison for life.

Died of cancer in prison 2017

3 Gary Stevens - Jason's dad

From London.

Alarms expert.

Became principal prosecution witness and entered witness protection with his family.

Murdered after a security leak gave away his new identity.

Nobody convicted of his murder.

4 The driver

????????????????

5 The Fifth Man

????????????????

I was fairly sure the row of question marks honestly summed up what we knew of the last two. Right, where do I start?

"Let's start at the very beginning," I said out loud. Great, now I had Julie Andrews singing in my head for the day.

I searched online for Danny O'Neill. It was easy to confirm the facts from Jen's notes but harder to reconcile the character that emerged to the image of a killer. After leaving the army he seemed to have drifted through a series of low paid jobs. At the same time he was a keen distance runner. I watched a clip of him in the BBC's London marathon coverage. He was wearing a shirt covered in poppies and carrying a collection bucket. The next BBC clip was from the evening news, showing a tent covering the front of his house after a police raid went wrong.

I googled Gabriel Thompson. It was tempting to go down the rabbit hole to see what a former child actor was doing now but this was the new me. On the second page of search results, I found something more promising — this was the Thompson I was after. It was a newspaper report confirming that our man had died in prison last year. Nothing new there. At the end of the report was a link to the story of his trial. For a murder trial it appeared to be very short — both the report and the trial itself. The trial lasted just two days with Thompson suddenly pleading guilty.

I was about to turn my attention to the next name on my list when I noticed the pencil drawing of the man in the dock. The style of the drawing looked somehow familiar. Last year I'd encouraged Dad to start drawing again. He produced the artwork for Joe's club. The shading around the eyes was very similar. There was no credit attached to the drawing. I did a reverse image search. Sure enough, the drawing was created by L Dale. I needed to speak to my dad.

5

After the initial adrenaline rush I couldn't stop yawning. By eight, I'd had enough breakfast news and retreated to bed.

Waking up feeling groggy at noon was not a unique experience. The warm spring sunshine almost knocked on the window, demanding to be allowed in. I threw the duvet to one side. That was better. I rolled onto my front and considered going back to sleep. Nothing to get up for after all. Thinking I could hear voices struck me as unusual. I closed my eyes just as the screaming started.

My naked buttocks prompted the screams. Things didn't improve as I leapt out of bed in full fight-or-flight mode. It was then I recognised the estate agent, ushering the screamer out of the bedroom and down the stairs. Following them required more trouser than I could manage. I called out, but they were gone.

I sat on the edge of the bed to get my heart rate back to near normal and braced myself for the inevitable slammed door. Instead, a male voice was shouting up the stairs. It was Rupert.

"Why was there a little old lady having a breakdown in your front garden, you monster?"

He was still laughing as I reached for my dressing gown.

Of course, that was in my suitcase, current location unknown.

"I need a shower. Why don't you grab coffees from the cafe and I'll see you back here in five?"

Rupert knew me well enough not to bother asking what I fancied. He turned to leave. Seconds later, the hot water was doing its thing, attempting to wash away the entire New York catastrophe. If only it were that easy. I was in danger of feeling miserable and tried to snap out of it. Then I realised I didn't have a change of clothes. My favourite attire was in a large suitcase, sunning itself in the States. Everything else had gone to the charity shop or was in the case in Jen's spare room. Commando, it was then. There wasn't even a stray can of deodorant to mask the three-day hum of my shirt.

Rupert was already at the kitchen table, bacon butty and hot, black coffee ready to save my life.

"Cheers, mate."

"You're welcome, but you could've got changed."

I explained my dilemma and agreed a shopping trip was high on the list of things to do. Bringing Rupert up to date with my disastrous trip to the States took longer.

"Wow. Why didn't you just bin the pills as if you were a normal human being?"

"I panicked, okay?"

"So what happens now?"

"Other than going to buy new boxers, I don't have a clue. I've got no idea if I've got a job. I suspect the incident with the estate agent means I've got somewhere to live, so it's not all shite."

I pulled my phone from my pocket, but it had long since died and I dropped it on the table.

"Need to phone Flic and Jen," I said.

"Joe spoke to Jen last night. She's still in France. She's hoping her dad will be well enough to travel before the end of the week."

"I'll call her as soon as I've charged my phone. Then again, my charger is in my suitcase. The shopping list is getting longer. Anyway, enough about me. What about your assignation with the mystery woman last night?"

"Well, that's an interesting tale. I won't go into all the details. We'd be here all day. The edited version is that her name is Angel. Until two days ago, she was sharing a cell with my beloved sister. She came bearing a message. Prepare yourself. Robbie's desperate for you to visit her."

"You're joking. After the mess she made of everything."

"That's part of it. She sees it as wanting to make amends, or at least make a start repairing things."

"So why send this Angel woman?"

"To be fair, she's tried writing to you." I looked guilty at this point. I had ignored several requests to visit Robbie. "Angel is quite a character and, how shall I put it? Passionate about helping her friend. To be honest, she scared the bejesus out of me."

"Scared you?"

"I suspect she can be persuasive if she put her mind to it. You'd save a lot of hassle by getting in touch with Robbie."

I didn't want to do that. Robbie had hurt me more than I cared to acknowledge.

Rupert had gone off to work. I was mulling over going to the pub when I remembered my phone. How could I get it charged? The office! Why didn't I think of that before? Maybe this broken sleep pattern was dulling my brain. Ten minutes later, I was at my desk, a cup of tea, two penguins and my phone charging. It felt strange being back here, especially without Jen. I called her, but it went straight to voicemail. She'd gone from enjoying a family holiday based around our film being shown in Cannes to sitting by her dad's bedside in the hospital.

I was about to leave a message when another call came in. I realised too late that it wasn't Jen.

"Hello, Flic."

I regretted answering. I meant to rehearse this bit. What would I say? Sorry, I can't come into the office for a year. Was it worth feigning illness? Somehow, I doubted a sniffle would cover this.

"I tried calling the hotel last night, and they said you hadn't checked in. Is everything okay? Are you ill?"

I was about to do the croaky voice, then decided against it.

"Bit of a problem. Nothing to worry about. Well, it might be — something to worry about, that is."

"Frankie, you're making no sense. Short of you being in prison, we're expecting you in the office next Monday."

I tried to laugh.

"No. I'm not in prison. Not any more, anyway."

"What?"

"Well, it wasn't prison. More of a holding cell at the airport, kind of thing."

I told her the whole sorry story. By the end of my tale, we were both reduced to tears. We were laughing so much.

"Sorry, I shouldn't laugh," she said, despite the merriment.

"It's okay. I recognise I was stupid. Not to mention lucky. They could just as easily have prosecuted me."

"It's not that. I meant I shouldn't laugh because my boss is going to go up the wall when he hears. He's planning a whole series of business announcements around your appointment. The team have lined up press and TV interviews, the lot."

"How do you think he'd feel about me working in the UK?"

"I think he'll come after you with a shotgun. No, Walter Guthrie is more likely to call a lawyer than a hitman."

"I'm sure I can appeal the ban and get everything sorted,

given a bit of time."

"You don't realise who you're dealing with here. The guy has a hospitality box in the New York Civil Court building. They frown on breach of contract by foreigners."

"Breach of contract?"

"This could be eye-wateringly expensive, Frankie."

"You know him. Couldn't you work your magic?"

"I think I'll need more than magic. I might be just ahead of you at the job centre. At least I've got a couple of hours before I have to call him."

"Don't suppose you fancy the job? That might appease him?"

"He suggested it, but I'd rather keep the Atlantic between me and him. Rumours are he's a bit of a sleaze ball — more hands on than you'd want."

"But you're happy for me to work for him?"

"You're not his type. Too old as well."

I saw a glimmer of hope.

"Shouldn't we go to the police about him?"

"Believe me, I'd love to, but there's no proof. They won't act on rumours, and I don't think any of the people involved want to risk everything to nail him."

The glimmer of hope collapsed, and I was back to impending doom.

"Do you need me to do anything?"

"I think you've done enough, don't you? You could start looking at your finances. I suspect you're going to need cash, lots of it. Let me try to talk to him, see if I can rescue this. I'll call you later."

That went worse than expected and I'd assumed it would be a shitshow. On top of everything else, I needed to buy underpants. It was then that Flic's comment registered like a punch in the chest. This could be expensive. Could they sue me for breach of contract? Who am I kidding? They were

American, they could sue me for running out of clean underwear.

I soon wished I hadn't searched for examples of US court settlements. This job was meant to make me wealthy. Instead, it could bankrupt me. I wasn't rich by any means, but neither was I skint. Even without recovering what Robbie stole, I'd earned plenty over the last year. Reaching for a notepad, I listed my assets. There was the office, for a start. It had been a tiny cottage before I bought it and had it converted. Selling it would be awful. It was where I worked with Jen on the script for the film. So many memories.

Then there was my house. It was small, but it was mine and a definite step up from the rented flats. Selling that would be counterproductive — I'd still need somewhere to live. I had an OEIC, whatever that was, and a steady but declining flow of royalties from the series of children's storybooks I'd written. We were yet to see any return from the film.

Even without an expensive lawsuit, with no job or writing partner, could I survive? An income was a priority. I needed a list. Stuff I need:

1 - Not to get sued

2 - Make some cash

3 - Pants

All I could do was cross my fingers for the first one. The second was important, but I had cash in the bank, so maybe not urgent. The third was both urgent and important. I needed pants.

6

Getting the train into Leeds was still a bit of a novelty. The local station had opened a few years ago, but I was so used to driving in, it rarely entered my head. Now, without a car, it seemed obvious. As I sat on the platform, I called Jen. Voicemail. She'd be at the hospital with her phone switched off.

"Hi, Jen. Just checking in to see how you and Ben are getting on. Call me when you get this. It's Frankie, by the way. I suppose you knew that. Speak later, bye. Oh, hang on. I've made a start on trying to turn your book into a TV series. I have questions but you concentrate on your dad for… got to go; train's here." Smooth.

Just over half an hour after arriving in the city centre, I'd bought myself a new wardrobe. Well, enough to get me through the next week, at least. Thanks to a quick visit to M&S and the changing rooms in trendy shop in the Victoria Quarter, I had even remedied the commando situation. Pleased with my lightning quick shopping spree, I decided coffee was in order. I claimed one of the half a dozen seats outside Starbucks and settled in the spring sunshine. Whilst I freely confess to hating clothes shopping, I love a good people-watch.

After a few minutes, I registered the busker, gathering quite an audience outside Boots. I couldn't see her, but she was belting out a more than passable *Creep*. She followed that by playing to the home crowd with The Kaiser Chiefs anthem *I Predict A Riot*, greeted by loud cheers. She eased into a story about being inspired to play guitar by Jimmy Page after playing her dad's albums as a kid. I knew how she felt. The version of *Nobody's Fault But Mine* that followed was excellent.

I finished my coffee, gathered my bags, and was almost knocked over in the scramble to fill the vacant seat. I tutted and set off to investigate the voice. Imagine the shock as I got closer. The source of this joyous music was wearing a white vest, a tattoo extending down one arm and across her back. I felt uncomfortable and edged my way through the crowd, heading for the station.

"I'm dedicating this next song to the bloke who seems determined to walk away from me this week."

Had she spotted me? Did she mean me? She launched into the first line of *One More Indian Summer*, the song I'd written with Toni that featured on the closing credits of the film. She meant me.

I rejoined the back of the back row and listened. Her voice was stunning; similar to Toni's, but fifty years her junior. It had a warm, velvety texture but with a vulnerability that suggested it may crack at any minute. It was impressive. What the hell had she been doing sharing a cell with Robbie? The song was over.

"Thanks, guys. I'll be back real soon."

People drifted away as the warm applause faded. I decided I couldn't really just sneak off, so I shuffled forwards. Angel scooped coins into a small leather bag and registered that I was there.

"So, Mr Dale, where are you taking me for a bevy?"

"I wasn't aware that I was."

"Course you are. Why else did you come back? Here, grab this and we'll go to the Scarborough Taps."

Suddenly, I was carrying a small speaker and a mic stand, heading for the pub.

"How did you recognise me in that crowd?" I asked as we walked through the early afternoon shoppers.

"I think familiarity burned your face on my memory forever." That sounded ominous. "Don't worry. Robbie has pictures of you above her bed. I saw them every time I peed." That was nice to know.

The gods of outdoor seating were with us again. Angel pushed a chair towards me as I got back from the bar with two pints of bitter.

"Cheers Mr Dale."

"You're allowed to call me Frankie, you know."

"Is that what your friends call you?"

"Yes."

"So, I'm your friend then?"

The look she gave me was off-putting. I could see why Rupert found her intimidating.

"It depends why you're here, I suppose." She downed half the pint in one before answering.

"I'm just a messenger. One with the voice of an angel, granted."

"Actually, I'll give you that. I'm flattered that you sang *One More Indian Summer*."

"Had to. Got your attention, didn't it?"

"You did. So, this voice of an angel thing. Is that how you got your name?"

"Nah. My mum was a fan of bloody *Rugrats*. On my birth certificate I'm Angelica." I smiled, but fear evaporated any smart-arse comment before it came out. "Breathe a word of that to anybody, and I'll slit your throat and pull your nuts up through the hole." Terrifying! Then the huge belly laugh. "Don't look so feckin scared, I wouldn't, really. Or would I?" The belly laugh again. I managed a small grin. "Come on, drink up. Then you can get another round in and I'll pass on my message."

"Aren't you supposed to get the next round?"

"Me? An unemployed ex-con, striving to rebuild her life from the shattered ruins? I can't go spending what little I've got on afternoon boozing. Away with you. And I'll have a bag of salt 'n' vinegar seeing as you asked. Ta."

I did as I was told, even though I was likely to be unemployed shortly. When I got back, Angel was openly going through my shopping.

"Do you mind?"

"Mind? Nah, very snazzy. Oh, I see what you mean. Sorry. I just thought, now that we're friends…"

"You thought you'd rifle through my bags?"

"Just interested. Nice shirt — the blue one. The brown one looks a bit like shite. You should take that back."

"I like the brown one. At least, I did."

"Nice boxers too." I snatched the bag back, pushing the boxers to the bottom, away from the looks of passing strangers. She laughed again. "Anyway. Bit extravagant innit? Six shirts, six pairs of boxers, jeans — the lot. You minted or something?"

"Quite the opposite." Despite myself, I ended up telling her the story of my weekend and lack of clothing. I left out my previous commando status.

"Poor you. So we've both come from cells fairly recently?"

"Keep your voice down. I was hardly Al Capone. It was one day and they let me go. Anyway, if it's not an indelicate question, how did you end up inside?"

"It was a case of mistaken identity," said Angel, looking hurt.

"Of course. I bet they all say that."

"It was. I firebombed the wrong fucking house. It had CCTV — got me bang to rights. I meant to get my useless ex-boyfriend's place next door but one. Would've got away with it then cos he didn't have bloody cameras."

"Life can be harsh." I said.

Angel looked at me, trying to decide if I was taking the piss. She decided I was and let out a shriek of laughter.

"Too fecking right, it can. Mind you, if I hadn't gone down I wouldn't have met your fiancée."

"Ex-fiancée."

"Don't say it like that."

"Like what?"

"Like it's over. Done. It doesn't have to be. Robbie still loves you."

I took a big slurp of my pint, coughed and spilt some on the table.

"She just had a funny way of showing it. Clearing out the bank accounts, jilting me at the altar, that sort of thing."

"Robbie was right. She said you'd get a bit arsey about that."

"Arsey? The police thought I was in on it. If they'd had their way, I would've been in the next cell."

"Never gonna happen."

"And how do you know that?"

"Women's prison. You wouldn't last five minutes in there. They'd eat you for breakfast." Angel dabbed a tissue at the pool of beer on the table. I laughed, calling Angel an arsehole under my breath. "That's more like it," she said. "Robbie said you had a sense of humour. She was right about the cute bit too, when you're not being a prick."

I took a sip without mishap this time. Placing my glass on the table, I folded my arms and sat back, crossing my feet. Angel laughed.

"What's funny?" I said.

"She said you might sulk as well."

"Not sulking," I said, but we knew I was.

"What's up then?"

"You accused me of being a prick," I said.

"Cos you're being a prick. Look, what I'm saying is, Robbie wants to see you. She knows you haven't forgiven her. She just wants a chance. Wants to talk."

"What if I don't want to?"

Angel gave up trying to mop the beer spill but just looked at the soggy mess on the table. She pulled a pack of cigarettes and a lighter from her jacket.

"That would be… unfortunate." She clicked the lighter, watching the small flame for a second. "Robbie's my friend. I want her to be happy. You could make her happy."

I shivered. Was my imagination working overtime, or was there a hint of a threat behind her words? I waved away the offer of a cigarette. Angel lit one for herself, blowing the plume of smoke towards me, repeatedly clicking the lighter.

"Just talk to her, please. Make my friend happy."

I was back at home, thinking about Angel and feeling a little uneasy. I admit she'd been good company. We'd sat for over an hour over a few pints, enjoying a laugh. But, and it was a big one, just like Rupert had said – she frightened the bejesus out of me. There was something about her. Firebombing her boyfriend's house was a sign. I suppose, technically, she firebombed his neighbour. Scary.

Then there was Robbie. I'd been head over heels for her before she betrayed me. I flicked through the photos that were still on my phone. Was I just being a coward not speaking to her? I'd told myself that I'd ignored her letters because she was part of my past. Jen was my future — hopefully. Right on cue, Jen called.

"Speak of the devil," I said, trying for over the top cheerful.

"*I'm* the devil? It's you that turned into Pablo Escobar the minute I turned my back."

She'd heard.

"It was two pills. I panicked. How did you hear?"

"Jason just called. He got the full tale from Flic. In fact, Joe's trying to call me now. You've caused quite a stir. Hang on a second."

I heard muffled cursing.

"Everything okay?"

"Yes. Sorry. Just sending Joe a text. I'll have a natter with him later. I need cheering up."

Hang on, shouldn't I be the one cheering her up? I'd come back to that later.

"How are things over there? How's your dad?"

"Oh, he's on the mend. They should discharge him tomorrow and we can head back home."

"That's good news," I said. "You must've been worried."

"I was, at first. Once he responded to the antibiotics, it was just boring. Sitting at a hospital bedside while the rest of the population was enjoying the French sunshine."

"Couldn't you take it in turns with your mum?"

"That's what she said, but it didn't seem fair. Besides, I said I was taking a year off to spend time with him. I can hardly leave him to it at the first sign of trouble. Anyway, talking about my year off. It begs the question, if New York is out of the picture and I'm taking a break, what are you going to do with yourself?"

"I'm worried that I'm going to need huge amounts of cash to get a fancy American lawyer. If I get sued…" I was afraid my voice was about to crack. Jen sensed I was upset and spoke calmly.

"You'd tell me to worry about the things I could affect and ignore the rest. Give Flic time to speak to her boss. Maybe she can sort everything out. Maybe she could make sure there's no court case. You need to occupy your mind. There was loose talk of creating a TV series out of Jason's life story. What about a pitch for that?"

"To be honest, I've already started. But you wrote that book. I assumed we'd work on the pitch together."

"I know, but I'm out of the picture. You can do this. If it comes to needing money, it would be far better to have a project ready to go rather than sitting in the pub with Rupert and moaning about how unfair life is?"

I was about to argue, but she was right.

"Fair enough. I'll crack on. What about you? Knowing you, you'll have things so well organised that you'll be writing all the time you're away." There was a murmur of what could've been agreement from Jen. "You've started something, haven't you," I pushed.

"Let's just say I've got a couple of ideas I'm kicking around. I want to let them mature a little before I share. Besides, it would appear I have another major challenge coming up."

"What's that?"

"Well, I had a long talk with Dad last night. He's obviously been doing a lot of thinking. He knows the treatments will one day run out but hates the term *bucket list*. Says it's just ticking stuff off before he snuffs it. But there are things he wants to do. Sounds a lot like the definition of a bucket list to me but, if it makes him happy…"

"I take it you're getting roped into one of them?"

"Yes. He wants to do the coast to coast walk, from St Bees to Robin Hood's Bay. I said I would do it with him."

"I've always fancied doing something like that. How far is it?"

"About 190 miles."

"That far? Sounds like a lovely father and daughter

opportunity." At least my u-turn was quick and decisive. That sounded like hard work, particularly with my current lack of sleep. Besides, I was going to be desperately trying to earn enough to fund a rich lawyer. Jen laughed.

"Don't worry. You don't have to do it. Anyway, sounds like you're going to be busy with your new project."

We talked for another hour. Mostly, it was effortless, relaxed and normal. Just once, I sensed the tension lurking in the background. Jen was worried about her dad, working through the thought processes that tried to make sense of him not always being there. I wanted to do more to comfort her, but she assured me I was doing well. We agreed to get together for a meal once she was back in the country.

I'd forgotten that Jen was an hour ahead. Her stifled yawn was a signal to wrap the call up. It felt good to speak again, and we'd get to meet up in person later in the week. Then I switched thoughts to the future.

Working on a new project seemed so simple, with Jen beside me. She gave me the confidence to do stuff. It didn't particularly matter if I was out of my depth or in danger of screwing up big style. Jen would know what to do. It was the same with the actual writing. Okay, I had a series of children's books that had sold well, but Jen had edited all of them. We'd worked together on the film script and the website. *The Hubberholme Syndrome* and *The Woman In The Yellow Raincoat* had both become successful, but I was in no doubt that Jen's contribution was immense. Could I do this without her?

Then again, what was the alternative? Sit and do nothing while Jen was on her extended break? She'd talked about a year, but nothing was certain. As usual, when faced with thoughts like this, I decided a beer was required. Then I remembered the empty fridge. I checked my watch. The pub closed five minutes ago. There was nothing else for it. A cup of tea, then bed.

I was exhausted. My all too brief stay in New York meant that I never adjusted to the time difference, so jet-lag was not an issue. The stress and worry, however, combined to make me both jittery and exhausted.

I went to bed, hoping to get a solid twelve hours. I managed four.

7

Half an hour after retrieving my car from the storage unit, I parked as instructed and walked towards the water, taking the right-hand path at the fork. This was all very cloak and dagger. I saw Flic on a bench just ahead.

"An unusual place for a meeting."

"Hi, Frankie. What can I say? I like ducks."

"We need pancakes and plum sauce."

Flic smiled and shook her head, relaxed in the evening sunshine.

"How can you say that? Look how cute that one is."

"Looks like he's plotting something. I take it cute ducks weren't the only reason for you to be so far from your natural habitat."

Flic was about to answer, but paused as the roar of jet engines filled the air. To our left, a Jet 2 flight climbed from the runway that bordered the park. Her eyes followed the plane as it climbed.

"I should've been flying to Paris this evening, but things kinda changed."

"I take it you've spoken to your boss?"

"Ex-boss, it turns out."

Ducks fled as my voice rose.

"Oh my God, Flic. Not because of me?"

"Let's just say the conversation started there and escalated quickly." She patted my leg, eyes still on the vapour trail in the sky. "Don't worry, not about that anyway. It'd been coming for a while." Now I was worried. "There is good news and bad news."

"I take it I'm fired." Flic gave the slightest nod. "So, what's the good news?"

"Sorry, that is the good news." I was about to ask how that news was good, but Flic continued. "The bad news is that he *is* talking about a lawsuit."

My heart was about to burst out of my chest. I clutched at the only straw I could see.

"Only talking about suing? Nothing definite?"

"No. He's got three other cases on, two as suer and one as suee. I know that's not a word, it's been a long day."

"Should I call him? Do a bit of grovelling?"

"No. That's the last thing you should do. Let him calm down, see what happens."

"So, I'm unemployed, but what about you?"

"We mutually agreed that my position was untenable." Flic laughed. "Around ten seconds after I told him to shove his job up his creepy, litigious arse."

"Flic! No. You can't do that because I was an idiot. Call him back. Apologise."

"Don't worry Frankie. The earth has continued to rotate and I'm actually quite excited about the future. I've been mulling over a plan for a while. Today I went for it."

"Go on."

"Well, it would appear that I am at a crossroads with no job and, thanks to last month's annual bonus, a wheelbarrow full of cash. You dipped your toe into being a producer with *The Hubberholme Syndrome*. Would you be interested in starting our own production company — partners?"

"But I've already got the company with Jen. Then there's Jason."

"I confess, I'm slightly ahead of you with Jason. I spoke to him an hour ago. He's up for leaving his job and coming in with us."

"What about Jen? She's taking some time out, but I can't just abandon everything."

"Certainly not. I'm talking about five of us. Equal partners. In fact, it would make sense for you to keep the separate partnership you already have as Vince Taylor. That way you can continue to write together and sell stuff to the new company to produce it, whether it's TV, films, stage — whatever we want. We'd call the shots. Tell me you'll at least think about it."

"It sounds like a wonderful idea, but…" I tried to focus on the words. "If I have to pay for lawyers, I'm going to need all my cash. How could I invest now?"

We both fell silent. Flic fussed over an inquisitive cocker spaniel, showing off its brand new stick. The dog owner smiled and shook her head.

"Actually, I just thought of something else. If Guthrie sues… I'm not saying he'd win, or anything like that, but if he did, he'd likely take your share. Him as a partner is the last thing I want. Maybe we need a rethink."

We sat in silence. In the space of thirty seconds, I'd gone from being Vice President of Production (New Markets), to unemployed, to partner in a new business, and back to unemployed. It was difficult to keep up. Was I careering out of control? I managed a laugh at the old joke.

"What's funny?" Jen asked.

"Nothing. Ignore me."

"Okay. Plan B. The rest of the plan stands. We put your share on hold until Guthrie has gone away. Then you invest and become a full partner. Until then, you come and work for us."

"As what?"

"I don't know. Head of paper clips or something. You're the creative one. I just want you and Jen around. This way, we get your talents from the off and you don't tie up all your capital. We also go for a quick win to help with funds."

"How do you mean?"

"I have a friend who has twin girls."

"Nice. How old?"

Flic looked at me like I'd asked a dumb question.

"I don't know. They're about this big." She held a hand out in front of her. "Does that help?"

"Probably about six. Unless there freakishly tall. Or short for their age. Tell you what, I'll shut up."

"The point is, they love your stories. They want one read to them every night. To save her sanity, my friend would pay anything for an audiobook. That way she can play them as often as needed, and she gets to sit with a G&T while they listen. Then, I thought, why not get somebody to read them on TV? If we can sell the idea to the BBC, we're onto a winner. Quick turnaround, as the stories already exist. What do you say?"

"Sounds perfect. I'm pretty sure my publishing deal is just for the illustrated hardback. I'll get onto it."

"The day started badly, but things are looking up. You should know I took a flier on this and signed a lease on new offices just over there." Flic pointed over the runway. "You're welcome to claim a desk there whenever you need it. *Burning Down The House* is your number one priority. Right, I need to make some more calls."

"Hang on," I said. "You said five partners. You, Jason, Jen and me…"

"Can't say at the moment, but you've heard of them. Right, you've got research to do."

* * *

It is amazing how half an hour sitting on a park bench can change your entire attitude towards life. Earlier, I'd spent a constructive morning feeling sorry for myself and watching daytime TV. I'd even thought briefly about becoming an expert at buying and selling tat. Now, with a genuine threat of a massively expensive lawsuit hanging over me, I got my finger out. Flic's encouragement could be a lifeline.

A call to my publisher confirmed I owned the rights to market an audiobook, but they'd be happy to produce one. Flic was already working on a pitch for the children's stories to the BBC.

My so-called research for *Burning Down The House* was tortuous. I'd been trying to track down Gabriel Thompson's widow. I wanted to know why he'd changed his plea to guilty after a day of his trial. I knew from the newspaper account that her name was Elizabeth. That just made things harder. Would she be Liz? Beth? Betty? Liza? It was a bit of a needle in a haystack. What if she'd re-married or changed her name? After all this time, she could be anybody or anywhere.

I was about to give up when it hit me. If she had remarried, there would be a marriage certificate. Surely that would have her formal name on it? I got to work. Half an hour later, I was convinced I'd found her. Kind of. I had a name, Liz Wilkinson. I even had an address but no phone number. The bad news was the address. It was in New Zealand. I was hardly going to get on a bus and visit. Without a phone number it was a dead end.

I rubbed the back of my neck and decided coffee was required. As I returned from the kitchen, my phone was vibrating a samba across the desk. I reached out just in time. Not recognising the number, I answered hesitantly.

"Hello, Frankie speaking."

"Frankie. Hello, love. It's Geraldine, Jen's mum."

"Oh. Hello. Is everything okay?"

I must've sounded a little panicked.

"Don't worry, Ben's fine. He's had his first dose of chemo. He seems to have coped well with it. No, it's Jen."

My heart almost stopped. Jen? What the hell was wrong? Before I could respond, Geraldine continued.

"Sorry. Jen's fine. I didn't mean to worry you. No, she's perfect. In fact…" I could sense hesitation. Geraldine always struck me as the perfect mum to Jen and granny to Charley. Kind, caring, well spoken, even demure. "… she's too bloody perfect. I know we've only been back a few hours but we had a week in France. She's a wonderful daughter and we both love her to bits, but, to be honest, Frankie, she's doing my fucking head in."

The language stung, but the sentiment behind it was even more shocking. I chose my words carefully.

"Is she sort of, kinda, you know?" You could tell I was a writer.

"Taking over? Yes. We love she wants to do so much, but unless she backs off, I may have to murder her. Brutally. Sorry, that sounds awful."

"Your daughter has many wonderful qualities. She'll do anything for anybody, but has a tendency to take over." I felt disloyal even saying that much. "Have you spoken to her about it?"

"I tried, but she just thinks I'm trying to put a brave face on things, telling her I can manage. Look, you must help me. For God's sake, get her back to work, at least part-time. You're my last hope."

"I could try."

"No." I jumped at the severity of her voice. "Sorry, that was sharp but, no. There is no *try*, only do." Now she thinks I'm a Jedi. "Please Frankie. Use your charm on her. Drug her. Kidnap her. Do whatever it takes."

How could I say no? After a quick chat about Charley and the plans for Ben's treatment, we said our goodbyes. The notes spread across the desk gave me the perfect excuse to call Jen. I just hoped, for all our sakes, that I was up to the task.

My first instinct was to call Jen straight away. The telephone equivalent of ripping off a plaster. Then again, that usually hurt. Better to think about it. I looked at my watch hopefully. Five to four. Too early to go to the pub. I was supposed to be working. I looked again at the scattered notes and sighed. Right on cue, the phone vibrated again. It was Jen.

"Jen, hi. How are you?"

"She's doing my fucking head in."

Whoa. What?

"Your mum, by any chance?"

"How did you guess? I love her dearly. You know I do. But sometimes she just does my bloody head in."

"You said," I said, trying to appear neutral. "What's she done now?"

"Nothing. That's just it. I said I wanted to help. She took that as a signal to pile up thousands of jobs for me. Would you mind just? Could you just? We could do with… It never ends. Help me!"

"How about I come around tonight? A takeaway curry after I've read Charley's bedtime story? You can sit with your feet up and do bugger all. Let me look after you."

"That sounds nice. Can we have ice cream too?"

"I'm on it. Whatever you want."

"Chocolate chip, rum and raisin, cookie dough and strawberry cheesecake."

"You'll be sick."

"Don't care. You'll clean up. You said you'd look after me."

"I will. What time do you want me?"

"About seven? Time to chuck spaghetti hoops on a plate for Charley. I'll have her more or less docile by the time you get here."

"Okay, and don't worry. It'll be fine. I promise."

Returning to the task in front of me, I picked up the trusty pack of Post-its. Faced with the same picture as before, I sighed and swore under my breath. I was getting nowhere finding the two missing gang members. I was stuck. Playing with Post-its was my primary plan. Jason would be useful, but he'd taken a few days off ahead of a book tour to support the paperback release. I upped the volume on the music and joined in with Robert Plant and Alison Krauss.

"Please read the letter that I wrote."

It was hopelessly off key, but it didn't matter. I had an idea. I could write to Liz Wilkinson. Not as instant as a phone call but better than nothing. How long had it been since I wrote a letter? Typing the words was easy. An envelope was a different problem altogether. A trip to the post office was in order. Where was the post office? The internet, as always, came to my rescue.

I was about to grab my jacket when there was a knock at the door. I looked at it, slightly confused. That had never happened before. The only visitor was the Amazon man, who often stuck his head around the door. Placing the pen behind my ear, I paused the music and shouted, "it's open".

"Hello, Ben. Fancy seeing you here. Come in. Is everything okay?"

"They're doing my fucking head in. Thought I'd hide here."

"I'll stick the kettle on."

It was funny. Only in the last few weeks had he become Ben rather than just Jen's dad. He'd mistrusted me at first. He probably saw me as a potential weirdo, sniffing around his daughter. It seems I had won him over with my natural charm. Chocolate biscuits seemed to help, judging by how many he was getting through. He must've noticed my glance.

"Sorry. It's the chemo. I have a constant craving for sweet stuff. Ironic that diabetes could kill me before the cancer." Ben didn't miss my slight flinch. "Quite a shock when people talk about death, isn't it? We do anything to avoid talking about it. Don't worry, I'm coming to terms with the fact that I won't be around forever. I still get angry — why me? That sort of thing. Then I thought, why waste my energy? Make the most of what's left. Spending time with my wonderful wife and daughter. Trouble is, they're doing…"

"Your head in. I got that bit," I said with a grin.

"It sounds daft but, spending time with them is not the same as them doing everything for me. They're also winding each other up. I used the excuse that I needed some exercise to sneak out for a walk this afternoon. They argued about coming with me, so I escaped out of the back door. Sent them texts from the park to explain what I'd done."

"Would it help if I tried to coax Jen back to work? Maybe part-time?"

"I'll leave everything to you in my will if you do."

"No need for that. I need her back, to be honest. Let me see what I can do. Now, tell me about this coast to coast walk."

Ben's eyes lit up. His enthusiasm about the whole thing — even the wet and windy conditions — shone. Although it wasn't for me, I understood the drive to achieve something like this. She was on the naughty step, but he still wanted Jen by his side. He accepted my offer of logistical support. We agreed to sort out details later, but I would do things like meeting them at a pub along the route to deliver a change of clothes. I would also be on hand to offer a ride back from Robin Hood's Bay when they were done.

An hour after his arrival, Ben admitted to feeling more able to face his nearest and dearest. I promised a steady supply of biscuits when he needed them, but pointed out that, with luck, his daughter would spend more time here over the next few weeks. Waving from the doorstep, I looked at my watch. The research could wait. I had to post a letter.

8

"How come, if tomorrow is publication day for the paperback, you aren't doing interviews and book signings till your arm hurts?"

Jen laughed.

"You're a partner in two businesses involved in this and don't know the answer?"

"Fair point, well made," I said. I continued my steady, rhythmic movements.

"Half an inch down… Bingo! I'm benefitting from being anonymous. All the interviews just use written replies to the same questions. Rupert has done a great job handling the social media side. With a bit of luck, he'll keep the publisher happy and the rest will take care of itself. Ow!"

"Sorry."

"Go back to doing… Yes, perfect. I needed this so much. You are wonderful."

Jen leaned back on two cushions, a look of bliss on her face. I switched my attention to the other foot. This was still as physical as our relationship had got, and I would do anything to please this woman.

I had read bedtime stories to Charley. We'd cleared away the debris from the takeaway, loaded the dishwasher, compromised on two flavours of ice cream to avoid actual danger to health, then settled on Jen's sofa. James Taylor was serenading in the background, and the foot massage had been on top of Jen's wish list by a mile.

"You're so good at this. Just the two hours, please. Any longer and I'm not sure how I could repay you," said Jen.

"There's one way," I said. Jen opened one eye and frowned. "Not that. Unless you're telling me, you can't resist me any longer, in which case I'm willing to oblige. I'm told the feet can be very effective erogenous zones."

"Careful, I could kick you in one of yours."

We both laughed. We knew how we felt about each other, but Jen was still not over losing Sean. I continued with the foot rub.

"Don't worry," I said. "I know you're working through a lot just now. It's nothing like that."

"Tell me you don't want a foot massage. Not sure I could cope with that."

"What's wrong with my feet?" I was pretty sure they were clean and my socks were hole-free.

"It's not your feet specifically. It's feet. They're weird. No offence."

"None taken. Anyway, it wasn't what I had in mind. I need to pick your brains."

"So it's about the book?"

"Am I that obvious?"

"Don't forget, I have special powers. Then again, so do you. You can write a script without me. You're very talented."

"Oh, I know I could." I was bluffing. "It's digging out more of the story than appears in the book."

"You mean the other two gang members?"

"Yes. What happened? Why are they left out?"

"It was the publisher's legal team that blocked it. Everything pointed to there being two more. There was a driver. He got them out of trouble at times. Then there was the organiser and fence. I couldn't prove that they actually existed, even though they had to. I just came up with a complete blank when I tried to identify them definitively. In the end, we ignored them. Nobody seemed to care. The authentic story was the killer and Jason's dad turning on the others, going into witness protection."

"This whole witness protection thing. It's bugging me. Why would the authorities go to all that trouble if only two of the gang were incriminated?"

"I asked Jason about that. The official line was that there were credible threats made against the family. They were innocent so needed protection."

"Official line?"

"Jason suspected that his father provided information on something else, unconnected to the gang. It was all hushed up, nothing in the press. He says he has no evidence to back it up, just a hunch."

"Flic thinks the TV companies won't commission the script unless we can name the other members."

"So, how does the detective's hat fit?" said Jen.

"Useless at the moment. I'm not getting anywhere. Although, you'd look rather fetching in a deerstalker."

"Ah. But I'm taking time out to be with Mum and Dad."

"How's that going?"

"Ouch."

"Sorry." Had I upset her? "It's just that you seemed tense, a bit. Would it be so dreadful to come back to work?"

"What about the coast to coast walk? I can't just abandon that."

"That's two weeks. Three at the most. How about a deal? You come back part time. Twice a week I come with you on a longish walk to get you to peak fitness. I'm sure your parents will shout if they need you to help with hospital visits and stuff. They'd have time to adjust to everything and there's less chance of you all killing each other."

"Have they said something to you?" Jen glowered, but didn't withdraw her foot from my massage.

"We may have had a little chat. They instigated it — not me. Look, this is an exciting time for the business and we'll make sure Ben has everything he needs to get through this. What do you say? Will you think about it?"

Jen sighed and pondered.

"I have one condition."

"Name it."

"Foot rubs after every walk."

"Okay. As long as you shower beforehand."

"You drive a hard bargain."

"Take it or leave it, pal."

"I have one more condition," she said.

"That's cheating. What is it?"

"You open a bottle of wine. We've got an investigation to discuss."

"I can live with that. Do we have a deal?"

I reached out for a formal shake. Jen held onto my hand.

"You're a good man, Frankie Dale." She kissed the back of my hand. "Now shift your arse and get me Merlot, and lots of it."

9

Jen was due at the cottage at around eleven. She was planning to visit her parents and break the news to them she was coming back to work. I'd made an early start, which largely comprised staring at the whiteboard. Scrawled across the top, in what I later learned was permanent marker, was 'FENCE—DRIVER - who?'

"What's a fence driver?"

The loud voice came from behind me.

"What the hell are you doing here? You scared the shite out of me."

"Charming," said Angel, dropping uninvited into Jen's seat. "I just thought I'd pop in and see my mate. Not exactly a friendly greeting."

"I'd say come in and sit down, but you already have. How long have you been there?"

"Long enough. You really shouldn't scratch there in public."

"I wasn't in public. I was all by myself in the privacy of my office. How did you know where I worked?"

"I find things out. It's a gift."

She tapped the side of her nose like I didn't want to know. She jumped to her feet.

"Where's your kettle?"

I knew it was feeble, but I simply pointed to the kitchen. My legs were like jelly. I shouldn't have to face this much stress after four hours of sleep.

"Sit down. You look pale. Let me get you a coffee. Black and strong?"

"Yes please," I mumbled. "How did you know that?"

Angel tapped the side of her nose again and skipped off to the kitchen. Instead of this office being just for me and Jen, it seemed I now had to cope with the idea of people just dropping in. I really ought to lock the door behind me. My heart returned to normal speed after the shock of finding Angel standing behind me. She plonked a coffee on the desk.

"Couldn't find any biscuits. Funny, could've sworn you'd have some," she said.

"An unexpected visitor scoffed them all yesterday."

"I should've brought some. As a gift, like. Next time. You seem nervous."

"I'm just not used to unexpected visitors. I'm used to this space being kinda private," I said.

"You should have some security kit."

"I didn't think I needed it until you arrived."

"Leave it with me. I'll sort something out for you."

"No need, honest. Nice to see you and all that, but I have a lot of work on," I said.

"Surely you can spare ten minutes for a friend? It's not as if you're dashing off to the prison to visit Robbie."

So — the reason for the visit. I must admit, I'd put my ex-fiancée right out of my mind since Angel had first delivered her message.

"As I say, I've been very busy," was my defensive reply.

I noticed Angel was holding a cigarette lighter, deftly passing it over one finger and under the next, backwards and forwards across her right hand. She broke the silence that followed.

"So, what *is* a fence driver?"

Despite wishing to get rid of her, I answered.

"It's not a what. It's a who. Two people probably. It's a script I'm working towards, based on a true story."

"Could be fun. Tell me about it."

"I can't. It's a work in progress."

"What? Do you think I'm going to steal your idea, write a script and become a celeb?"

"No, of course not."

"Actually, it sounds like a great plan."

I wasn't sure if she was joking. Then again, I was stuck. What harm could it do? She might just have an idea what to do next. I ran through a synopsis and explained the problem of identifying them.

"Sounds like an interesting puzzle. What's the book called? The one it's based on?"

"Have a look in the bottom drawer."

I knew Jen had a few copies the publisher had sent through. Angel took one and held it up, reading the blurb on the back.

"Keep it, assuming you read books?"

"Course I can read. What do you think I am?"

"I didn't say that. I asked if you read books, not whether you *could* read. Many people don't get beyond magazines or Twitter these days."

"Honestly, it got me through prison. That and having Robbie as a friend. I ended up doing an A-level in English Lit. Got an A-star. So, yes, I read books." She looked again at the cover. "So who's this Vince Taylor?"

"It's a pen name that me and my partner use for publishing."

"Your partner being the glamorous Jen?"

"Yes. She wrote that, but we always publish under the joint

name."

"Like Lennon and McCartney. Doesn't matter who wrote what, you share everything."

"Exactly."

"So where's Jen today?"

"She's due any time now. I don't want to be rude…"

"But can I sling my hook? Time I was off anyway. Besides, I've got a book to read."

The cottage had a lot more familiar feel to it. No visitors. I'd stocked up on chocolate biscuits and Jen was back in her seat. We'd spent the last half hour going over the notes on the two missing gang members. It was Jen who called a timeout. She pushed her seat back from the desk and stretched out her legs.

"Could we make this easier for ourselves?"

"You know me. I'm all for a simple life," I smiled, helping myself to another biccie.

"It's just that the book was a biography. I was determined it would be factual. This is a dramatisation based on the book. Can't we use the phrase 'in the interests of telling a good story, we made up the bits that we couldn't prove,' or something like that?"

"That would be a brilliant move," I said. "I've seen something like that so many times and never questioned it. Flic says the commission depends on finding the mystery men. I suppose the series would have a much bigger impact if we discover who these people were. If the police got to arrest them it would make front-page headlines. Finding the truth would lead to much more interest."

"Okay, in that case, we should have a chat with Jason."

"Fine. I'll call him."

I picked up my phone. Jason answered on the first ring.

"That's keen. Were you poised just in case I rang?"

"Hi Frankie. Obviously, I spend all day poised for a call from you. I was just about to call you. Is Jen there as well?"

"Yeah, I'll put you on speaker."

We chatted for five minutes about the new company. Jason was enjoying the chance to work from home in London most of the time, rather than at our new office in Leeds. Then I explained the reason for the call. He sounded delighted that we were trying to fill in any blanks in our knowledge of the facts.

"I'm in Leeds tomorrow. Why don't we get together for a couple of hours and see how I can help? Although, I'm not sure I'll be able to add much more to what you already know."

"Thank you," said Jen. "It's worth a go."

"No, thank you. I mean it. Thanks for sticking with this. The book is brilliant, but I still feel there's more to come. I know what happened to me and Mum, but I don't really know why. I want to know who was behind everything," said Jason.

Before wrapping up the call, I remembered what Jason had said right at the beginning.

"What were you going to call us about?"

"Well remembered. It's good news, honest."

"Why am I worried by that reassurance?" I laughed, despite feeling uneasy.

"No. It's good. We made a second pitch for work and it's now agreed. CBBC wants us to make a series based on your children's books. They want us to put together eight episodes, with an option for another eight next year. They wanted the format to be a mix of a story teller speaking to camera and actors playing the lead characters. Now they are favouring straight story telling. We can hammer the detail out later. This should be easy and generate cash. Could you draw up a provisional list of eight stories and see if any need abridging to fit twenty minutes? They'd like to have that in a couple of weeks. Doable?"

I was close to ruling it out, but Jen interjected.

"Leave it with us, Jason. We'll have something ready."

"Great. I've got another call coming in. Speak soon."

Jason had gone. I turned to Jen.

"Sounded like you have a plan for how we achieve the deadline," I said.

"Not a Scooby's. Just thought we needed to sound confident," said Jen with a grin.

"Blind panic and late nights it is, then."

"That's a plan. Glad to be back. I'll put the kettle on."

While I was waiting, I checked the social media accounts. The launch of the paperback was creating quite a stir. Rupert was a social media genius. I was still reading the comments about the book as Jen returned with coffees. One comment caught my eye.

Enjoyed the hardback, but how come Uncle Pete never gets a mention? He was our hero when we were kids.

"Playing with Twitter does not count as research." Jen offered me a Penguin or a KitKat. I pointed at the former, but the look on Jen's face convinced me I was wrong; she loved Penguins.

"This could count as research. Thanks," I said, picking up the mug.

"What is it?"

I read the tweet out loud, then clicked on the user page. Kittens — lots of them, but the location was interesting. Jen was flicking through her notebook.

"She's from Bradford. Could her uncle have been our driver?" I asked.

"Hang on. Here it is. The bit that I couldn't prove. His initials were PP — Peter Parker."

"No way."

"Straight up."

"So the getaway car was driven by Spiderman? Course it was."

"Not that Peter Parker, obviously. Would've been cool though, wouldn't it?"

"I suppose it would. So, what do we do now?"

"Some detective you are," said Jen. "Send her a message. We need to talk."

I did, then sat back, staring at the screen.

"No reply."

"Give her a chance. Some people have other things to do."

I whooped — our first proper lead — and I had a KitKat.

"Hello, love. How're Charley and Jen?"

Typical, not how are you? Or you're looking well.

"Hello, Mum. They're both well. Jen struggles a bit with her dad's illness, but otherwise..."

"Give them our love. Shame you didn't bring them with you. Sit down, I'll put the kettle on. Do you want a sandwich?"

"No thanks, Mum. I'm fine."

"It's no trouble."

"No, honest, I'm not hungry."

"Probably just as well."

"What?"

"Well, you've put weight on while you were in America. All those sizeable portions, I expect."

"I was only there six hours."

"Good job you didn't stay a couple of years then. What exactly happened?"

I couldn't face the whole drug thing. I'd never hear the end of it.

"I decided Jen needed me here. She's got a lot on and I wanted to help," I said.

"So, will my hat get an outing after all?"

"I've told you before, we're just good friends."

"Are you sure you won't have a sandwich?"

"You just said I was putting weight on."

"Well, a sandwich won't hurt. I've got a low-fat spread."

"No, thanks."

"Biscuit? Go on, have a biscuit."

Seconds later, she was back with a plate of chocolate hob-nobs. I gave in, just to please her.

"Where's Dad?"

"Playing football. I ask you — at his age? Dozy beggar'll have another heart attack, then what?"

"What does his doctor say?"

"It was him that suggested it. He plays as well. Here, look." She pushed a small flyer towards me. It was for a weekly walking football session at the local sports centre. "They do all sorts there these days. You could come to my keep fat class tonight. That would sort the weight out. Are you sure you don't want a sandwich?"

I just shook my head and Mum launched into a convoluted tale of one of the class members and the aftereffects of Guinness. When there was a lull, I saw my chance.

"What happened to Dad after the fire?"

We'd only recently talked about the fire at the house when I was a teenager. It's how I got the scars on my back. My dad's prized record collection went up in smoke. When I finally made some money from my writing, I bought him a replacement collection. He was again listening to the music he'd loved.

Mum fidgeted, then poured more tea from the pot.

"He wasn't well. Not for a long time. His nerves were bad. I suppose these days they call it depression."

"How come I didn't know this?"

"You were busy being a stroppy teenager. You hardly spent

any time in the house. When you did, you were in your room. Then college and you moved out."

"How bad was he?" I could see that she was trying not to cry. "Sorry, if you don't want to talk—"

"No. It's fine. You two have sorted things out between you now. I'm surprised he hasn't told you himself. He lost his job. It was a struggle for a while. Eventually, his counsellor tried to get him drawing again. It was two years after the fire before he touched a pencil. She encouraged him. She got him some part-time work. That's when he improved. What makes you ask, anyway? Why now?"

"I think I saw one of his drawings online. Was the job at the newspaper?"

"That's right. They asked him to sit in court all day, drawing the people at some big murder trial. It was on telly and everything. Anyway, he got to know the manager at the print works and they offered him a full-time job. Not drawing, though."

"So that was how he became a typesetter?"

"It was. Right until it all went computerised. Ask him yourself, he's here."

Sure enough, the front door opened and in walked the ageing footballer. How did she do that? Some special sense after all these years?

"Ask him what? Hello, son. Thought you were in America."

"Been there, done it."

"Fair enough."

"We were just talking about when you worked at that murder trial, drawing the killer."

"Gabriel Thompson? He was no killer. Stitched up, right from the off."

"What makes you say that?"

"It was fishy. I said then it was a fit up. No way did he do it. Trial lasted one day. It was terrible.

"Terrible?"

"Terrible! I was counting on being there for weeks. My big chance of a new career. Then, first thing Tuesday morning, he changed his plea to guilty. Totally out of the blue and I was out of work again."

"Any idea why he changed his plea?"

"Like I say - fishy. I've got a book about it somewhere. You should read it. Vince, somebody or other. My lad's a writer. Do you know him?"

Mum kicked me under the table. I looked at her, but she just shook her head. She turned to Dad.

"Why don't you get showered and changed? All that football must've made you hungry. I'll start making tea when you get back."

"Okay. Nice to meet you, young man."

When he'd made his way upstairs, I looked at Mum.

"That's what it's like. One minute he's fine. Next minute, somebody's turned the lights off and he's not there anymore."

"But he could remember every detail from twenty-five years ago, then not recognise me. How do you cope?"

"It's not a matter of coping. I love the daft old bugger. What else can I do? Well done, not correcting him."

"I picked up on that when you went all Vinny Jones on me."

"He gets frustrated if he realises he's getting things wrong."

She pushed herself up from the kitchen table. I didn't know what to say. She dropped a bag of potatoes in front of me.

"Make yourself useful and peel those. I take it you'll stay for tea?"

"Won't Dad find it confusing if he doesn't recognise me?"

"Stay. Sausage, chips and beans, okay?"

"Lovely. I thought you said you had a keep fat class tonight?"

"I do. Need my strength for that. Don't cut the chips too thin. And put those biscuits in the cupboard. Don't want you ruining your appetite. Honestly, I don't know where you put it."

Any response would be futile. Dad was back by the time I'd laid the table.

"Hello, Frankie. I didn't hear you come in. I thought you'd be coming at the weekend. How's my little mate Charley?"

He was back with us as if nothing had happened.

10

Jen had taken Charley to the dentist. I was with Jason in the office. It was his first visit to our new home.

"So, this is what's costing the money?"

"It's enormous. Do you think we'll fill the place?"

"Don't worry," said Jason. "Flic's hard at work on the recruitment front. Before long, we'll be knee deep in projects."

We wandered around the empty spaces, chatting, then grabbed coffees and sat at a table in the kitchen.

"Do you mind if I ask you a personal question?"

Jason looked worried.

"Depends what it is."

I ploughed on.

"When we spoke yesterday about the research into what happened to your dad… You sounded quite emotional. It still hurts?"

"It does. And it makes me angry. Yes, Dad did some bad things. Nobody wants to find out the man they looked up to all their lives was a criminal. But, he was my hero. Then, just as he was rebuilding his life, he gets murdered."

"What was he like?"

"He was Dad, you know. He was a complicated character.

It hurt when he packed me off to boarding school. I thought I'd done something wrong. Now I suspect it was just that he wanted the best for me. By sending me away, they shielded me from the strange double life he was leading."

"Double life?"

"Yeah. He was a pillar of the community. Locals thought he was some kind of saint. Lots of charity work, sponsoring stuff. They even named a suite at the local hospice after him. Obviously, that changed when they found he was part of a gang that robbed jewellers. Proper little Robin Hood, stealing from the rich and giving a chunk to those that needed it. Okay, he must've kept a lot as well. That sort of house and lifestyle wasn't available to everybody. As I say — complicated. But he was my dad. He didn't deserve to be killed the way he was."

"And no conviction for his murder?"

"No. The American police saw him as a gang member getting what he deserved. The investigation found nothing and everybody went back to their lives. Everybody except me and Mum. They shunted us off to another life, another country."

"It would mean a lot to you to sort this out, wouldn't it?"

"It's not just the killing, it's all of it. The chances are that whoever was the mysterious Fifth Man that organised the jobs was also the one responsible for killing Dad."

"I don't suppose you've remembered anything else since the interviews with Jen? Any clues?"

"Sorry, mate. I asked my mother again last night over the phone. Neither of us have anything."

Jason seemed to collapse in on himself. He looked smaller than the Jason I knew. Yes, it would make a compelling TV script, but it would help my mate. Sometimes that was more important. We had to do this. I turned to go back to my desk to allow him to collect himself.

* * *

I'd recorded demo versions of the stories to see how they fit into the twenty-minute guideline. I'd stayed late last night working on the edits. Progress on *Burning Down The House* had stalled as our other deadline loomed.

Jen had brought croissants for breakfast.

"Don't you tire of eating nothing but pizza?"

I looked at the half a croissant in my hand — the rest clung to my shirt.

"This isn't pizza."

"True, but it hardly makes up a balanced diet."

"I often eat the pizza with my left hand. Does that count as balance?"

"When did you last eat a vegetable? And no, breaded mushrooms don't count!"

I gave it some thought. Even I was ashamed of myself when I couldn't remember the last green thing I'd eaten.

"That pause tells me everything. No arguing, you're coming to my place at the weekend and I'll cook us a proper meal. No cardboard boxes, foil trays or plastic chopsticks allowed. You're having green stuff and liking it. Any requests?"

"I'll tell you what I've fantasised about for almost a week."

"Steady tiger. I'm very impressionable."

"Roast beef and all the trimmings."

"I make a mean Yorkshire pudding."

"Throw in gravy that stands on its own two feet and you've got a deal."

"Let's do it straight after work on Friday. I can stick the meat in the oven on a timer. Be ready when we get back. You bring the wine."

"I thought we were being healthy."

"We are, but there are limits. We're not savages."

* * *

Jen left the office mid-afternoon each day, picking Charley up from school and calling in to spend time with her parents. With Jen being more of a daughter than a carer, they were getting on so much better. She'd been gone about ten minutes when Angel arrived.

"I love this book, but it only tells half the story. Put the kettle on then."

I took the pencil from my mouth and grinned at her.

"Good afternoon Angel. Nice to see you too. I'm very well thanks, how about you?"

"Is that sarcasm?"

"Not at all. I'll put the kettle on."

When I returned with tea and biscuits, Angel was sitting with her feet on Jen's desk.

"So, you read the book, then?" I said.

"Devoured it. Your mate Jen can certainly tell a tale, even if it's only half of it."

"To be fair, she was commissioned to write Jason's story. He wasn't part of the robberies."

"No, but that's the juicy bit. I can see why they're pushing you to update it for the telly. How far have you got?"

"It's complicated."

We both knew what that meant.

"Not far then?" I was about to get in a huff and invite Angel to bugger off and leave me to it. "Let me help," she said.

"How can you help?"

"Told you, I find stuff out. Where do you want me to start?"

There were only so many times I could turn down help without looking a complete arse. Progress had been slow, to say the least. I sighed.

"Danny O'Neill. Shot by the police when they went to arrest him. From what I can work out, Gary Stevens named him to the police. Reports suggest he was having a beer watching football on the telly. Somehow he ended up with three bullets in his back. There was an inquest — open verdict. Nobody held accountable, just filed away and forgotten about."

"Sounds a bit iffy to me. I take it he was married?"

"Yes. Two kids."

"What does the wife have to say? Was she there at the time?"

"No idea. How would we even find her?"

"And you thought about not accepting my help? I'll find her. Can I use your laptop?"

"Why not use your phone?"

"Yeah, cos that'll work."

Angel reached into her pocket and held up a phone.

"What the chuff is that?"

"Don't dis the Nokia 103. All the rage just before I got sent down. Updating to the latest mega phone hasn't been a priority for me since I got out. Now, shift over and I'll find Mrs O'Neill."

Reluctantly, I eased out of my seat and allowed Angel to take control. She tapped at the keyboard as I leaned across, trying to look over her shoulder. She angled the laptop away from me. I leaned further across. Again, a slight nudge of the laptop. My next lean went beyond the patience of gravity. The wheels on my seat gave up and I crashed to the floor.

"Serves you right," said Angel. "Look, I can't work with you hovering. Don't you have work to do?"

"Kind of difficult when you've got my laptop."

"Give me five minutes. You must have emails to answer. Use your phone."

I was about to remind her that this was my office, my investigation and my, — even in my head, I struggled for another example — thingy. Angel picked up her phone. Who was she calling? Before I could ask, she spoke.

"Hi, mate. Yeah, good. I need an in for Liverpool council." Angel typed as she listened. "Thanks buddy. I owe you one. Ha, no chance." She ended the call. "Dirty bas—" More tapping at the keyboard. "Gotcha. She still lives at the same house. At least she pays council tax there. Don't see why she'd do that if she didn't live there."

"How much of what you just did was illegal?"

"How would I know? Don't have time to work out percentages. Now, do you want this phone number or not?"

"You've got her phone number and address? How?"

"Told you — I find stuff out. Do you want to ring her or do I have to do everything?"

"I'll do it," I said.

I got to my feet. Angel looked up at me.

"What? Oh, you want your seat back? I apologise. Can't expect the boss to make a call from the other seat. That would be stupid."

I let that go — I had my seat back. What would I say to Mrs O'Neill? I didn't even know her full name. Then I looked at Angel's scribbled note. Bernadette O'Neill. Okay, so I knew her name. Maybe using it was too informal. What would I say?

"Get on with it," said Angel.

"I'm just deciding what to say."

"What about starting with hello? Then explain that you're working for a TV company and want to talk to her about her husband's killing. Tell her you want to expose the people who killed him, get her on your side."

That all sounded reasonable. Why was my heart pounding? Come on, Frankie. You can do this. I took a deep breath and dialled the number. It rang. I waited. It rang eight times until the answer machine kicked in. I panicked and disconnected the call. Angel shook her head and glowered at me.

"What?"

"So now you're scared of answering machines?"

"I need to think what to say."

"Say exactly what you were going to say if she's answered. Leave your name and number and ask her to call back. Numpty."

She may have a point. This time, I called and left a message that was clear and concise. Okay, it was confused and waffly but got the essential stuff across.

11

We were heading for the main office for a meeting with Flic and Jason. We'd distributed the proposal for the structure of the children's series together with scripts for the first two stories. All of this needed to be agreed ahead of the press release to kick start the publicity. It was Jen's first visit to the office.

We were chatting happily as I pulled into the car park.

"Cheeky bugger," I muttered.

"What's up?"

"Some git has parked in my spot."

"Does it matter? There seem to be plenty of others."

"It's the principle. And they're parked over the white lines. That's two spaces."

"Well, I presume one of them is mine and I've never used it and you haven't used yours for ages. Let it go."

I stopped by the white van and glared at the words.

"Penelope's Parcels. Parked like a complete…"

Still chuntering to myself, we made our way to the office.

Flic and Jason were already in the main meeting room. We were the sole occupants of the huge building — using a separate room seemed odd. An office manager was due to start soon, once the work increased. A group hug marked us all being in the same place for the first time since Flic started the company. It reminded me of the first day back at school after the holidays. Flic didn't seem to care that I still hadn't come up with a job title. She simply treated me like a partner already.

Everything settled down when Jason ran us through the list of smaller projects that he and Flic had been busy kicking off. However, the main one was the children's TV series.

"We've been looking at who could tell the stories."

This was exciting. For our previous film we'd used mainly unknown actors, apart from taking a punt on the ageing Roddy Lightning. He became a great friend, and it broke my heart when he died. I told anyone who would listen that casting Roddy was my idea and a masterstroke. This made me think I would be good at coming up with names for the new series. I'd had a few daydreams about casting Tom Hanks and Lily James, but reasoned that may be on the ambitious side. The picture on the screen piqued my interest.

Demus Wolf was one of the hottest character actors on TV. He had one of those faces that everybody knew but couldn't always put a name to. His appearances triggered long, involved conversations about what he'd been in and whether it really was him under all that makeup. They often cast him as the bad guy, scarred and sinister looking. The man was a genius.

"Could we really get him?"

It was Flic that answered.

"I think we can. I met him for drinks last night. He seems quite keen."

"Hold on. You went for drinks with Demus Wolf? How did that come about?"

"I called him. He was at home in Manchester, so we met up."

I was open-mouthed.

"You have Demus Wolf's phone number and know where he lives? How?"

"We worked together a few times. I actually know his wife well. Remember the woman with two kids that were into your stories? We started as runners at the same time. Little black books are extremely useful in this business," said Flic. "And it gets better. I took a leap and talked to him about *Burning Down The House*. If we get the green light, he would be interested in playing one of the lead roles."

"Wow! Really?" My response was pathetic, but all I could manage at short notice. This was brilliant news.

"Don't forget, none of this happens if you can't find the two missing characters. Any progress on that?"

Jen responded.

"Nothing concrete yet. We're getting together with Jason later to have another crack at his memory!"

"So, Jason," I asked. "Who've you lined up for playing your good self?"

"That's a tricky one. We'll need two, don't forget. Young me and slightly less young me. We're still working on getting two fabulous looking blokes who are up to it."

"Don't forget the air of modesty as well. That's gonna be tricky," I grinned.

Flic got us back on track. The next couple of hours saw us move on from the children's stories and discuss potential locations for *Burning Down The House* (New York deemed too expensive), potential directors (Jen threatened violence when I suggested she could do it), and a schedule that saw us film late next year. Again, this all depended on filling in the rather large blanks. When the meeting ended, Jen left to pick up Charley from school. Angel and I were heading for Liverpool.

My knowledge of this area was almost entirely sports related. An annual trip to St Helens in the Bradford Bulls glory days and one forgettable (and expensive) day at the Grand National at Aintree. It was only when I pulled up outside the house that I realised I'd been here before. Not the house, the car park at the end of the road. It seemed like another lifetime now. A day with my ex-girlfriend, posing next to the statues on the beach before taking shelter in a pub.

Despite my garbled message, Bernadette O'Neill had called back. She was happy to meet. I assumed it was her at the front door, pointing at the drive. I took the hint and pulled through the open gate.

"Better to park on the drive. You must be Frankie."

"Hello, Mrs O'Neill. This is Angel."

"Please, it's Bernie. My mother-in-law insists on Mrs O'Neill, we don't need two of them. Angel, lovely name, come through. Tea?"

"Lovely, thanks."

"Sorry about the cooking smells, by the way. I've been doing another batch of lasagnes for the food bank. I take it as a compliment that we get complaints if I don't make them at least once a week."

Bernie left us in a bright, tidy room with views to a well kept back garden. I was drawn to the pictures which almost covered one wall. In pride of place was the Premier League trophy, flanked by Kenny Dalglish in a suit on one side and the happiest red-shirted man alive on the other. Except he wasn't alive. Not now. I recognised him from the newspaper reports. Danny O'Neill in happier times. My eyes moved across the wall. Every picture featured the same broad smile. It was like a shrine to the man who'd been killed, presumably in this room.

"My late husband loved that team," said Bernie.

She placed a tray on the coffee table and took the armchair beside the unlit fire.

"He looks like a real character," said Angel. I sat beside her on the plush sofa.

"You can say that again. He'd do anything for anybody."

We all stared at the photograph. It was Angel that broke the silence.

"Thanks for agreeing to speak to us, Bernie."

"I should be thanking you. It's about time somebody got to the bottom of what happened. We tried, of course, but…"

Bernie produced a tissue from the sleeve of her cardigan.

"I can't imagine how difficult it must be," I said.

"It is, even after all this time. Every time I look out of that window it all comes back. The kids are always on at me to move, start somewhere new. I know they're probably right. It's the memories though. The reason for staying is exactly the same as the reason for leaving. He's here, in every room, every tree in the garden, every brick. How could I go somewhere else? Maybe if you unearth the full story I'll get — what do they call it — closure?"

I held up my phone. Before I could ask about recording, Bernie just nodded.

"Tell me about Danny."

"He was the kindest, most gentle man you can imagine. If it wasn't for the robbin' he'd have been up for a sainthood, I reckon. After he came out of the army he was a bit lost. He fell into thieving through his family. A long line of villains. All of them loveable rogues."

"You said on the phone that you didn't believe the official story, the result of the inquest."

"Not a word of it. Complete cover up."

"Maybe you could talk us through what happened on the night?"

"We were watching the match. It was a Monday night, the patio doors were open like now. I was here and Danny was where you are. I heard something out the back, rustling in the shrubs. Danny said he'd go and check but I told him to carry on watching. There was only five minutes to go and we had a corner. He picked up the remote to turn the sound down. I went to the door and noticed one of the panels on the fence was broken, like somebody had been climbing over and snapped it. Next thing I know, the front door's off its hinges, noise like you wouldn't believe and three gunshots. Bang. Bang. Bang. Danny still had the remote in his hand but there was blood…"

I looked at Angel, not knowing how to react. She jumped up and knelt in front of Bernie, trying to console her. I couldn't help glancing at the garden. Sure enough, the top of one of the panels was still missing. Bernie took a deep breath.

"Thanks, love. I'm okay now. The police enquiry was a joke. They said Danny had a gun but it was the remote. They said that the officer that fired all three shots was acting in self defence. I recognised his face at the inquest, but he couldn't have been the shooter."

"How could you be so sure?" I asked.

"Because he was standing by the front door when the shots were fired but Danny…" Again Bernie took a deep breath to collect herself. "The blood sprayed towards the door. He was shot from the back garden. I saw somebody drop the gun and go back over the fence. They were all lying. Whoever the shooter was, it couldn't be the copper they said it was. Somehow, they convinced the judge that their version was right. Said I was in shock, unreliable witness. If that's the case, who broke my bloody fence panel?"

Was that why she'd never had it repaired after all this time? Somehow, it was still evidence.

"Believe me, Bernie, we'll do everything we can to find out who was behind the shooting. Could I just ask you something else? Was Danny the one who planned the jobs, fenced the gold and diamonds?"

"You're kidding. Danny? Strictly a squaddie, not officer

class. He took orders, blew safes and legged it quickly. Genius with a sewing machine too. I told him he should do that for a living. He said there wasn't enough money in it. Don't suppose we'd have a house like this if he'd been making show dresses."

"Show dresses?"

"Irish dancing. Both of our daughters loved it. Once the other parents knew Danny had made their dresses he was deluged. Spent every spare hour on the dresses. Raised thousands for charity over the years. As I say, a saint. Apart from the safe blowing."

"So you have no idea who the ringleader was?"

"None. They were very secretive. I'm not even sure he knew. It was just a job. Get told where to go. Blow the safe. Scarper with the stuff," said Bernie.

I looked at Angel. She didn't have anything to add. My stomach let out one of its famous rumbles.

"Sorry, Bernie. I think on that note, we ought to leave you in peace. You've been very helpful."

"Just make sure you nail them. I need it after all this time."

"We'll keep in touch. Thanks again."

We said our goodbyes and went back to the car. Angel went to the roadside to check that I was okay to reverse out. There was a tap on the window.

"Here, a couple of lasagnes for later."

She pushed a carrier bag through the open window and waved to us all the way to the corner.

12

"Excellent press release, by the way. Jason just confirmed that it's in this week's Stage magazine and one of the Sunday papers is running a special on Demus as the family man and storyteller," I said, dumping the wine carrier on the table.

We were in Jen's cosy kitchen. I ruffled Charley's hair. She didn't even look up from the picture she was drawing with a disturbing green wax crayon.

"Hiya dude." She gave me a high-five and switched to a red crayon. Jen broke off from peeling carrots and looked over her shoulder.

"Need I ask where she got that from?"

"Must be the school. You know what kids are like," I said.

I earned an eye roll from the five-year-old.

"I know what big kids are like. Make yourself useful and set the table. Just the two of us. Madame here has already eaten. Tell uncle Frankie what you had."

"Fettuccini-al-Charley."

"That sounds nice. You must be very important to have an entire meal named after you."

"Too right," said Charley. She was five going on fifteen.

"She'd live on pasta if I'd let her," added Jen.

"A lot of kids are like that," I said.

"Maybe, but few kids insist on pesto, olives, and anchovies to go with it."

"Respect."

That earned me another high-five.

"This is for you." Charley held out the picture.

"Thank you. What's the green thing?"

"It's you, silly."

"And the red thing?"

"Mummy. You're holding her hand."

"And is that you?"

"Don't be silly. I'm in bed. That's your wine glass."

"But it's bigger than Mummy."

Charley just nodded and collapsed in a fit of giggles. Before she recovered, Jen had swept her up and was halfway to the bathroom. Once teeth cleaning was complete, they would summon me for story duties. I had to admit. I liked this set up. This house felt warm and welcoming, and I loved spending time here. I wouldn't have asked to be drawn green, but I liked the size of the wineglass.

It was always an interesting decision about which story Charley would demand. Tonight it was a rerun of the one I'd made up for her on one of my early appearances. Ziggy Stardust And The Spiders From Mars may not have been the version that David Bowie had in mind, but Charley loved it. She just about lasted to the end before falling fast asleep. It was on our list for the series.

I crept out of the bedroom and headed for the kitchen, hesitating before entering. Jen was singing. I hadn't heard her sing before except on stage at Joe's club, and that didn't count, as we were all drunk. She was singing alongside Clive Gregson and Christine Collister. It was the Merle Haggard song, *Today I Started Loving You Again*. Perfect. Was it creepy to stand in the hall, just behind the door? I didn't care. I had to hear this. Closing my eyes, I leaned against the wall and listened.

I felt a hand on my shoulder.

Nabbed!

Jen must have heard me and come to investigate. I expected to get a hard time for spying on her. Instead, she steered me into the kitchen, continued to sing and we embraced, swaying to the music. Please let this never end.

"Shit. The broccoli."

Jen sprinted across the kitchen and rescued the pan that was boiling over. I've never disliked green vegetables as much as I did at that moment.

"Almost ready. Yorkshire puddings are rising."

I knew how they felt.

"Why don't you open a bottle and grab a seat?"

The spell vanished without even a puff of smoke. Or had it? As I poured the second glass, Jen walked up behind me and tenderly kissed the top of my head.

"Horseradish?"

"Pardon?"

"Would you like horseradish with your beef?"

"God, no. Can't do with the stuff," I said.

"Good answer, cos there is none."

I lit the candles as Jen served up the food. She switched off the overhead light before she sat at the table.

"This is all beautiful," I said. I meant every word.

"It's been ages since I cooked a roast like this. Never seems worth it for me and the pasta queen."

"Believe me. Yorkshire puddings like this are always worth it."

"Well, it's nice to be appreciated," said Jen.

"I am in awe of your puddings. I'm also very glad you came back to work. It's been brilliant working together again."

"It has, but I still feel guilty that I'm not spending all my time with Mum and Dad."

"You shouldn't feel guilty. They'll shout when they need anything. Ben seems to cope well with the chemo."

"Touch wood. It surprised me. I thought it would wipe him out, lose his hair, all that. But, so far, so good."

"I don't think there's a standard reaction to it."

Just for a second, Jen glanced across the room to the picture of Sean, Charley's dad, lost very young to cancer. She recovered and chatted about the scripts and the likelihood of working with Demus Wolf. Flic had signed him up to narrate all eight stories. The series would even be called Wolf Tales.

"I still can't believe he's agreed to read my dinky stories that I made up for Charley," I said. "Even better if we can get him for *Burning Down The House*. We can have a bit of fun, making him very sinister. Give the makeup people a challenge."

"You're not allowed to make him look like Gollum."

"Maybe not that far, but…"

Over the next hour, we discussed how we could dig deeper into the mysterious figures who'd made a career of robbing jewellers. There'd been no response to the message about Uncle Pete. Perhaps it had been a long shot. We were struggling to get anywhere with the mystery.

Jen slapped the table.

"Right, enough about work. It's Friday night and high time we had more wine," she said.

"You go through and get comfortable. I'll stack the dishwasher and open a bottle."

"Let me help."

"No. You cooked a superb meal. Let me look after you now. Pick some wonderful music."

Jen shrugged and, for once, did as I said. Within seconds, I could hear Scott Matthew. Jobs done, I joined her on the sofa.

"Do you mind if I put my feet up?"

"Of course not. It's your sofa, after all."

I was expecting the feet to come my way for a foot rub. To my surprise, Jen swung her legs the other way and hooked herself under my right arm, her head resting on my lap. I was very aware of the roast beef making bubbling noise deep in my stomach, but Jen didn't seem to mind. She balanced her wine glass with care, only realising the long stem caused a problem when she tried to drink.

"Help!"

I slid my hand under Jen's back and tipped her forward enough to drink from the glass.

"Ta."

I lowered her back to the horizontal. This nice little routine continued for almost an hour.

"Bugger."

"What's up?" I asked.

"I need the loo."

"Well, I can't help you with that."

Jen thought for a moment.

"If you loved me, you would."

"I do love you, you know that."

She squeezed my hand and wriggled a bit.

"I need to go. Sorry."

I helped her to an upright position. When she'd left the room, I thought about what had just happened. I told her I loved her. More to the point, had she engineered it? Either way, she hadn't run a mile. Luckily, the bathroom wasn't that far away. I heard the flush and realised I could do with going myself. When Jen didn't return, I made my way upstairs. The bathroom was empty. As I came out, Jen was standing by Charley's bedroom door.

"She's sparko. You tired her out."

"I do my best," I whispered. "More wine?"

"Not yet."

"That's not like you."

She just grinned and took my hand, steering me across the landing and into her candlelit room. Then the entire universe changed.

13

At just after five o'clock, I wondered where I was. Then I sensed rather than saw Jen, fast asleep, just inches from my face. So, it *did* happen. There was a chink of light coming from the gap between the curtains. Desperate not to disturb her, I eased out of bed, doing my best to gather up my clothes. I slipped out of the bedroom, conscious that Charley could arrive at any minute.

Once downstairs, I tidied away the glasses and other signs of our evening and its drastic change of direction. Over coffee, I reflected on last night. Without sounding too weird, it was the best night of my life. We'd both accepted that Jen wasn't ready for a close relationship. Sean's death had left such deep scars. She always said she'd let me know if things changed. They seem to have changed big style. At least, I hoped they had. What if this was just a fumble? No, too depressing to contemplate. Obviously, I contemplated it for about half an hour before giving myself a severe head waggle. Jen wasn't like that. Kindness shone from her. She was caring and smelt nice and made me float on a cloud of sweet, shimmering Barry White strings. I was smitten.

By the time I'd finished my coffee, I was wondering what to do next. I couldn't sneak out and go home. That seemed rude in the circumstances, but I didn't want to wake Jen. Opting for more coffee, I checked my phone. In particular, I wondered if there had been any social media reaction to yesterday's press release. There had. The tweet announced Demus as our storyteller for CBBC. It hinted he was the favourite to star in *Burning Down The House*. Clever, no confirmation of a green light, but enough to ramp up the publicity. The book had sold well and keeping the interest levels high could only help.

Any other time, I'd be all over our social media. I'd had other priorities last night. Rupert had done a good job. The tweet about the press release was gathering momentum. I scrolled through the various comments. On the whole, they were positive. Everything was a mix of congratulations and speculation about who could play other roles.

"Good morning you." I almost leapt out of my skin. Jen moved like a ninja, not making a sound. "Any coffee left in the pot?"

"Yes. Sit down, I'll get it."

"No. Stay where you are. I want to look after my man."

So, not a drunken fumble. It looked like I was her man. I almost cheered. Should I mention last night? I wasn't sure of the etiquette. I needn't have worried.

"Sorry I jumped on you last night. It just seemed right."

"Don't apologise. I had a lovely time."

That earned me a kiss as Jen sat beside me at the kitchen table.

"It was fun, wasn't it?"

I took a chance.

"Fun enough for a rematch?"

"Oh, I suspect that is a possibility, but not this morning. This morning is ballet class," said Jen.

For a moment I had a horrible vision of me pulling on tights. Jen saw my look.

"Not you, idiot. Charley. She'll be up and about soon. Good job we tidied away your sleeping bag from the sofa." She raised an eyebrow, and I knew what she was getting at. Explaining the new arrangements to a young, enquiring mind could come later. "What have you got planned for today?"

"Me? I'm not sure. I might call into the office later."

"No. It's the weekend. Leave that. Go home for a bit. Change your shirt and whatever else needs changing, but why don't you come back here this afternoon? Dad's coming round to plan the coast to coast walk. I thought you could help with that. Mum's taking Charley out for the afternoon. I thought I would bribe her to keep the little mite overnight. We could go out for a meal. Then we could, you know…"

For once, I caught on quick.

"I suppose the research can wait until Monday. I'll book somewhere nice."

Jen dropped me off at home, a very excited Charley waving from the back seat. I still couldn't believe how things had changed over the last twelve hours. It looked like everything I'd hoped for over the last few months was coming true.

"Bring a toothbrush tonight," Jen whispered as I left the car.

I floated through my front door, nimbly avoiding the pile of mail trying to block my path. It was no match for me. I was soon in my armchair with yet more coffee. That was as far as the plan went.

I switched on the TV. My Sky Q box appeared to be creaking at 95% full. That was good, in a way. It showed I was doing other stuff rather than bingeing on telly. I wondered what was taking up all the space. The answer appeared to be three months' worth of *Countdown*.

Countdown had been my guilty pleasure. When Dad got the dementia diagnosis, the doctor had recommended keeping him sharp by watching the show every day. We'd watched a few together, and I got hooked.

"Obviously not hooked enough to watch the eighty-four episodes that are stacked up," I said out loud.

At least I could make a start. My competitive nature always took over. Each show was a battle. Today was the opposite. Some freak of nature opened with nine letter words in the first two rounds against sixes for me.

"You can fuck right off," I said and zapped the telly. Instead, I settled on a soundtrack of Paul Buchanan and opened the *Notes* app on my phone.

In a supreme act of optimism, one note announced itself as *To Do*. This was my attempt to make sure I didn't miss those annoying minor tasks that were dropped when shiny things caught my eye.

1 — Bank statement.

I was meticulous about understanding every transaction and where my money was going — ever since Robbie. Bolting the stable door after the horse has buggered off with all the cash, but it made me feel more secure. I ought to get it done. Then again, it meant logging onto the bank site, downloading the statement, stuff like that. I yawned. The bank could wait.

"Think I'll save the excitement for later." Talking to myself suggested excitement had been in short supply until last night.

2 — Open post.

What can only be described as dread surged through me. I closed my eyes and crossed my fingers.

"Please. No stuff about being sued. Keep the post free of legal threats and I'll take my empties to the bottle bank every week."

I'm not saying there is a god of all things postal, but if there is, it pays to keep in with them. Small sacrifices like this must help.

I received little that wasn't junk these days, but a recent close shave involving council tax non-payment prompted the reminder. I ought to tackle this, given the mountain by the door. With the pile safely moved to the desk, I upped the volume on the music and began sorting.

Most stuff went in the recycling bin — a recent purchase after a bollocking from Jen. The rest included a letter from the council, thanking me for signing up for its online service.

"You couldn't email that? Save another tree."

Only one left. No US stamps. A visit to the bottle bank was confirmed. I'd saved the cheap-looking brown envelope to last. I ripped it open.

"Bollocks."

It was from the prison. Robbie had arranged a visit. She was serious about me getting in touch.

"And this is the thanks I get for sorting the post?"

Simply, I didn't want to go. I pushed the letter to the far corner of the desk. That would sort it.

Then I remembered I needed to sort out a restaurant booking for tonight. That was more rewarding. This needed some thought. I really wanted to go to Aldo's, the local Italian. The trouble was, I'd taken Robbie there at the height of our romance. Should I take Jen to the same place? Typical Robbie. She robbed me blind and was supposed to be out of my life. Now she was affecting my first proper date with Jen.

"Jen!"

The big, soppy smile came back to my face, and it banished all thoughts of Robbie. Five minutes of sitting and grinning culminated in booking us in for tapas. Who says I can't decide?

I didn't stop there. The decisions just kept coming. A bath rather than a shower; trousers and jacket not jeans; lucky blue boxer shorts from the recently returned suitcase (no point tempting fate); and ham rather than tuna sandwich for lunch (tuna can give me wind).

With decision making like this, it was no mystery why both personal and professional lives were going from strength to strength (assuming Guthrie didn't sue and bankrupt me).

I arrived back at Jen's at around three. Ben was already there, surrounded by maps, notebooks, and biscuits. I volunteered to put the kettle on before joining the planning session.

It was good to see them so relaxed together. They were back to normal after the tension of the last few days. Their affection was obvious, as was the enthusiasm for the walk ahead. It almost made me want to join them. Almost.

Ben's chemo schedule largely dictated the plan. His logic was that he would get weaker as the cycles took their toll. We pencilled in a date just four weeks away. The natural pessimist in me assumed that the chances of booking accommodation close to the route at short notice would be pretty much non-existent. I was wrong. I got the job of trying online booking for our chosen stops. When the computer said 'No', Jen hit the phone. She used her charm to get recommendations for nearby alternatives. In one case, the owner offered to bribe her teenage sons to stay with friends for the night so that they could make room. Only once did she resort to the tale about it being her dad's last wish. He rolled his eyes at that one and threatened to change his will. However, it worked, and two hours later, we'd booked the complete walk. To his credit, Ben didn't even flinch when Jen booked herself a double room for the midpoint when I was due to meet up with them.

Jen created a very detailed breakdown of the plan. When Ben went to the bathroom, she told me quietly that I was on emergency callout if anything went wrong.

"Don't worry, I can be at any of the stops within a couple of hours."

The plan was complete. They'd marked up maps. There was even a copy for me. Jen went off to get ready for our night out. It was Ben's turn for the lowered voice.

"I wanted to thank you, Frankie."

"There's no need. I'll enjoy coming over to meet you mid-walk."

"I didn't mean for the walk, although I'm grateful. No, I meant getting Jen back to work. I suspect we would have murdered each other if you hadn't. Also, I'm glad you seem to be, you know, getting closer." I don't know which one of us blushed the most. "She's been alone too long. You two are good together. You both deserve to be happy. Mind you, if you do the dirty, I'll break your bloody legs. Okay?"

He disintegrated into manic laughter. I think he was joking, but I had no intention of finding out.

14

 I'd spent the entire wonderful weekend at Jen's. The tapas restaurant had gone down well and we'd hardly stopped laughing throughout. By Sunday evening I was back at home. We agreed that Jen and Charley should stick to their normal routine for Sunday evening. I had vague plans for a drink at Joe and Ambrose's club, but for now, tea and antiques was fine. This week's roadshow was from Kettlewell in the Dales. It felt strange seeing the village that had played such a big part in our film, *The Hubberholme Syndrome*.

 As the director picked out several glorious views, the memories came flooding back. As one middle-aged woman sat at the table, I caught sight of the colossal figure of Ted II looming over her shoulder. He looked less than impressed by what he saw. I never found out how much the hideous doll collection was worth. The knock at the door was loud and insistent.

 "Angel. How did you know…? Silly me. You find stuff out. You'd better come in."

 "Nice place. Does it have any beers?"

 "Have a seat."

 Angel propped the guitar case in the corner and I went to the kitchen to grab a couple of beers. I was gone maybe twenty seconds, but during that time, Angel spotted the letter from the prison. Not bad from that distance.

"Cheers. I couldn't help notice the visiting order."

"How the f–? Never mind. Yes, it came on Friday."

"Does that mean you're going?"

"No. Well, I don't know. What good would it do?"

"It would help Robbie, you know, the woman you were going to marry. The one having a hard time in prison."

"And why is she in prison? Oh, silly me for forgetting how she committed huge scale fraud and wiped out my bank account. Not to mention leaving it to me to cancel an entire wedding."

"She said you could be a selfish prick sometimes."

"Me? Selfish? Look, I was quite happy, sitting watching Antiques Roadshow and quietly fancying Fiona Bruce. I didn't need you coming round here giving me a hard time and calling me a selfish twat."

"Prick."

"What?"

"I called you a selfish prick. Anyway, I was merely quoting Robbie."

"Oh, that's okay then. Worth giving up my Sunday evening for. What are you doing here, anyway?"

"Again, not entirely friendly. You could do with working on your anger issues. Maybe a chat with Robbie would help? Look, don't get your Calvin Klein's in a quiver. I bring information."

"What information?"

"Just wind your neck in and I'll tell you, ungrateful arsehole."

"Thought I was a selfish prick."

"You're multi-faceted and an ungrateful arsehole. Do you want to know the name of your getaway driver or not?"

Now she had my interest. I leaned forward.

"How did you do it?"

"I told you. I find stuff out. Very resourceful, me. Anyway, his name was Peter Parker."

"I know," I said.

"Leave it out. Why didn't you tell me?"

"Sorry. I wasn't aware I had to report back to you. You've confirmed what me and Jen found. The question is: how?"

"Don't ask me that. I'm like the Pope — never reveal my sources."

"I'm not sure the Pope is who you mean."

"Oh, but it is."

She tapped the side of her nose and winked.

"Tell me what you know about him."

"I got it from the woman who knew him as Uncle Pete."

"Hang on. I contacted her through a direct message. How did you—"

"Look, we're on the same side? Does it matter that I had a quick peek at your Twitter account? While we're on the subject, you need to use stronger passwords." I struggled to put my annoyance into words. Angel took my spluttering as a signal to carry on. "Okay, I didn't hack your account, but the look on your face suggests I'm right about the passwords. All I did was contact the woman who'd replied to you. While you were asking nice polite questions, I tracked her down through the pictures she's posted. She's called Karen and lives less than a mile from here. Turns out after a few drinks she's quite chatty."

"So why didn't she reply to my message?"

"I told her not to bother, that I'd bring you up to speed. Which is why I'm here. Worth another beer, or are you going to throw a wobbly?"

"Help yourself," I said, on the verge of a wobbly.

Angel returned with two more beers.

"How come this Karen is happy to talk about her uncle if it

looks like he was involved in breaking the law?"

"I think the way she sees it, everybody was breaking the law back then . Besides, he's not her real uncle. All the kids just called him Uncle Pete. He seems to have known every family on the estate. Dead popular as well. By the sound of it, if your telly packed up or there was more week than money, Uncle Pete would step in."

"Loan shark?"

"No. That's the thing. He took nothing for it. Seems he just enjoyed helping people. Karen remembers him drinking with her mum and dad in Mary's Bar, just up the road from here. When he did, the local kids would ask if they could wash his car. He always had pound coins for the kids at the end of the night."

"Was he, you know… dodgy?"

"She says not. Just genuinely cared about people. Anyway, he's in his eighties now. Lives in a care home near Huddersfield. The only driving he does is a mobility scooter around the grounds once a day. He had a stroke a couple of years ago. It left him struggling to speak clearly and now his left arm is pretty much useless. Nice old bloke, though, slightly touchy-feely, but remembers enough about his previous job."

"You mean you've spoken to him?"

"Greeted me like a long-lost friend when I went for the second time. Spent all afternoon with him. Filled in quite a few of the gaps."

"Did he give you the name of the bloke who fenced the jewels?"

"Ah, the infamous Fifth Man. No. I'm pretty sure he remembered, but he clammed up. I'm certain he was terrified, to be honest. Wouldn't talk about anything for ages. We ended up doing a jigsaw for the rest of the afternoon. By the time I was ready to leave, he'd got over it. Asked when I was going again."

"So, when are you going back?"

"I'm not sure I am. Why should I put myself out to visit somebody who sees the same four walls every day? Not much in it for me. Know what I mean?"

It was all too clear what she meant.

"If I went to see Robbie, do you think it would help you see why you might visit again?"

"Who knows? Acts of kindness bring their own rewards."

"I thought the saying was that no kind act goes unpunished?"

"That's very cynical Mr Dale."

Angel reached into her jacket and dropped an envelope on the coffee table.

"I wrote up some notes for you. No progress on identifying the dirty cops involved in covering up Danny O'Neill's killer. That might take a bit longer. Can't stop now, though. I'm on my way to sing at Joe's club. Are you coming?"

"Sorry. Can't tonight. I've got work to do."

"Another time, eh?"

"Sure. That would be good."

Angel finished her beer, picked up the guitar case and was gone, just as the muted Fiona Bruce was saying goodbye.

Should I have gone with Angel? I'd kind of planned to go to the club anyway and her singing was great. However, the lure of the envelope sitting on my coffee table was too strong. I needed to know more about the mysterious Peter Parker (Spiderman or not).

I killed the TV and flicked the music to random. Lindsey Buckingham's *Trouble* filled the air. As I opened the envelope, I hoped it wasn't an omen.

15

On Monday morning at ten o'clock, I was at the new offices. Flic had called a meeting. At least it meant seeing Jen for the first time in almost eighteen hours. Parked outside the office, her car glinted in the spring sunshine. To my intense annoyance, parked next to her was the same white van. Parking there once was bad. This was taking the piss. Frustration boiled over and I blasted the horn. That'll show him. Nothing happened. Muttering lots of swear words, I reversed into one of the three empty visitors' spaces opposite.

I swore again at the van as I walked to the office. The van didn't seem to care. Bloody thing. In contrast to my grumpy mush, the face that greeted me was fresh, smiley, and professional looking.

"Good morning. You must be Frankie. I'm Melanie, the new office manager and occasional receptionist."

Melanie stood and stretched a hand towards me. I did my best to change the grump into a smile. It ended up just looking creepy.

"Pleased to meet you, Melanie. Sorry, I don't always harrumph like that. There's a white van parked in my space. I just got annoyed."

"Oh. Let me sort it for you."

"That's okay. I'm in a visitor spot now. I'm only here for a couple of hours. Welcome aboard. It'll be an exciting place to work."

"It is already. I can't believe he's coming this morning."

Did she mean Jason? If anything, I was the celebrity around here. I'd been on *'The One Show'*. That was from before we opted for the anonymity of working as Vince Taylor.

Melanie continued.

"The others are in the boardroom." I hesitated. Where the hell was the boardroom? Melanie's professionalism was impressive. She swept her arm towards the stairs, making it obvious where to go. I gave what I hoped was my winning smile and made my way upstairs.

I could see the others through the open door. So this was the boardroom. Jason was on coffee duties. As he was pouring, Flic grinned at me.

"Jen was just telling us you two have got it together at last. Congratulations."

I thought about feigning outrage that the secret was out, but I couldn't. The beaming smile on my face was instant and heartfelt. Jason handed me a coffee and added his congratulations. It was quite a start to our meeting. I picked a seat and settled in.

Daydreaming through meetings was my speciality. It took a moment to realise the room had gone quiet. That was a sign that I'd missed a question aimed at me. Before I could decide who I needed to ask to repeat themselves, I realised everybody was looking at Melanie. She had her phone to her ear and was nodding. That was a bit much, wasn't it? Taking a phone call in the middle of an important meeting. It got worse. She nodded at Flic, stood up, and left the room.

My first impressions of Melanie had been very favourable. She didn't make a fuss when Jason had given me the Elsa mug. Turns out it was a gift from her *Frozen* mad daughter. She'd seemed perfect. Now she was wandering off in meetings. How wrong could I be? I would have a word with Flic later.

"I think that's a good point for a comfort break," said Flic, rising from her seat. Five minutes later, Melanie was back in the room. The only way to describe the figure beside her was to say it glowed. Not in a Rudolph sort of way. In an 'I'm a star' sort if way. Demus Wolf was in the building.

He floated across the carpet and hugged Flic like the old friend she was. Flic introduced him to Jason (firm handshake) and Jen (hug and Jen almost exploding with joy) and then, me. I managed not to make a complete idiot of myself, even though I suspect I held onto his hand just too long. When Demus spoke to the group, it was strange. The voice was so familiar, yet odd to be coming from somebody standing in our office. Sonorous — was that the word?

"It's fantastic to meet you all. In my defence, it was Flic's idea to keep today's visit secret. She thought it would be funny to see your faces. She was right." Demus laughed and pointed at me. DEMUS WOLF WAS POINTING AT ME!!! I did my best to act cool, but Demus Wolf was in our office and joking with me. Okay, I was star-struck. He continued. "I'm so happy to have the chance to work with you guys. I loved *The Hubberholme Syndrome*. The performance you got out of Roddy, the story — everything. I loved it and I'm very excited to get my hands on the script for *Burning Down The House* as soon as possible."

Flic was next to speak.

"Demus has agreed to present all eight of the children's story series and record them for the audiobook. In addition, one thing we are keen to do is use Demus in the pitching of the entire *Burning Down The House* project. His face will sell this series. It's early days, but we want to get some photographs, maybe even a short video with Demus in full makeup. Even if the image changes for the actual drama, it will help us with the sale. I thought we could agree on some of the character points. Maybe Jen and Frankie can come up with some dialogue to allow Demus to work on the voice. That kind of thing. We've laid on a working lunch. We have the man for an hour, so let's work him hard."

Demus laughed. "Flic's right, use me and abuse me for the next hour. Then I fly to LA for a meeting. It's a hard life. The key to this is the illusion. Get the audience to see what you want them to see, nothing else."

We'd got to work. I never even considered the range of food that Melanie had wheeled in. Jen and I scribbled some notes. We kicked around ideas for accent, pitch, mannerisms —everything that would bring the character to life. Then the magic happened. Taking a deep breath, Demus transformed. A shiver ran down my spine as he spoke the words. Jen and I exchanged looks. This was it. He was our lead character. Now we just had to work out who he was in real life, then write six hours of gripping television. Bring it on.

16

On Monday night, Jen was once again running the writer's session at the community centre. Despite everything, she turned up every week, giving encouragement to new writers. It was how we'd first met and where I took my first Bambi-like steps at putting words on paper. Well, on a laptop anyway.

"Do you want me to come and help?"

"You're off the hook. I'll see you tomorrow. Relax for the evening. See if Rupert can play out or something."

"If you're sure."

A pint with Rupert sounded good, but I had some thinking to do. It wasn't just the usual 'what's for tea' type of thinking. Deep, meaning of life type stuff.

I stared again at the letter. Tomorrow at 3pm I would sit opposite the woman I had been due to marry. The voice in my head screamed.

Run away. Head for the hills and keep going.

I returned to what Angel had said. Robbie was stuck, staring at the same four walls, day after day. Could it hurt to sit for half an hour and listen? I had loved her at one time. Fair enough, she'd stolen all my money and trashed my whole life, but...

I was too busy with the research. If Guthrie went ahead with his threat… She'd be disappointed, but hey, she disappointed me when my wedding got called off.

"Bollocks to it. Decision made. I'm not going."

I would spend the afternoon with Jen, working on something important. Our writing world was comfy and warm. A haven where only good things happened. And we had biscuits.

Then again, there was Angel. She would get annoyed if I bailed out. That was scary, but what could she do? I was a grown man. An adult sometimes. Nobody forces me into anything I didn't want to do.

So, on Tuesday afternoon, I sat in the visitors' car park of the prison, clutching my piece of paper. I'd invented a dental checkup to explain my absence from the office. It was a white lie, but still bad.

Jen and Robbie had history, having been close friends at one time. Not now though. In line with my mood, the weather had changed in the last half hour. A perfect spring day had been replaced by fine rain. Was the world telling me something? It was almost time to go in. *Way Back Home* by Junior Walker and the All Stars was playing. I couldn't cut this short. I'd listen to the end of this song, then go in.

The windscreen misted over. Somehow, the building in front of me seemed even more depressing. The building itself was modern, two storeys, concrete, drab. All topped off with the coiled razor wire on top of the walls.

The music took the piss, moving on to *The Letter* by The Box Tops. I still held the scrunched paper. It looked battered now. I knew how it felt. Okay, if I wait until this song finishes, today goes well. One minute fifty-two seconds, according to the playlist. I watched the seconds counting down. Fourteen, thirteen, twelve…

Right, whatever song comes next, I take it as a sign… three, two, one… Four Tops - *You Keep Running Away*. Now that wasn't my fault. The universe is telling me something. I turned the key in the ignition and slipped into reverse. I couldn't go in. Levi Stubbs sang his heart out for a lost love; I buggered off, heart pounding, and ran away from one of mine.

It was silly, but I just couldn't step into that place. I was a coward, and I was doing what cowards do best; legging it. I drove for ages, with no idea where I was going. I saw the sign for Skipton. The friendly welcome waiting at the pub in Kettlewell was what I wanted. Jim, the landlord, wouldn't judge me for running away, especially if I didn't tell him I had.

Twenty minutes later, I was nosing the car into a parking space. Memories of filming came flooding back. We'd made some good friends here. I needed to get better at keeping in touch. Before leaving the car, a thought hit me: how would I explain my visit here to Jen? I was at the dentist, not having beer in the pub. I'd already lied to her once and tried to keep a secret. No way was I adding to that. I started the engine again and headed back home.

All the way back towards home, I was muttering to myself.

"How could you lie to Jen?"

It was a bad way to start our new relationship. Angel had annoyed me too. What did she know? There was no way I was still in love with Robbie.

I looked at my watch. It was just gone five. Jason had been due at the office today. Would he still be there? I wanted to chat to him about whether he'd heard of Peter Parker before (the driver, not Spiderman).

The office was on my way home. I pulled into the near deserted car park. There was only one space taken. The white van was there again. The day's anguish welled up. I screeched to a halt inches from the rear of the van and blasted away on my horn. Had I paused for a second, I may have recognised how demented I must've looked. At that moment, I didn't care. What gave this idiot the right to park in my allocated space?

Huge, dark storm clouds had replaced the fine rain of earlier. The car park resembled a scene from Blade Runner. A loud rap on the window.

Where did he come from? A hooded figure didn't look too pleased. I pushed open the door and tried to leap out, almost throttling myself with the seat belt. By the time I untangled myself, some of the impact was gone. Also, I was nose to chest with a very solid and angry looking man.

"Do we have a problem, pal?"

The accent seemed local, but the shock of red hair suggested Viking raider. Blind rage was confusing my brain, making me think I was braver than usual.

"Don't call me pal. Yes, we have a problem. What gives you the right to park in my spot? Every time I turn up, there you are in my space. It's not a hard system, you arsehole." I pointed at the disk attached to my windscreen. "There you go. Official parking permit. F Dale number six."

"And you're F Dale are you?"

"Yes. Of course I am." I was almost screaming now.

"Well, that's very nice for you. The trouble is, my permit says Penelope's Parcels, Number nine. And this is number fucking nine. Number six is over there, tosser."

He pointed to his right. Even through the torrents of rain, I could see the markings now. Eight, seven… six.

Bugger.

Of course, Flic and Jason's cars had often occupied two of the spaces.

Double bugger.

A fraction of a second before I continued shouting, my brain caught up with my mouth.

"Shit. Sorry. I am very sorry. It's just…"

"Like I said — arsehole. Now, are you going to shift your car or am I reversing into it?"

I got back into the car, legs shaking. I stalled the engine on the first attempt before reversing. The white van shot backwards, screaming to a stop an inch from my bumper before roaring off into the rainy afternoon. Waiting until he was out of sight, I headed for home, as Jason wasn't in the office, anyway. Could today get any worse?

As I reached home, my heart sank. Sitting on the wall, arms folded, was Angel. She did not look happy. The suspicion that I caused the unhappiness almost made me run away again. This running away business was getting ridiculous. I decided against, in part because Angel was now standing behind the car, blocking any speedy exit.

"Angel, what a delightful surprise. You should've called. I almost went out for the night."

"Don't give me that, you swivel-eyed, treacherous scumbag."

As I thought — not happy at all.

"How do you mean?"

I tried to keep my tone light and cheerful, but my legs were like jelly.

"You know very well what I mean. Why on earth didn't you turn up this afternoon?"

"But… I did, kind of."

"How can you kind of turn up? You either did or you didn't, and I say you didn't."

"What makes you think, I mean, how do you know?"

"I find stuff out. Remember?"

Of course. She always knew everything. Impressive, but so

intimidating.

"Cup of tea?"

"No. I'm too fucking angry with you just now. I might not keep myself from damaging you, big style. Robbie is in bits. She somehow thought that you'd be man enough to see her. Let her explain what happened and why. Takes guts that. Whereas you are a coward. Twat!"

"I'm sorry," I said. "Let me try to explain."

Then I realised, as Angel's staring eyes tried to bore a hole through me, I couldn't explain. .

"Well?"

"Sorry," I mumbled again. "I think you're right. It makes no sense at all."

"I still think, somewhere in that tiny, neanderthal brain of yours, you still love Robbie."

"No. You said that before and it's still no." The sharpness of my shouted response shocked me. "I'm very much in love with Jen. She's my future. Robbie is my past."

"You sure about that? Have a think about it. I'll email you some more notes about your getaway driver. Don't know why I'm still helping you. Think again, otherwise..."

I rubbed at the pain where Angel had prodded at my chest. She marched off up the road. Should I call her back? What would be the point? I let myself in, locked the door behind me and sat on the bottom step, staring into space. Had Angel just threatened me? Don't be daft. She's just frustrated that I was messing with her friend.

I needed Jen, just the two of us, curled up on her sofa. I was just about to call her when I remembered she was spending the evening with her parents at some kind of family do.

A beer and *James Brown At The Apollo* was my compromise. I remember hearing *Think* then waking up just after ten. I poured the remains of the beer down the sink and went to bed. I gave up on sleeping just after four. This was getting silly.

17

I parked in my spot without making an idiot of myself (again) and entered the office with no drama. He couldn't be a great parcel man if he's always parked out front, unless he's so quick at delivering that he spends most of the day with his feet up.

Melanie was her usual smiley self. We chatted at the reception desk.

"I can't believe how much I love coming to work. Will he be back in the office?"

Her crush on Demus Wolf seemed to be as intense as mine. Flic had been working with the actor to produce what she called a sizzler — a short trailer to help sell the series. Today, we got to see the result. It was quite exciting, if I was honest. The script for the trailer was short but punchy and satisfying.

Jen swept through the front door. She kissed me then was straight into an involved conversation with Melanie, like they'd known each other for years. I wandered off in search of coffee.

Flic and Jason were in the boardroom, looking pleased with themselves.

"Good morning. Do I take it you have good news for me?"

It was Flic that answered.

"We sure do. Hi, Jen."

I handed over a coffee to Jen, and Melanie did likewise for Flic and Jason. We all sat around the table. Flic continued.

"As you know, we engaged a young director called XS to work on the sizzler. He was quite open that he would do it on the understanding that it's an audition for *Burning Down The House*. He's come up with something special."

"XS? What kind of name is that?" I asked, sounding more like my mum than I'd ever done.

"He's all about the brand. His real name is Jeremy, but he gets a bit upset if you call him that, apparently. He uses X for short."

"I suppose you can't get much shorter than that," I said.

"But he's good and keen to work with us," said Flic. "If this impresses you as much as me, we've found our director."

"So, we have the clip?"

"We do. Jason, do your stuff. I'll get the lights."

The big screen on the wall was solid black. Then that voice kicked in. It sounded like Demus was sitting a couple of inches from my ears, speaking only to me. I knew the script by heart.

"This is the story of over-powering ambition: mine. It's a story of friendship, at least between the other four men. It's also a story of cunning, treachery, and deception."

I realised the camera had been pulling back. A closeup of the black suit that Demus was wearing had provided the black screen. His face, half in deep shadow, emerged. He turned to the camera, a slow, unhurried move, revealing a face scarred by burning. The voice dropped to a whisper.

"This is a story of revenge. Mine."

The shot cut to red wires connected to a black box. The explosion was as unexpected as it was loud. A blinding flash followed by an orange fireball before the screen faded again to black. Melanie's scream was still ringing in my ears.

"Sorry, sorry. It just scared the life out of me," said Melanie, trying to regain her composure.

"It was a fantastic reaction," said Jen, sounding delighted. "I think it proved that it worked. I want to see this already."

"Suppose we'd better get our fingers out and get it written then," I added. "Or at least discover who our characters are."

Flic switched the lights back on.

"I take it you agree we've found our director?" Flic smiled, and we all nodded. "Melanie, could you set up a meeting as soon as possible?"

"I'll do it now." She picked up her notebook and left the room.

"So, how is the investigation coming along?" asked Jason.

"I think we're making genuine progress," said Jen. "Frankie's new friend, Angel, seems to be quite a star at digging up information and filling in the gaps of our knowledge."

I explained how we ended up with Angel's research. Flic seemed very interested.

"Why don't we get her on the payroll? If she's that good, we could use her."

"I'm not sure," I said. "She's somewhat abrasive."

"She scares him," said Jen with a grin.

"I'm not scared. Okay, maybe, but don't tell her."

"Look, we'll leave it in your court. If you think we should make her an offer, let me know and we'll make it happen."

Before I could reply, Melanie's scream got all our attention. She was downstairs at reception, her distress clear. We all charged for the stairs. I was first to reach her.

"What is it? Are you okay? You look very pale."

Melanie sobbed and pointed at the reception desk. She'd just opened a large Jiffy bag. I edged the corner open.

"Careful," whispered Melanie.

I froze as I looked inside. Two red wires attached to a black box.

"Shit." I dropped the edge of the bag and looked at the others. "I think we need to call the police. It appears to be a bomb."

We all gathered outside. The blue flashing light appeared in the car park within minutes. I was quite pleased to see the long arm of the law in the familiar figures of Smirky and Tinkle. PC Paul "Smirky" Newhouse and PC Kate "Tinkle" Smith had become friends of mine after a shaky start, even appearing in several scenes in *The Hubberholme Syndrome*.

We exchanged pleasantries before Smirky got down to business. He adopted a very similar approach to mine, lifting one edge of the Jiffy bag.

"Shit." He dropped the edge of the bag and looked at Tinkle. "I think we need to call Cagney. It appears to be a bomb."

Great. Let's get the entire team here. We'd had dealings with DI Cagney and DS Casey, too. At least they'd stopped seeing me as a chief suspect in every crime they came across. As Smirky made the call, I wondered if we should alert the people in the other offices. The thought of getting our white-van-man to evacuate his premises was not very appealing. I'd leave that to the authorities. Smirky suggested we all wait outside in the car park. Before I left, Tinkle tugged on my sleeve and raised an eyebrow. I pointed to the far side of reception and she disappeared towards the sign marked *Ladies*.

Cagney arrived, sporting a new, full-length, black leather raincoat. Whatever image he was trying for, it hadn't worked. Casey took up his customary position, hovering a couple of yards behind his boss.

"Casey, have a look and confirm Newhouse's theory."

If looks could kill, Cagney was in trouble. He edged a few

yards further back as the younger officer edged towards the Jiffy bag. His reaction was predictable.

"Shit. I think we need to call the bomb squad."

Cagney was making the call before Casey finished the sentence. They dispatched Smirky and Tinkle to evacuate the rest of the offices. Casey got busy with a roll of coloured tape to keep back the crowds. Cagney had at least stopped calling me Mr Dale.

"So, Frankie, any idea who would send you a bomb through the post?"

I shook my head before Melanie cut in.

"It didn't come through the post. The package must've been hand delivered when I was upstairs in the boardroom. It was here when I got back."

"Any CCTV?"

Melanie looked at me. I looked at Jason and Flic.

"We've only just moved in, it's on my list to get done," admitted Flic.

Whatever else I felt about Cagney, he was a master of the withering look. I could hear sirens in the distance. As they got closer, I could see a crowd, maybe a hundred people, shuffling to the edge of the business park. A large van with the magic words on the side accompanied the police car — 'Royal Logistic Corps - Bomb Disposal'.

Two figures dressed in camouflage gear got out of the van. After a brief word with Cagney, they entered the building. It was then I realised that everybody else had moved at least a hundred yards away, but the five of us from our office still clustered around Cagney. I was relieved when we got the order to move back.

Cagney perked up as another white van pulled into the car park. He straightened his tie. We were going to be on telly. I guided Jen away from the others. Out of hearing range, she looked at me.

"What's up?"

"Maybe nothing," I said.

"Go on."

"It's a nagging thought. I sort of pissed off Angel last night."

Jen looked a bit confused. Then, she saw what I was getting at.

"Are you saying you pissed her off enough for her to be responsible for this?"

"Well, she does kind of have form. Don't forget she fire bombed her ex cos he upset her."

"Jesus, Frankie. What the hell did you do? And before you say anything, if you cheated on me I'll feed—"

"No. Nothing like that," I said, crossing my legs. I took a deep breath and told her the full story of the letter and my absence yesterday.

Jen listened before asking her question.

"Why the hell did you run away?"

"I… I suppose it… it just felt wrong. And the place scared me. I know, I know. I'm pathetic. But, after everything, why would I want to see Robbie again?"

Before we could go any further, Cagney was waving at me. He wanted to speak to me from the look on his face. I walked towards him.

"The bomb squad wants a word with you."

"Me? Why me?"

"Think they've seen you on '*The One Show*' and want an autograph? How do I know? Come on."

"Hang on. Can't they come to us? Maybe it's not safe for us to go to them."

"It's not a bomb."

A couple of stomach muscles relaxed. We entered the building. One of the team was already loading their kit back into the van. The other was waiting by reception.

"Have you opened your mail at home this morning, sir?"

"No. You don't think there's another bomb at my house, do you?" This came out almost as a squeak. I was panicking.

"There's no bomb, sir. We found this note in the envelope."

He pushed a handwritten note across to me.

'*Frankie, you ungrateful twat. This is the CCTV system I mentioned in my other letter. Love Angel x (You're still an ungrateful twat.)*'

"You are familiar with somebody called…" He paused and looked again at the note. "Angel?"

I nodded.

"And, sir, did you, by any chance, receive a letter at your home address telling you to expect a package?"

"No! Maybe? I don't always open letters when they arrive, so, I don't know. It's possible."

"Would you do me a favour, sir?"

"Anything."

"Read your mail before you call us out next time. Have a nice day, sir."

I sensed a certain lack of respect in the final 'sir'. He marched off, having a brusque word with Cagney on the way. Cagney issued a quick bollocking to Casey, who strode off to administer career advice to Smirky. I could see Twinkle in the distance, waving the crowd back into their respective offices. Today's entertainment seemed to be at an end. Melanie came over, still clutching a tissue.

"I'm so sorry if I caused a panic," she said, sounding worried.

"Please, no, don't apologise. It's not your fault. I thought it looked suspicious. Better safe than sorry."

"I think it was the sizzler that freaked me out."

"Shows it was effective. A huge coincidence that the wiring looked so similar. Why don't I put some fresh coffee on?" I said, glad of something to do. "This can go in the back of my car, out of the way." I gathered up the Jiffy bag and made for the car park. Twinkle dashed past me, sprinting across reception. A tall red-haired, white-van-man was limping past our front door.

"Dickhead," he mouthed.

Not nice, but I suppose I can let him have that one.

18

We caught up with Smirky and Tinkle over coffee, then Jen and I said our goodbyes and headed for the cottage. I couldn't resist calling in at home. Sure enough, there was an envelope waiting. The same rushed handwriting as before. I scooped it up, and five minutes later, was with Jen at the cottage.

She was already sitting at her desk, staring at the Post-its on the wall. This had become a regular start to our working day, reviewing the latest timings for the eight episodes, and having a natter about the stories. We weren't far off finalising all the scripts. Every day, we'd settle down for a solid couple of hours of writing before I qualified for lunch. Today was a late start, but I knew better than to challenge the system.

On my desk was a brown package, about the size of a shoebox. The familiar scrawl on the label had the word 'ungrateful' then a squiggle. I could guess what that said.

"Thanks for bringing this in," I said to Jen.

"Bringing what in?"

"The box. I presume it was on the doorstep."

"What box?" I pointed at my desk. "Never seen it before," she said.

How the hell had Angel got inside to put the package on

my desk? Maybe I didn't want to know. I opened the envelope first. It contained some notes about what Angel had created. She used the term Raspberry Pi twice. I made a mental note to Google it later. We had detective work to do.

Thanks to the earlier notes from Angel, we fleshed out the story of the getaway driver. As we'd covered our whiteboard in small yellow squares for the children's stories, I adopted a high-tech approach for our gang research. We were now using Stickies, the online equivalent of Post-its. This gave us the added advantage that we could access them from both offices. For once, technology was making life better.

"Can I ask why you discounted Parker originally?"

"It was the legal team from the publisher. I wondered at the time if somebody had leant on them, but they were adamant that we couldn't release his name," said Jen.

"What made him so special?"

"Apparently, he's very well connected. Before he had his stroke, there was talk of him being made mayor."

"Really? How come?"

"Charity work. Over the years, he'd donated hundreds of thousands to local causes. He was some kind of saint."

"But the evidence points to him as the getaway driver for a vicious gang of thugs."

"I'm still convinced he was the driver. The vicious thugs bit may be a bit of a stretch."

"But they killed Jason's dad, that —"

Jen cut me off.

"It sounds daft, but until that point, they appeared to be perfect gentlemen. With all the jobs they carried out, not a single threat of violence. Nothing. Then a shotgun gets used and everything changed."

"Where did the donations came from?"

"It seemed genuine. His delivery and removals firms did well, and he was terrific at getting publicity for sponsored walks and events. He always had a steady flow of celebrities to endorse stuff or sponsor him."

"There must be some dirt on him."

"We need more facts about this guy," said Jen, throwing a pencil onto the desk.

"I think you're right. Besides, I'm too hungry to think."

"We agreed we'd do two hours before lunch."

"It must be about two hours. How long have we done?"

Jen looked at the screen.

"Twenty-seven minutes."

"Like I said, almost two hours."

I sat back and clutched my stomach.

"Go on then. We can't have you wasting away to nothing."

I almost ran to the kitchen. I already knew we had a treat lined up. We'd got into the habit of taking turns to provide lunch. No sad ham sandwiches today. Jen always played a blinder.

"You still think it's funny to put mine in a Peppa Pig lunchbox?"

"I take pleasure where I can," she said.

I slid the Cinderella lunchbox across the desk to her and focussed on the pig. My box was full to the brim. A baguette, stuffed with pastrami, cream cheese and sun-dried tomatoes, cut neatly in half, two mini pork pies and a banana arranged as a smiley face and a small bag of dates. She'd once again reinforced that she was the woman for me.

"What do you think about the idea of making Angel official? She seems very… resourceful."

"That's a good word for her," I said through a mouthful of sandwich. "We still haven't worked out how she got in and delivered the package."

"Well, maybe that's another reason to have her inside the tent pissing out."

"Yeah, I assumed she was still angry with me, but she still

delivered it."

"Flic thinks we can put Angel to good use. Maybe you should have a word. "

"Why me?"

"You're the one who knows her but, if you're too scared of her…"

"She doesn't scare me. Okay, she does. But, yes, I'll approach the subject next time she breaks in."

"What is it she's made?"

"It's some kind of CCTV system for the offices."

"You mean in case somebody breaks in?"

"Yeah. Funny that. I'll have a play with it tonight." Jen looked over her glasses at me. "What?"

"I was kind of assuming you would have your hands full tonight," she said.

"What did you have in mind?"

"A nice steak, salad, and maybe something exciting for afters."

"What if I'm not that kind of bloke?"

"Oh, you are. You most definitely are. My place at seven."

"You're on."

I could squeeze in an hour's playtime.

I didn't need to work that long. Jen left the office mid-afternoon to pick up Charley. At five o'clock, I could wait no longer and opened the latest letter from Angel.

I'd already Googled Raspberry Pi. Why didn't she just say computer? I realised I knew the concept behind them. I'd just never had the patience to make anything. My background was in building websites, not gadgets, but it intrigued me. She'd basically rigged up a two camera system for the cottage. Motion sensors triggered it, just like a commercial security system. The clever bit was, besides video footage, the system would take a picture of anybody moving around. It used facial recognition software and decided if it knew the person or not. During the day, the system added any unfamiliar faces to the database. Outside office hours, a stranger would trigger an alert to my phone, stashing photographs of anybody who shouldn't be there. Ingenious. Borderline illegal, but bloody clever. Where was she getting the facial recognition software from? Had she done all this herself?

Within half an hour, I had rigged up the cameras. One pointed at the door, the other at the window. After a bit of trial and error, known to us IT professionals as buggering about, I got the system to recognise me and add my photo to the database. Angel's note said that she was still working on the phone app, but she provided a way of accessing the photos on my desktop. All I needed now was a stranger to call, and I could test it properly. I looked at my watch. Correction. What I needed was a shower, a change of clothes and to get my arse to Jen's.

"So, you played with your new toy?"

"How did you know? I mean, what makes you think that?" I couldn't stop the grin.

"Since when can you ignore a shiny new toy and instead concentrate on achieving a deadline?"

"But it's brilliant stuff." I ran through the main bits of the system.

"Is it legal to take photographs of people and use facial recognition to identify them?"

"I wondered that," I said. "In the end, I reasoned we would be okay with normal CCTV. The dodgy bit is where she's getting the facial recognition data."

"I'd rather not think about that. Like you said, she's resourceful. Does it work?"

"I've only done the first part. It picked up my presence and added me to the database. I need to get somebody into the building outside office hours so that the system triggers an alarm. We need the phone app, but she's working on it."

"Maybe you should recruit her to work with your IT company."

"I thought that. She'd be useful on both fronts. "

"How does she make a living now?"

"That's a fair question," I said. "I've got no real clue. I know she busks in Leeds and she's done the odd evening at Joe's. Is that enough to make a living?"

"Maybe she has ill-gotten gains to fall back on," said Jen.

"Thought it was me who was supposed to make that kind of comment?"

"I apologise. I think we should sound her out. The info on Parker is great. We could do with her digging up the big guy now. The sooner the better. Anyway, you're not the only one with something new. Wait there."

Jen slipped out of the room. My mind wandered to the possibilities. She might return to model new underwear. I know, but I'm a writer. I have a vivid imagination. Jen called through from the kitchen.

"Are you ready?"

"You bet."

Jen burst into the room and posed. She looked the same. Stunning — but clothed. Panic rose. What had I missed? Jen took pity on me and pointed at her feet. I twigged.

"New walking boots! They look great." Not what I imagined, but I raised my enthusiasm levels.

"My old ones were getting tatty, so I thought I'd invest in these little beauties. I've been wearing them around the house to break them in."

"We could try a walk this weekend, a training session for the coast to coast. No need to go mad. We can stroll along the canal into Leeds and catch the bus back. It's about nine miles.

Plenty of opportunities to abandon and catch a bus if you get blisters."

"I take it the tea shop has nothing to do with your suggestion?"

"A piece of cake always goes down well."

"You know what — you're on. Too far for Charley. Why don't we do it on Saturday? I'll get Mum to pick Charley up from the dance school. You can buy me lunch in Leeds."

"Thank you very much."

"I have one condition. Don't look so worried. You need to visit Robbie."

A cold sweat appeared on my forehead. I thought, deep down, Jen would approve that I'd run away. She was no lover of my ex.

"But… I…"

"I know. It's a scary place, and you're not very good at conflict. I know she hurt you, but even Robbie doesn't deserve to be ghosted like this. It's one afternoon. Hear what she has to say. If you still want to ghost her after that, it's fine," said Jen.

"What if she wants me back once she gets out?"

"Is that what you want?"

"No, of course not. I'm spoken for." I reached out and took hold of Jen's hand.

"Then I've got nothing to worry about, have I? I suspect you'll end up sleeping better. I must admit, I'm worried about how little sleep you get these days. It can't be good for you."

"Do you think it will help?"

"It can't make it worse. Anyway, there's another reason you should go. We need Angel onside. If she's pissed off with you, she won't help us fill in the gaps with our story. If we don't find our Fifth Man, we don't get to make the series."

I was going to meet Robbie.

19

It surprised me that arranging a visit was simple. I rang the prison and spoke to a very helpful lady. I explained that I'd been due to visit, but an emergency had detained me. She'd laughed at her joke about being in the right place for it. She'd tapped away at her computer.

"How about today at 2.30?"

Who knew it was that easy?

The room looked familiar, like every visiting room in every prison drama on TV. I read somewhere that it's because they shot most scenes at the same disused prison. I picked at my thumbnail and looked at my watch again. The door opened and a steady stream of eager faces scanned the room, picking out loved ones and taking seats. Robbie met my eye and smiled, just as I was thinking she'd had a better offer. My heart flipped. I'd once fallen in love with that smile. I'd planned to spend the rest of my life waking up next to that smile every morning. She looked somehow smaller than I remembered, her skin duller, but still unmistakable. It was Robbie.

She slid into the seat opposite me. Neither of us knew the etiquette in this situation; not surprising. We spoke together after an awkward silence.

"Sorry," I said. "You first."

She smiled again, but her shoulders hunched.

"Thanks for coming. I wasn't sure that you would."

"You should thank Jen. She was the one that convinced me. And Angel, she terrifies me, if I'm honest."

"Don't worry about Angel. She's a very loyal friend, but harmless. Well, maybe not harmless..." Robbie took a deep breath and attempted to relax her shoulders. "Rupert tells me you and Jen are..."

"Yeah. It's taken a while but, you know..."

"So no hope for me then? I'll be out in two years. We could start again. Don't look so terrified. I'm winding you up. We both know I screwed things up."

I shuffled forward in my seat before speaking.

"Why so keen to see me?"

Robbie rubbed her face with both hands before leaning forward. Our faces were now just inches apart. I could see the faint remnants of a cold sore on her top lip.

"I needed to explain why I did what I did."

"You mean stealing all the money and ditching me just before our wedding?" Robbie looked as if I'd slapped her. "Sorry, there was no call for that."

"I don't blame you for being angry. Believe me, I loved you so much. Still do, if I'm honest."

"Then why?"

"I think I understand it now. I've been having counselling in here. The sessions have helped me to understand how corrosive my dad was. You know him, what he was like."

"There was no way to say no to him," I smiled.

"And you saw him, from an adult viewpoint."

"Steady on," I said.

Robbie smiled.

"You're more grown up that you give yourself credit for. You should be more confident. But imagine how I felt. From being tiny, all I wanted was to please Dad. I lived for his approval. Now I realise he just controlled everything in my life. I worked in his business. I lived in an apartment next to his house. Whatever he said, I did it."

"You could've chosen not to. We were building a life together, had money. We'd bought our first home. You could have said no."

"But that's just it. Nobody got to say no to him. The police only know a fraction. He controlled dozens of legitimate businesses and many more that were illegal. Dad cultivated people in high places. He always had something, leverage to get what he wanted."

"But he didn't have that kind of lever with you, did he? You made a conscious choice to help him."

"I suppose I did, but it always came down to needing his approval. In the end, I was neck deep in the corruption. I had no alternative."

"There's always an alternative, Robbie."

I could see tears welling in her eyes. We both leaned back in our seats, taking deep breaths. Just as I thought we were done, Robbie spoke.

"I read in the papers that you were working on this new TV series."

"How did you know that was us? We work under an alias to keep our privacy."

"Rupert mentioned it. He said you were having trouble tracing one of the gang members."

"Yes. He was the leader, planned the jobs, fenced the stuff. He seems to have disappeared without a trace."

"It's just possible I could help." I looked at her, open-mouthed. "Dad kept records. Very detailed records of everybody he came into contact with. He had something on everybody."

"And you think he knew this gang? Bit of a long shot, isn't

it? How many criminal gangs were there?"

"It might surprise you. It sounds like these guys made lots of money. Anybody making lots of money from crime would've interested my dear father. As I say, he had a lot of contacts."

"So, where are these records? The police crawled over his property."

Robbie looked around her before leaning forward again.

"He used a solicitor. Very private, very discreet. Very respectable, on the surface. He controls the files. They used to be in old-fashioned ledgers until his daughter pushed him into the 21st century. Now it's all digitised. I was only part way through building an index for them when we skipped town. Those documents would be priceless. A writer might find inspiration in them for a lifetime's work, and specific details on certain individuals. Explosive stuff, in the right hands."

"And this solicitor will just hand them over to me, will he?"

"No. But he'd hand them over to me if I asked. I made sure that his little secret was in a separate file. When it comes to dirty tricks, I learned from the master. That's why I was desperate to see you. I hope, in some small way, I can make it up to you by handing the files over. Are you interested?"

"It all sounds dangerous, to be honest."

"If nobody knows you have the files, it's safe. Just be very careful how you use them."

"And what's in it for you?"

"Peace of mind. Knowing that I've paid you back. Although, when I get out of here, I'll need to make a living, so I want a copy too. Oh, and there's a section that's got extra security. That's for my eyes only — no trying to crack the encryption. What do you say? Do we have a deal?"

What the hell was I getting myself into if I agreed? Could I decline the offer?

"In theory, if I agreed, how would you get the files released?"

"I'd speak to Rupert. He could contact the law firm and we'd go from there. Are you in?"

I sighed and gave the slightest of nods.

There was a general scraping of chairs. The visiting session was over. Robbie glanced around before standing. I reached into my jacket pocket.

"Here, I almost forgot. I brought you a present."

I handed over the Crunchie that had gone soft. Robbie smiled.

"And you asked what was in it for me? Take care Frankie. Please come again soon and give my love to Jen. Tell her… I'm sorry for what I did to her, too. I should've believed her."

Driving away from the prison, my stomach churned. Was I doing the right thing? It could make the difference, and the script for *Burning Down The House* would be a tremendous success. Robbie wanted to speak to Rupert before I did. She would look after her brother.

Would Joe be at the club yet? The sun was over the yardarm and I could do with a drink. I needed to contact Angel, but had no way of doing so. She'd always just sort of appeared. I dismissed thoughts of the film Beetlejuice. Angel was singing odd nights at Joe's club. He must have a phone number for her. I made my way through the rush hour traffic before pulling up opposite the club.

A locked door barred my way.

Bugger.

As I reached into my pocket for my phone, the door buzzed and clicked. A metallic voice told me to enter. Joe was making his way across the dance floor as I reached the bottom of the stairs.

"Good to see you, Frankie. Come through. Ambrose has just poured us both a loosener. I take it you'll join us?"

"So, this is what you get up to?"

"The long hours need some rewards." said Joe. "Beer?"

"Yes, please."

Joe was married to Robbie's brother, Rupert. He co-owned the club with Ambrose. My three best friends are under one roof most of the time. The setup was working well with Ambrose running the record shop with cafe attached during the day then, at night, the same venue became a supper club, music venue and record shop run by Joe. It seemed to be a growing success.

Ambrose appeared and the three of us settled into a booth.

"Rupert's coming over later," said Joe. "Why don't we make a night of it?"

"Don't you have to work?" I asked.

"The team can run this place with their eyes shut," said Joe.

Ambrose laughed. "He watches them like a hawk."

"I can still do that and have a drink. Come on, what do you say? It's been a long time since we all got together."

"I've got the car outside," I said, sounding feeble.

"It'll be fine there. Smirky and Tinkle are on late this week. They'll check on it. Anyway, you need to tell me all about your bomb scare."

I squirmed, which appeared to be hilarious to Ambrose and Joe.

"I suppose Tinkle told you all about that?"

"Yeah. They call in so she can use the facilities."

"Makes sense."

Sitting here with my friends was very appealing. I wasn't due to see Jen until tomorrow, so a distraction tonight would help. I just needed to make sure they didn't lead me astray — again.

"Joe, before I forget, do you have a contact number for Angel? I could do with speaking to her."

"Sure, I'll send it to you, but she's due in tonight. She's on stage at nine."

I convinced myself that I was saving the cost of a phone call by settling in to wait for her. Only three hours till stage time. How much damage could three hours do?

"So, how's business?"

Ambrose raised his bottle.

"Best deal I ever did." He and Joe clinked bottles. "I can't believe how well the two businesses go together. Record sales are way up and we pack this place at least four nights a week. This man is a genius."

"I wouldn't quite go that far," said Joe. "Gifted entrepreneur with a rakish smile, maybe. Anyway, part of the success is down to Angel. She's packing 'em in at the moment. Great voice. Why do you need her?"

"To be honest, I was going to offer her a job."

"Whoa! No stealing the talent. The way we're going, this time next year, we'll be millionaires."

"All right, Del Boy. There's no reason she couldn't do both. I want her for some consultancy. She seems to have some very special talents."

Joe agreed and signalled for another round of drinks. For the next couple of hours, we sorted out the problems of the world. It was only when nature called I realised I had a bit of a wobble on. When I got back to my seat, Angel had joined us. She smiled as I sat down. Joe had been called away to deal with a minor crisis behind the bar. Ambrose and the recently arrived Rupert were deep in conversation.

"Thank you," said Angel.

"What for?"

"Going to see Robbie. She called me earlier. You made a big difference to her mood."

"I did nothing."

"You turned up and listened to her. That's all she wanted. Not that hard, was it?"

"Suppose not. Listen, thanks for the camera system. It's quite something."

"Not quite a bomb, though?"

"How did you hear about that?"

"I find stuff out, remember?" Is there anything this woman didn't know, or couldn't find out? "Do you think I'd hand deliver a bomb to your offices?"

"No, not at all," I said.

"Loads of better ways to do it. Calm down, it was a joke. God, some people get jittery when bombs get mentioned."

"Can we talk about something else, then? How's the phone app coming along?"

"Pushed for time, but I've made a start."

"I might help with that."

I explained I was still a partner in an IT firm, then realised that she'd already found that out, obviously. She accepted my offer to hook her up with Spud to speed up the development work.

"I have another offer," I said.

"I seem to be very popular."

"We, that's me and everybody at the production company, have been talking about you. Your detective skills have impressed everybody. Are you interested in some consultancy work?"

"What kind of consultancy?" asked Angel, looking dubious.

"Finding stuff out."

"Sounds like me. Does it pay well?"

"Depends what you find out," I said.

"Okay, you're on."

Angel spit on her hand and held it out. She roared with

laughter at the look on my face and held her palm up to prove she hadn't spit on it. I shook it, and we were in business.

"Seeing as I'm now on the payroll, I've got something for you. I went to see my mate Peter this afternoon at the care home. He had another visitor, his grandson. Turns out he was a constant companion when he was a kid. Grandad told him all kinds of stories. Grandad's stroke means he struggles to tell those stories anymore, but the grandson remembers every detail."

"You mean he knows about the gang?"

"He was hinting at that. Was coy. I suspect he's looking to, how shall I put it… benefit from the knowledge."

"So he wants cash?"

"Don't we all."

"Could you find out how much?"

"I'm meeting him tomorrow afternoon."

I swigged the rest of my beer. Angel stood up and walked to the stage. She picked up her guitar and launched into an acoustic, slowed down version of Edwin Starr's *25 Miles*. It was incredible.

The rest of the evening followed the same blurred pattern. Joe calling for more drinks, Angel singing like — well — an angel, and Rupert gazing at Joe. He was well smitten.

"You'll wear him out, staring like that. At least save a bit of him for another day," I teased.

"I know some of it is beer goggles, but he just presses every button for me."

"Uugh. Get a room."

"We're married. We can do it in any rooms we fancy."

"Too much information, mate."

"Keep it under your hat, but I've just arranged another room for us! It's his birthday next month. I've booked a surprise week in Spain. A few days in Granada. Moonlit tour of the Alhambra, dinner on the terrace of the Parador, the works. Then lie on a beach for the rest of the week."

"That sounds fabulous. He's a lucky man."

"No way. It's me that's lucky. I can't believe how much life has changed."

"I'm pleased for you. When are you going to tell him?"

"Just as soon as I've told Ambrose."

"Ambrose? Ah, you need to break the news to him. He's running this place by himself for the week."

"Got it in one. I'm sure it'll be okay."

20

This did not feel good. My head hurt. Joe was definitely a bad influence. I had no idea what time I left last night or how I got home. It was daylight, but at this time of year, that didn't narrow it down much. I pulled back the bedroom curtain and my heart sank. Outside the house, parked neatly, was my car. No way had I driven home. That was a line I would never cross. Drinking-driving was a big no-no. Somehow, the car got home. I needed coffee.

I went downstairs — mystery solved. There was a note on the table.

When did you last service the car? I'll have a look at it for you when I get a minute. Hope hangover bearable. Took me all my time to get you upstairs. Nice boxers. Just flick the switch on the coffee machine. Angel x

Should I feel relieved or be sick? It looked like Angel had driven me home and put me to bed. The car key was beside the note. I shuffled across to the coffee machine. There was water in the reservoir and fresh, rich coffee in a new filter. I flicked the switch. She'd even positioned a mug next to the machine. This was gold standard looking after. Maybe she was okay after all.

The magic coffee seemed to take forever to drip its way

through the filter. Could I justify a glass of water and go back to bed? My phone registered a new text which answered the question for me.

Where are you? Your Stickies are going cold and this bacon butty won't write itself xx

Despite everything, I managed a smile. Jen was in the office. Of course I would go in. Drastic action was called for. Ten minutes later I'd showered, dressed and poured the jug of coffee into my special *Tim Peaks* travel cup. I had a five-minute walk to work, so no driving required.

When I arrived, Jen was in the kitchen. I joined her and leaned in for a kiss.

"Oh dear. No offence, but you stink."

"I just showered."

"The body's fine. The breath is like a brewery toilet floor. Sit down, I'll stick your butty in the microwave."

I did as I was told and shuffled my pathetic body through to my desk. With a supreme effort, I lifted the cup to my lips and the life-giving coffee transfusion began. It was hot and strong. It seemed to understand the size of the task it was embarking on. As the microwave dinged, I took another sip.

"Can I have tommy sauce?" I croaked, emphasising my suffering.

"You mucky pup!"

"What?"

"Look at your shirt."

I risked looking down. My pristine cream shirt was now sporting a large dark stain, starting just below my chin. Closer inspection of the cup revealed I hadn't got the lid on right. Every time I'd taken a sip, I'd dribbled coffee down my front.

"Bugger."

I unscrewed the offending lid and placed it on the desk. Jen arrived with a roll of kitchen towel and dabbed at the stain.

"Not got my magic stain stuff here. That'll have to do for now."

"Thanks."

I raised the cup to offer a toast to Jen. I somehow caught the lip of the cup on the lip of the idiot and poured most of the contents down my shirt. Jen rolled her eyes and pushed the kitchen roll across the desk.

"I spend my whole life cleaning up after small children," she said, shaking her head in disbelief.

She didn't seem to have tremendous sympathy. The coffee was hot, and I ended up doing a weird dance, trying to lift the shirt from my skin and stop the pool of liquid that was oozing its way towards my keyboard. Five minutes later, order restored, I'd remembered an emergency T-shirt that was stashed in my desk drawer. I kept it pristine throughout the latest coffee and the bacon butty.

"Does sir feel better now?"

"Yes, thank you. Much appreciated."

"Need I ask how you ended up in that state?"

"Joe."

"Enough said. Maybe not a great idea on a school night?"

"No. You're right but, I made some progress."

"Okay, I'm all ears."

About to make my lame joke about them not being that big, I stopped when the raised eyebrow silenced me. I told Jen about Angel and how Parker's grandson might help, for a price. I held back what Robbie had offered, as it could take some time to get hold of the files.

"So he wants money for helping?"

"Yes, but that's nothing compared to the TV series and sales of the updated book. It would be satisfying to work out who he was after all this time — get some kind of justice for Jason. All those years and the police haven't solved his dad's murder. We could do it."

"Sounds bloody dangerous to me." I must admit, I'd been worried about that bit. "I wouldn't want to do anything that puts Charley in danger," said Jen.

"We won't. If we're getting in over our heads, we back off and hand everything to the police."

"We have to make sure we're ready to film the CBBC shows."

I nodded.

"Go on then Sherlock. Pay the man."

My phone rang. It was Angel. Jen went back to her laptop as I answered.

"Morning sunshine. Got your trousers back on yet?"

"Yes. My trousers are on."

Jen looked over her glasses at me and just shook her head. I made a sort of shrugging gesture and Jen went back to typing.

"I've been busy this morning. Assuming you are up for paying him, Parker's grandson is up for a meeting."

"When?"

"Five o'clock, your new office."

"Today?"

"Yes, today. I thought you had a deadline. Can you get a grand by then?"

"That's steep, but ..."

"Right. I'll meet you there."

I was nervous. Parker had asked for a grand to help us with our story. I'd seen enough telly to know you didn't just hand the cash over. The offer would be £300 today and the rest when we have the full story. Besides, the cash machine limit is £300 a day, so it would have to do.

Let's face it. A grand on this would be nothing if I ended up being sued for breach of contract. Losing that would wipe me out. I had to take the risk. Making a success of this was my best hope.

It was strange that Angel wanted to meet at the new offices. I'd pictured a drive to some industrial estate or multi-storey car-park. Some cloak and dagger would've been nice for my money. At least the office was convenient. My parking space was empty. Then again, it always had been. I pushed through the heavy doors, expecting Melanie to be behind the reception desk.

"Hello Mr Dale. I'm Tom, Melanie's new assistant and receptionist."

Since when did Melanie have an assistant? Tom must have seen the question mark on my face.

"I just started this morning and recognised you from the photo Melanie gave me."

I shook the outstretched hand.

"Pleased to meet you Tom. So many fresh faces at the moment. I'm expecting a couple of visitors in the next few minutes. Angel—" I realised I didn't know Angel's surname. "Just Angel, no surname. Like Madonna. Like A Virgin?"

Not a flicker. Nothing. What do they teach them in schools these days?

"Never mind. Anybody else here today?"

"Melanie is in the open plan office. Flic is in Leeds at the BBC and Jason is working from home. Jen is…"

The notepad in front of him didn't know where Jen was.

"Don't worry, I've just been with Jen at the cottage. I'll pop in and see Melanie. When the visitors arrive, could you bring them up to the boardroom?"

"Certainly. Would you like me to do drinks?"

"Tea please, that would be great."

Ten minutes later, after a quick chat with Melanie, I was at the boardroom table. The door burst open, and I heard a familiar voice from outside.

"And the afore-mentioned dickhead should be…"

I was about to object to being described like that in front of our mysterious source. The face I saw knocked the wind from my sails.

"You?"

"I believe you two have met informally," said Angel, relishing the element of surprise. "Al Parker, this is Frankie Dale. He's not really a dickhead. Not all the time, anyway."

The tall, redheaded white-van-man looked as uncomfortable as I felt. We both managed a quick handshake, and I gestured for them both to take a seat. This was awkward. What were the chances that our neighbour was so connected with the case? His limp was heavy as he moved to a seat.

"Are you two going to play nice or do I have to keep you apart?" said Angel. She was enjoying this far too much.

"I'm sure we can get along just fine, assuming Frankie has the cash for me," said Parker.

I opened my notebook and slid the white envelope across the desk. Parker took the envelope and resisted opening it. Instead, he left it on the table in front of him.

"Looks light to me," he said.

"All I could get at short notice. You get the rest when I'm convinced that what you have is worth paying for." I hoped I sounded like some badass gangster. Maybe not.

"This is a waste of time."

Parker pushed his seat back. He was going to leave. Angel stepped in.

"Come on Al. That sounds reasonable. I thought you wanted this cash to do something nice for your grandad and the residents at the care home?"

That seemed to work. He pulled forward again. Angel nodded at me and I picked up my phone.

"Are you okay if I record this? It will save taking notes."

"No. No recordings."

"Okay."

I made a point of folding my large notepad to a fresh page, writing the date and underlining it.

"Before I tell you anything, I want your agreement that we protect Grandad. He's an old man. His health is not good. I can't tell you anything if that puts him in danger of prosecution."

"Mr Parker, I'm not from the police or the crown prosecution service. I can't offer immunity or anything like that. All we want is to clear up a mystery from twenty-five years ago. I'm sure that, given his age and health, the authorities would act accordingly." I had no idea if this was true, but I needed answers. "Why don't you tell me about your family and we'll go from there?"

There was a tap on the door. Tom wheeled in a trolley with flasks of tea and coffee. Angel poured and passed around the biscuits. Parker stirred in two sugars and took a sip.

"My dad upped and left when I was seven. Just legged it one night. A few weeks later, Mum crashed her car, killed instantly. My grandparents took me in."

I was making notes, but already felt awkward. This seemed difficult for him to talk about. What right did I have to ask? Then again, we had a TV deal to chase.

"Grandad tried really hard, but it was difficult for him. He wouldn't talk about Dad. He was a Pete as well. Three generations, all called Peter Parker. Al is my middle name. Whatever other skills the family had, picking names wasn't one of them. Whenever I asked about Dad, my grandad just sort of clammed up."

"It must've been tough for you."

"At first it was, but my grandparents doted on me. Grandma was a superb cook. She tried really hard to make sure I had everything I needed. Grandad was away at work sometimes. When he was at home, he used to let me help him around the car, cleaning it, changing the oil, that sort of thing. As I got older, he taught me how to strip the motor down. I was driving by the time I was twelve."

"What did he do for a living?"

Parker shifted in his seat. I thought he was going to clam up again.

"I think you know what he did."

"He drove the getaway car for a gang of jewel thieves."

"Granddad was a driver. He would act as a chauffeur. Sometimes he made deliveries, others he was more like a taxi. A quick taxi." Parker smiled without confirming or denying my statement. "He had a series of very nice cars. They were his pride and joy. He loved driving.

"I need to ask the obvious question. Who did he work for?"

"Honestly, I've got no idea. I was just a kid. Would you know who your grandad worked for?"

"Fair point."

"Did you ever meet any of his friends? Did anybody come to the house regularly?"

"I don't remember anybody coming to the house. There was one night. I must've been eight or nine. Grandma was out. Bingo or something. He got a phone call and seemed to argue with somebody. When he hung up, he told me to grab my coat, we were going out. I sat in the back of the car. I just remember how quick he drove. It was brilliant. Fastest I ever moved. We drove for ages, then pulled into some factory yard. That bit was scary. He got out. Told me to stay where I was and keep the doors locked. He was gone for ages. Later, he looked like he'd been in a fight. There was something wrong with his hand and blood on his face. He told me not to tell Grandma. He winced as he put the car in gear and we drove back more slowly."

"And you have no idea who he'd met."

"None, but it was the first time I wondered what his job was. He'd been a nice bloke who gave my piggy backs. Now he had a darker side."

"How much does he remember?"

"Most of the time, not a lot. Every now and again he'll say something, mention a name or a job, but there's no way of knowing if it's something true from his past or whether he'd seen it on the news ten minutes ago. That's why I don't want you talking to him. He's unreliable. My main concern is to protect him."

"I understand that, but to be fair, you've not told me a huge amount. You must have more."

He took a deep breath, weighing up how much he could tell me.

"I don't know a lot. There are bits and bats that I've pieced together over the years. You're not the only one who wants to be a detective. I've been looking into my old man. I need to know why he left. Look, I've got notes at home. I'll put something together for you. Hopefully, you'll think it's valuable. I would be grateful if you could give me any information you find out on where my father disappeared to. I'm still keen to track him down, get to know him."

"Okay."

I gave him a card with all my contact details and walked him to the door.

After he'd gone, Angel was subdued.

"Sorry about that," she said.

"How do you mean?"

"I thought he'd be more useful than that. It felt like he was more concerned with tracking down his errant father than with helping us. Good job you kept most of the money back."

"I'm not too downhearted. Let's see what he has. Have you thought any more about working here?"

"Have you got enough for me to do?"

"Let's get the phone app finished, then we can talk. Have you spoken to my mate, Spud?"

"Not only spoken to him, we met up this morning. We should have a demo version for you by the end of the week."

"That's great news. Spud's a good guy. His work is top-notch."

"Cute too. Don't tell him I said that."

"Your secret's safe with me."

The word cute is not one I'd have used to describe Spud, but I suppose Angel had been locked up for a long time.

"Something I've been meaning to ask," I said.

"Shoot."

"I know the fire bombing was mistaken identity, and you got the neighbour rather than the boyfriend, but why do it?"

"Cos he was a dipshit."

"Yeah, but by that logic, most of the south of England would be ablaze."

"He lost all our savings. We'd been saving for a house. He bought a wreck without consulting me, just so he could be on that stupid show about renovating crappy houses. Idiot made it so open-plan that the lot fell down. Well, near enough. Ended up selling it for next to nothing. Like I said — dipshit! Fancy a pint?"

"Better not. Too much the other night. Thanks again for getting me home."

"No problem."

"Can I give you a lift?"

"No thanks. Think I'll walk. Nice evening. Shame to waste it. Laters."

With that, she was gone. I realised I still didn't know where she lived.

Melanie was still at her desk, and she assured me she would lock up. I wished her goodnight and headed for the car. I looked both ways as I reached the main road, but Angel was nowhere to be seen. She just disappeared. A very interesting character and useful to have around.

Down the road, I looked to my right and saw Angel heading across a field. She appeared to be singing, not a care in the world. Not a bad way to be.

21

Friday morning saw me in the cottage early. The predicted showers were due to move away by mid-afternoon, so my plan was to make genuine progress on the research early. With work done, Charley might enjoy the play centre in the beer garden down by the river. If her mum and I had to wait for her, we may as well have a beer or two. We could round it off with something and chips before heading back to Jen's.

Patience was not one of my virtues, and I was desperate to see what Al Parker could add. I didn't have to wait long. The snap of the letterbox almost gave me a heart attack. A white envelope had appeared on the doormat. Scooping it up in one hand, I opened the door with the other. This achieved two things. First, I cracked my knee against the door, which hurt — a lot. Second, I saw that whoever had posted the letter had scarpered. Of the deliverer, there was no sign.

Slamming the door more heavily than was necessary, I hobbled back to my seat, rubbing the painful knee and swearing like an expert. Who says men can't multi-task? I soon tore the envelope open, along with the skin on the inside of my index finger. I once read that paper cuts were more painful than gunshots. My suspicion was that this was bollocks, but it stung a bit. This detecting business was dangerous, but surely Miss Marple never got damaged like this.

After much finger sucking and more swearing, I extracted the sheet of plain white paper. It looked like someone had removed them from a printer or photocopier. I remembered an incident in my brief career at the call centre. My boss had despatched a colleague to the photocopier for some blank sheets for a meeting. When he didn't return, they sent me to find him. He was standing next to the machine as it printed out one hundred copies of a blank sheet. I amazed him when I showed him how to open the drawer and extract a wad of pristine paper.

Anyway, that wasn't important now; the note from Al Parker was. The hand-written sheet was neat, with the text double spaced. Not much for a grand. When I read the note, it seemed an even worse deal. It was polite and business-like, but the message was very clear. Parker had changed his mind and wanted nothing to do with us. We were to have no further contact with his father and he considered the matter closed. No mention of my £300, cheeky sod.

I threw the note on the desk. How could he take my money, then tell me to bugger off? I grabbed my jacket, determined to march into his office and tell him what I thought of him. For good measure, I'd punch him in the face and take my money from his wallet. Then again, he was twice the size of me. I'd end up in the hospital or lose the rest of my money. I slumped back into my seat, determined to grumble at him from here.

"Why the face?"

It was Angel, standing by the door.

"Your mate, Parker, ripped us off."

"How do you mean?" I told her about the note. "I'll pay him a visit. Get him to think again."

"No. Let's not antagonise him any further."

"We might not need him, anyway. I've been digging."

Angel added two unfamiliar names under the row of question marks: Eddie Elgin and Dougie Dwyer. She pointed at the names and explained.

"When I was with the old man, I noticed a photograph. He told me it was him with a couple of mates from the old days — Eddie and Dougie. Told me if I ever needed to buy a car, Eddie was my man. I said I might be in the market, so he told me where to find him."

"Let's go," I said, getting excited at the thought that this might be a lead.

"Hang on. We're talking about a picture that was almost thirty years old. I checked out the site. It's now a hand car wash. Eddie was long gone. Parker told the story like it was yesterday. When Eddie had the site, it was a small petrol station. It had spaces for three or four cars at a time, with cheap window stickers displaying the prices. Grandpa didn't buy any of these, but the two of them did deals and new cars arrived."

"Any sign that he stole them to order?"

"No idea. Parker just said there was never a problem getting what he fancied. He even bought his first van for the removals business that way. Parker lost touch with him after a fallout. Wouldn't say what the fight was about."

"Is he in touch with him now?"

"Not seen him for years."

"Could be our man?"

"Worth putting him on the board, certainly. He had lots of contacts for getting hold of cars. It would be good to know what they fell out about."

"What about the other bloke? Dougie?"

"Dougie Dwyer. The three of them were regulars at *The Robin Hood* in Wyke. They met up every Thursday night to play dominoes."

"Have you checked out the pub, see if anybody remembers them?"

"Same scenario. It closed down years ago."

"Another dead end?"

"Not quite. One thing I know about old Dougie was that he was quite handy with his fists. Liked a fight, at least. He had a very obvious black eye in the photo. Parker just laughed and tapped the side of his head when I questioned him. Sorry, you'll need to excuse me. Dodgy curry."

I was about to object, but she was gone. I looked at the unfamiliar names on the board. Then I realised I didn't have a clue what to do next. Could one of them be a criminal mastermind? My first option for any project is Google, but I didn't know where to start. I typed in Dougie and Dwyer. What were the odds on it turning up the top result headed "Criminal mastermind living in Bradford". It turns out it was quite long odds. My search returned over 557,000 results. I might need to narrow it down a bit. There must be fewer results for Eddie Elgin. Wrong. Just over four million.

Detecting was harder than it looked. Luckily, Jen arrived bearing croissants, so I went to make more coffee.

"You've been busy," she called through to the kitchen.

I explained about Angel's meeting with Parker and the photograph.

"So, you think one of these two is our Fifth Man?"

"I think it's a bit early to say. It's a start," I said. "Oh and, you won't believe this, Parker turns out to be the owner of the white van that kept parking in my space at the office."

"Except he didn't," said Jen. "The complete swine parked in his own space."

"Technicality," I said, placing two coffees on the desk. "What were the odds of him being our neighbour?"

"So, do you have some kind of conspiracy theory? He moved in before Flic formed the company, somehow predicting that we would rent an office next door?"

"When you put it like that…"

"It makes a kind of sense that a courier has a base next to the airport. Makes for a quick getaway if the whole parcel delivery gig falls foul of the law."

"You think he's a criminal?"

Jen was laughing out loud by now.

"No, you idiot. Of course not. He's a respectable businessman who just has a dodgy grandad. You just don't like him because you made a tit of yourself over parking."

"Are those croissants just for show?" I think I'd made a good job of changing the subject.

Jen pushed the bag of goodies across the desk. I tucked in and returned to the Stickies.

"Robin Hood keeps cropping up," I said.

"How do you mean?"

"Well, your walk finishes at Robin Hood's Bay. Parker drank in the *Robin Hood*."

"Hardly a classic whodunnit pattern, is it?"

"No, but you discounted Parker because of the charity work he did. Jason mentioned his dad supported lots of charities. Could the entire gang have been some kind of modern day Robin Hood?"

"You mean stealing from the rich and keeping most of it?"

"Maybe not."

"Have you spoken to Angel about working for us?"

"I mentioned it, but nothing definite. She's working with Spud to finish the phone app. We said we'd discuss it again later in the week."

"For my money, we need to get her on board straight away. She's very… resourceful."

"She's here by the way," I said. I pointed towards the bathroom. Jen looked puzzled but continued.

"We could do with her checking out these two."

"Couldn't we do that?"

"Maybe. Have you forgotten we're due in the studio next week to record *Wolf Tales*? They want us there in case there are any last-minute changes."

"Next week? I thought that was ages away."

"Didn't you read the email?"

That could be it. The extra formality of running a proper production company had swelled my inbox to breaking-point. Clearing it would have to go on my *To Do* list. Come to think of it, checking my *To Do* list would help as well. I vowed to put it on the list.

"Fair point. I'll try Angel again," I said. "Although just mentioning her name seems to make her appear. I don't know how she does that."

"Like I said—resourceful."

At that moment, she reappeared.

"You decent?"

"We were just talking about you," said Jen. "Coffee?"

"Yes please. That would be nice."

"Frankie?"

I was just about to say that I already had one when I realised it was a suggestion, not a question. She smiled. I melted and made my way to the kitchen. By the time I returned, the pair of them were laughing like old friends. I placed the cup in front of Angel.

"What's so funny?"

"We were just discussing how important delegation skills in the modern workplace are," said Jen.

"You seem to have that nailed."

"You need to delegate, too. Angel agrees. Your priority has to be the series with the BBC. It's paying the bills. Angel has also agreed to join our happy little team and track down our missing gangsters."

"And how much are we paying Angel to do this?"

"That's detail. I'll ask Flic to put an offer together and we'll go from there," said Jen.

Impressive. I was less impressed when Jen offered Angel a croissant from the bag, reducing my potential consumption by one.

"All this and team croissants too. I could enjoy working here," said Angel, exploding crumbs everywhere.

"Actually, I don't wish to be rude, but it would be based at the big office. This is our scriptwriting hub," I said, with crossed fingers under the desk. Thankfully, Jen backed me up.

"He's right. It doesn't happen that often. It would make more sense for you to be based up there. Would that be a problem?"

"Not at all. It's closer to where I live. Suits me down to the ground. When do I start?"

"I'll call Flic now. If she's okay, we can drive up there this morning and get you started."

Jen got on the phone to Flic. I mentioned my half-baked Robin Hood theory to Angel.

"I'll check out Thompson and O'Neill, see how generous they were. Can't harm, can it?"

Angel started taking notes while reading our Stickies wall. Jen saw my hopeful look at the croissant bag.

"Go on, you can have the last one," said Jen.

She just gets better and better.

22

My plan for a late afternoon visit to the beer garden had come off. A second round of drinks had just arrived and the food order was in. I'd completed a short stint as swing pusher before Charley had spotted two school friends on a climbing frame. Jen looked stunning, her bare shoulders soaking up the sun. I was plucking up the courage to ask Jen's advice.

"There's something I need to tell you," I said.

"You're not pregnant, are you? I thought you were taking precautions."

"I'll have you know I keep my fingers crossed at all times."

Jen laughed and punched me on the arm.

"What is it? You look worried."

"Not worried. It's just something that happened when I went to see Robbie."

"Did she steal your dinner money? I'll get her for you."

"No. Nothing like that. She offered me something." This received a raised eyebrow over the sunglasses. "It turns out, her dad kept a little black book with the dirt on most of his contacts. Not so much a little black book as an online encyclopaedia."

"Crookipaedia?"

I smiled and nodded.

"Very good. We should use that in a script sometime. Anyway, she wants to give us a copy to help to track down our Fifth Man. She reckons it is so comprehensive there's bound to be something there."

"But you're afraid it could be dangerous?"

"Exactly. Who knows what we'd find?"

"But it would be useful. How would we get hold of it?"

"Robbie would arrange it through Rupert as soon as I say we want it."

"How about we keep it in reserve? Let Angel see what she can dig up."

"I knew you'd be the voice of reason."

Charley had just launched herself head first down the slide. Jen seemed unconcerned, but I was a nervous wreck. I needn't have worried. Cries of "again!" soon followed the giggles as she hit the soft landing area. In my day, the landing would be concrete, the cries real, and the next ride would be in an ambulance.

Jen's parenting skills were another thing I was in awe of. She wasn't one to fuss or be over protective but had some intuitive awareness of danger. I'm sure that just by thinking alone, she could steer Charley to a safer path. Despite approaching my fortieth birthday, I felt in no way ready for the responsibility of parenthood. It terrified me. At least this way, I was like an unofficial second in command. An understudy who spent the entire show eating crisps and drinking beer, safe in the knowledge that the star had it all under control. I finished the crisps just as our burgers arrived.

"Charley, food!"

Jen hadn't even raised her voice, but Charley's reaction was instant. She ran towards us, flinging herself into my arms. I swung her around in an arc and plonked her on the bench. I was quite pleased with myself for executing the move without damaging her, and even more pleased that she had sought me out like that.

The warm sunshine at the end of a working week felt great. Jen and I were relaxed. Charley beamed. We must've looked like the perfect family. Only I knew the torment affecting Jen at the moment. As a parent supreme, she was wrestling with an as yet insoluble puzzle of how to broach something to her daughter; uncle Frankie's potential move from the sofa and sleeping bag arrangement to something a bit more intimate. I wondered if Charley was far too young to question anything, but Jen was cautious. For once, she was about to be wrong-footed. Charley spoke loud and clear.

"You should sleep in Mummy's bed."

The remnants of my mouthful of burger shot from my nose, followed by explosive coughing. Through a shield of tears, I looked at Jen for backup. She was almost wetting herself, finding it all very amusing, if a touch embarrassing. It froze most of the adults in the beer garden to the spot. Jen composed herself.

"Okay, young lady, what makes you say that?"

"I like to watch Peppa Pig."

That was unexpected. Charley saved me the bother of asking her to explain.

"When Uncle Frankie is on the sofa, I have to shush and stay in the kitchen. And he poops a lot."

Charley collapsed in a fit of giggles. I was about to plead innocence, but I knew it was a fair cop.

"So you'd rather he was upstairs in my bed?"

"Yes. It's a giant bed. Then I can watch Peppa Pig."

Jen looked at me and shrugged. Looked like Peppa had just got me promoted. Nice one.

Later, as we walked towards Jen's house, I had that nice, contented buzz after sitting in the sunshine, reinforced by the knowledge that I'd remembered to use the facilities before we set off. Charley was just ahead of us, chattering to herself.

"So, given that my daughter has blessed us, are you staying over tonight?"

"That depends."

"Oh yes? Think you might get a better offer?"

"You never know. No. It's just that we have our long walk tomorrow. I need to make sure I get a good night's sleep. Remind me, how comfy is your bed?"

"Super king size, a memory foam mattress that is a foot thick and pillows that cost more than my car."

"Sounds acceptable." This got me a dig in the ribs.

"Besides, I've been thinking."

"Mmm?"

"How about, once Mum takes Charley, we sack off the walk and go back to bed for the day?"

"Will there be snacks?"

"Doubtless. Maybe even a band at halftime."

"What about getting fit for the coast to coast?"

"You saying I'm not fit?"

I recognised a trap when I saw one.

"You, my love, are as fit as the proverbial butcher's dog."

"You say the nicest things. It's a good job you've pulled already."

23

By the time my feet touched the ground again it was Sunday morning. Let's just say Saturday had been rather nice and leave it at that. For the first time since I was four years old, I hadn't watched the FA Cup Final. I'd been busy. On the way home, I called at the cafe and stocked up with the essential bacon butty and coffee combination, then settled in my armchair to watch the recording. With no idea of the result, I tried to convince myself it was live. Twenty minutes in, the final wasn't doing much for me. I was quite pleased when I got the text from Angel.

She knew I was at the BBC in Salford tomorrow. Did I fancy meeting in the office? She might have something for me. I was hooked and zapped the TV. Minutes later, I was pulling into the car park. Angel was already inside, now a trusted member of staff with her own keys. She was up a stepladder.

"Just in time. Pass me that screw. I dropped the little so and so and you'll save me getting down."

Better to do as I was told. The job took seconds to finish.

"Come on. Coffee's ready," said Angel.

I followed her into the office. Her laptop and phone were on the desk nearest the door.

"You look pleased with yourself," she said. "What've you been up to? Don't answer that. I think I can tell and I'm pleased for you. I don't deny, I envisioned you getting back with Robbie, but Jen's okay. She's good for you. Anyway, we don't have all day to chat."

I had contributed nothing to this chat, but she was off again.

"I just installed the three cameras. The first points at your bit of the car park. One in reception, another just behind you. Give it a wave."

I swivelled in the seat but struggled to see a camera.

"Where is it?"

"Tiny thing, in the corner," she said.

It was indeed tiny.

"Does that really give a useful picture?"

"Why don't we see?"

Angel picked up her phone and tapped at the screen.

"Voila!"

I looked at the screen. There was a perfect, detailed picture of me looking gormless, mouth open and scowling.

"That's pretty good. I take it you got the app finished?"

"Sure did. All tested and ready for you to install. I'll send you the link. It's pretty nifty if I say so myself. Spud's got a good team together. You pick your partners well. I'll add the cameras at the cottage too, so we can monitor them from the app."

"I'll give you the wi-fi password for the cottage so you can access them." Angel gave me a look. "Then again, knowing you, you've already hacked in."

"Now you're learning," said Angel, grinning.

Protest was pointless.

"That's brilliant. Thank you. I don't suppose you've made any progress on our other project?"

"Blimey, you don't ask for much, do you?"

"Sorry, I'm just, you know, keen," I said.

"I might have something. I'm confident I've got an address for Eddie Elgin. We should pay him a visit, don't you think?"

"And say what?"

"Ask him if he was the brain that planned robberies in the eighties and nineties? How do I know? You're in charge of this project." She grinned at me again. As if I was in charge!

"How did you find him? Wait. Before you tell me, did you do anything illegal?"

"More coffee?"

That didn't sound promising.

"Tell me how you tracked Elgin down," I said, deciding that worrying about how Angel got her information was pointless.

"Well, we knew that Parker senior bought cars from him for years. He gave me the address of the petrol station. There's a park just up the road. I spent a delightful afternoon at the bowling green. Had several cups of tea and had a chat with the bowlers. Friendly lot. Some of them had lived in the area all their lives."

"So they knew Elgin?"

"They knew of him. Seems he had a bit of a reputation for being dodgy. Nothing specific, just a general unpleasant smell. Didn't socialise in the local pubs. The one local place he was a regular at was Odsal Stadium. He was a big Bradford Northern fan, apparently. When they rebranded as Bradford Bulls in the nineties, rumour had it he put money in. He never joined the board or anything like that, but he bought several season tickets every year. Still does, as a matter of fact."

"And you know this because…?"

"I may have had a little peek at the database."

"A little peek?"

"Just a little one. Just enough to have his address now that he lives near Skipton."

"Sounds like he did okay for himself. Do you think we should pay him a visit?"

"I think it's the only way we're going to get answers."

"When should we go? I'm in Salford tomorrow at the BBC."

"I thought we'd go now."

"Now?"

"What else were you planning to do that's more important?"

"But don't we need a plan? Work out what we're going to say…"

"Plenty of time in the car. Come on."

The last time I'd been to Skipton was with Jen. We had a late night trip to the police station when Roddy was missing. I didn't need the satnav for this bit as I drove on the familiar road, passing the turning to Kettlewell where we'd made the film.

"It's funny that Elgin had connections with the Bulls. I wanted to turn pro with them when I was at school."

Angel looked astonished.

"*You* played rugby league?"

"Don't say it like that. Yes, *I* played rugby league. After music, it was my grand passion."

"You were good enough to turn pro?"

"In my head I was. They didn't quite see it like that. Besides, I gave the game up because of an injury."

"You got hurt?"

I shuffled in my seat.

"Not me. Our prop broke his nose. Blood everywhere. I passed out. My mates took the piss so much I told them to shove it. Never played again."

"You mean you gave up on your dream because some kids

laughed at you?"

"Pretty much. I didn't want to end up with a flat nose and no teeth like he did. That's why I'm so handsome now."

Angel's snort was uncalled for.

Minutes later, we arrived at our destination. Cars packed the narrow street down one side. Parking was at a premium. Business appeared to be booming at the local church. Our timing was lucky. Most parishioners were making a getaway towards the pub. Just ahead of us, a car was waiting to pull out. I flashed my headlights and received a wave from the window of the VW. I edged into the vacated spot and pulled on the handbrake.

"Is this going to work?"

"How many more times? Stop worrying. We're not accusing anybody of anything. We are researchers working on a TV show and just want to ask him some questions," said Angel.

I nodded, took a deep breath, and got out of the car. We dodged the steady stream of traffic, and walked back down the other side of the road, checking house numbers as we went.

"This is it," said Angel.

I opened the garden gate and stood back to allow her to go first. She gave me a firm push in the middle of my back and propelled me towards the front door. Angel reached around and pushed the doorbell before stepping back. I felt her hand on my back again. We waited. Getting no answer hadn't been part of the plan, proving my point that it wasn't much of a plan. I was just about to suggest we give in when there was movement in the house.

The door swung open in a smooth arc. It seemed almost creepy, then I realised it was an automatic door. I saw the woman in the wheelchair.

"I'm sorry to keep you waiting. I was in my studio. It takes a while to get here. How can I help?"

I hesitated, but received another shove in the back.

"We were hoping to speak to Mr Elgin, Eddie Elgin? Do we have the right address?"

"You do, but he's out just now. I'm Lyn, his wife. Maybe I can help. You'd better come in."

She spun the chair with ease and moved down the hall. We stepped inside and the door closed behind us. She led us to a large sitting room.

"Eddie will be here soon. It's a lot easier if I let him offer you a cup of tea."

"Would you like me to make it, Mrs Elgin?"

"Lyn, please. That's very kind of you, dear. The kitchen's just through there. Everything's by the kettle."

Angel skipped off to the kitchen. She turned at the door and made a gesture at me. I took it she meant for me to get on with it.

"So, Mrs Elgin. Sorry, Lyn. My name is Frankie Dale. I'm working on a TV drama based on a book that came out last year."

I heard the front door swinging open again.

"Oh, here he is. You can tell Eddie at the same time."

I stood to greet the newcomer in the room. The first thing I noticed was the dog collar, followed by the beaming smile. I shook the outstretched hand.

"Apologies for not being here when you arrived. Kind of busy on a Sunday. Hello, I'm Eddie."

"Frankie, and I'm sorry for intruding. I didn't know about the…"

I fingered my collar, struggling for the right word. Elgin chuckled.

"Do I take it you're not a regular churchgoer?"

I squirmed a bit, retaking my seat.

"Depends how you define regular, I suppose."

This time, he roared with laughter.

"Weddings and funerals? Never mind, plenty of time for me to get you on the side of the angels."

I smiled, even though I wasn't sure if he was serious. My position on religion had always been that I respected everybody's views until the point they tried to impose them on me. Just then, an angel appeared. This one was carrying a tray, teapot, and cups.

"Speak of the devil," I said. "Not that she's, you know… she's quite nice when you get to know her."

"Anybody making tea is fine with me," said Elgin, accepting the tray from Angel and placing it on the table.

"I think what Frankie is trying to say is that my name is Angel."

"Very apt, I'm sure," smiled Elgin as he shook her hand. Maybe Lyn noticed too, that he held onto Angel's hand a fraction too long. She addressed her husband.

"Frankie and Angel are working on a television programme. He was just about to explain when you arrived."

She leant across and poured the tea. I accepted a cup and turned to Elgin.

"Yes, it's a dramatisation based on a book that came out last year. We were hoping you may provide some of the background that was missing from the book. We believe you knew Peter Parker when you were younger?"

It was noticeable that the avuncular smile disappeared for a second and the temperature in the room dropped ten degrees. Adding sugar to his tea, he recovered his composure, before taking a seat opposite his wife.

"My word, that seems like a different lifetime. Yes, I knew Peter in my younger days. I haven't seen him in almost thirty years. He must be in his eighties now. Is he still —"

"Yes, he's still alive, although he suffers from the aftereffects of a stroke. He's in a care home. His grandson is very protective of him."

"They were very close, after his father disappeared."

"Have you any idea what happened to the father?"

"There were rumours, but nothing I would gossip about. Peter had some colourful friends. But then, you know that, or you wouldn't be here."

"We know he drove getaway cars for the gang that made a habit of robbing jewellers for a good five years before it ended in violence. The gap we'd like to fill is the identity of the fifth gang member. Somebody had to plan things, fence the jewellery, that kind of thing," I said.

"And I might know something about it?" I took another sip of tea. Then Elgin laughed again. "Hang on, you don't think it's me, do you? This thing," he said, pointing to his neck, "is hardly the uniform of a master criminal, is it?"

"I wasn't suggesting —"

"No, but you're wondering, aren't you?"

"Why did you fall out with Parker?"

"It was stupid, really. Italia 90. As a proud Scot, I got a bit carried away. I bet Peter that we would beat Brazil. Lost a grand, a huge amount in those days for me. I should've left it there, but he couldn't resist winding me up. In the end, I bet him five times that amount on the outcome of the semi-final. Italy beat his beloved England, and it was my turn to celebrate."

"So that led to a fight?"

"No, at least not with Parker. Lyn found out and went ballistic. Almost ended our marriage, but luckily for me, she gave me another chance — as long as I cut ties with Peter. So we didn't fall out. We just didn't stay friends. You may have noticed I had a change of career and lifestyle. I thought master criminals retired to Spain and lived on their millions? Few become vicars in a rural community and coach the under-11 rugby league team."

"The crimes were a long time ago. People change."

"Do you think I spent most of the eighties robbing jewellery shops? I had other things to do."

The expression on Elgin's face had changed. He crashed his cup onto the table, spilling some of the tea. Anger? Or about to burst into tears. Angel gave me a look that suggested I should hold off. Then Lyn spoke up.

"What Eddie is trying to say is that my accident changed everything. Saturday, July the 13th 1985. Everybody remembers that date."

"Live Aid?"

Lyn nodded.

"We were having a party at the house. Somehow we'd forgotten to buy rum. I remember watching Ultravox. When they finished Vienna, I set off to walk to the off-licence. I had to be back for Spandau Ballet and said that nothing would make me miss them. I was wrong. It happened in an instant. I stepped onto the road and a car hit me. When the ambulance got there, I was still holding one of the rum bottles."

Elgin stood, crossed the room and knelt in front of his wife, distraught. She gripped his hand.

"Both our lives changed that day. Eddie cared for me day after day while still running a business. He worked his fingers to the bone to keep us going. I can tell you now, he was at home with me every evening doing everything that I could no longer do myself. There's no way he was off around the country breaking into jewellery shops or meeting dodgy characters to fence anything. Whoever you're looking for, it's not Eddie."

"We can see that, Lyn," said Angel. "I'm sorry we bothered you."

Was Angel backing off already? Was that it? I'd had visions of my rapier questioning breaking down Elgin's resistance before I extracted the killer confession. Now it looked like it was time to go. We replaced the half drunk cups on the table and stood to leave. Angel had watched reruns of Columbo. As we reached the door, she paused.

"Eddie, I believe everything you told us except one thing."

"And what's that?"

"Why did you fall out with Parker?"

Elgin glanced at his wife before deciding. He took a moment to choose his words.

"I told you. Lyn thought he was a bad influence. Nothing more. Now, if you'll excuse us, we have an afternoon of shouting abuse at the referee and risking life and limb with a meat pie."

"Bradford Bulls by any chance?" I asked.

"Got it in one. We meet our daughters and their husbands, grandchildren. Big family day out."

"It's been a couple of years since I've been, but I used to be a big fan."

"You should give it another try. A club rising from the ashes."

I handed over one of my cards.

"These are my contact details. Please, if you think of anything that may help, just call. Thanks for your time."

Elgin showed us out. In the car, I looked at Angel.

"So, we rule him out as our suspect?"

"I think so, but why lie?"

"About Parker?"

"No. About why he wanted rid of us. The Bulls don't have a game this afternoon," said Angel.

"And how do you know that?"

"Because I was in Newcastle on Friday night to watch them. We won, actually. I never miss a game, home or away. Unless I'm in prison. That makes it tricky."

24

Charley was almost bouncing off the walls with excitement. The yellow tram was the best thing in the world. Jen had taken her out of school for a couple of days. The tram edged to a stop at the end of the line and we stepped off into Media City. After checking in at our hotel, we presented ourselves in reception at the BBC studios.

Within a couple of minutes, a young, fresh-faced production assistant called Emmy met us. I was about to comment about the appropriateness of her name for a career on TV, but she singled out Charley for special attention. Jen and I were just bit-part players. Emmy put herself eye to eye with Charley. There were questions about whether Charley would like to meet somebody or other. I had to admit the names meant nothing to me, but Charley's excitement notched up even further.

Jen watched as her daughter took the hand of her new best friend in the entire world. Emmy led down a corridor. Feeling old, I held onto Jen's hand as we followed. We emerged into a room that was full of bright colours. Two strange looking creatures sat behind a reception desk. It was just the right height for a five-year-old. The two puppets greeted Charley by name. Her eyes were like dinner plates as she approached the desk. To Charley it was the equivalent of when I'd spotted Keira Knightley across reception at a hotel in London. It was a memory I would always treasure and Charley would feel the same.

The surprises kept coming. Emmy took us to the studio. Filming of Wolf Tales was about to start. Just yards from where the cameras focused was a miniature director's chair with Charley's name on the back. Emmy got her settled before turning to the adults.

"We couldn't quite get chairs with names on for you two, but I'm sure you'll be comfortable. Demus is just in makeup, and this is Erin, our director."

Again, somebody half my age took control.

"Hi, Frankie, Jen. Pleased to meet you. We're ready to record, but I have a bit of a job for you on the third story. In rehearsal, it was a little long. Could you work your magic, do a bit of editing? We need to lose about 500 words."

Ouch. That was quite a chunk, but that was why I was here. Demus walked into the studio and every woman in the building stared. I had to admit; he had magnetism. He made a beeline for us, which made my head swell to twice its size. After a few seconds of chat, Erin was asking for quiet. Jen took a seat next to the still mesmerised Charley. Emmy showed me to a desk at the back. As everybody else settled down to listen to Demus tell one of my stories, I got to sit with my laptop and try to perform surgery on another one.

From where I was sitting, I could just see Jen and Charley. Both of them looked so happy and enthralled by the entire process. We'd come a long way in the last couple of years. Here was one of the biggest actors of his generation, reading my words in a TV studio. Even better, I was with the woman I loved. At that moment, more than anything else in the world, I wanted the three of us to be a family. Was it too soon to think that way?

I was still daydreaming about my mum getting the chance to wear her special hat when lights came on and people started buzzing around. It appeared the first story was complete. I looked at the word count. I'd removed eighteen words.

Erin appeared by my side.

"Everything okay with the edit?"

"Great. Almost there."

What was the punishment for lying to a CBeebies director?

"Good news. Demus nailed that first time. It means we can start episode two early. We may even squeeze in number three before lunch if you're ready."

"Great."

Crap. What was Demus playing at? Couldn't he be imperfect just once? He was supposed to be my friend. He was certainly my partner in crime when it came to arranging the special day for Charley. Not everybody gets this kind of treatment, but Demus had helped me to make it happen.

I needed help. Erin gave me a thumbs up and went to speak to Demus. I texted Jen.

Help.

I saw her take her phone from her pocket. She read the text, spoke briefly to Charley and, much to my relief, headed over.

"You stuck?"

"Yes. This is harder than I thought."

"Let's have a look."

Before long, Jen's fingers were flying over the keys. She highlighted passages, asked for my approval, then bang — they were gone. By the time they were recording the second story, we had a beautiful, well edited third. I emailed the updated document to Emmy and moved across to watch the action. Things were close to perfect, sitting in the dark with these two lovely people, listening to a bedtime story read by a

BAFTA winner. A bag of *Maltesers* would make life complete. As the wonderful John Cooper Clarke said, "You can't have everything; where would you put it?"

Jen leaned close and whispered.

"Thank you."

"What for?"

"Making all this happen for Charley."

"What makes you think it was me?"

"Emmy told me."

"What a blabbermouth. That was supposed to be our secret."

"You done good Mr Dale."

She squeezed my hand. I looked across and saw the tears on her cheeks.

"Hey, what's wrong?"

It took a moment to answer.

"It's just the sort of thing my dad would do for me if I was that age. I'm going to miss…"

This time the squeeze felt like it was breaking my fingers. It was a worthwhile sacrifice if it was comforting Jen.

25

As we producers say, *Wolf Tales* was in the can. Not that they used cans these days. It was all digital, but you get my drift. We'd returned from Salford after two magical days of recording. Charley's behaviour had been impeccable, even when the train home was delayed by an hour.

On Wednesday morning, we were meeting at the main office. Flic had laid on champagne and pastries for our small team to celebrate our first production. *Wolf Tales* was done. There was talk of a second series later in the year.

Jen brushed crumbs from the front of my shirt.

"Come on, Angel wants us in the meeting room."

"Can we get coffee first?"

"No time. She says she needs us now."

So Jen found Angel as intimidating as I did.

We entered the room and sat down. The array of flip charts, whiteboards and online Stickies that greeted us impressed me. Angel had been busy.

"Sorry to drag you away from the champagne. I thought it worth reviewing what I turned up while you were away."

"It looks like you've got quite a lot," I said.

"Not there yet, but here goes. For what it's worth, I think Elgin was telling the truth about looking after his wife. I tracked down one carer, Sue, who visited twice a day for a year after the accident. She confirmed Elgin was never far away from home. Sue would arrive to make lunch and find Elgin was already there, sharing a meal with his wife."

"You said she was there a year. What happened then?" Jen was taking notes.

"Lyn was becoming more independent. She had the chair and could look after herself. Sue said that they would all just sit around the kitchen table and chat. It was her that introduced the couple to God."

"Not in person, I presume," I said.

That just got me a look.

"She reckons they were just trying to come to terms with what had happened. Some people turn to drink or drugs, they went to church."

"Could he have been trying to make amends for past crimes? Cleanse his soul?"

"Maybe, but I don't think so. I think they're genuine and there's no evidence Elgin was involved, or that he benefited from crime at all. It looks like they were broke by the time his business folded, just after his argument with Parker. A month later, he got his first job in the church. Looks like he's good at the job and well liked by his parishioners."

"So, we're back to square one?" I let out a long sigh.

"Not quite," said Jen. "We've eliminated one person who could be our man."

"What about the other one, Dwyer?"

"He's proving elusive at the moment. I tracked down two regulars at the pub he used to drink in with Parker. Nobody knew him that well, but they mentioned his accent. Said he was a bit *ooh aarr*."

"A pirate?"

That got me another look.

"Not a pirate, numpty. From the West Country somewhere.

Also drank nothing but cider. They used to stock it just for him. The name of the cider is interesting."

"Dwyers, by any chance?" Jen looked quite smug.

"Give the lady a coconut. I'd never heard of it," said Angel.

"Back to my student days. It was the cheaper alternative and like rocket fuel. Stoked many a good night out. Not thought about it in years," said Jen.

"One reason for that is that they went bust after the big banking crash."

"Hang on," I cut in. "Do you think it's just a coincidence that they shared a name, or was he part of the family?"

"I've been working on the theory that he was part of the family. I've struggled so far, but there's one lead that I'm hoping will pay off. Have you ever tried to trace your family tree?"

Now, this is my area.

"I have. Very dull family. Hard to believe, but I'm descended from a long line of miners on Dad's side and fishermen on Mum's. No murderers or millionaires anywhere," I said.

"Well, you'll be familiar with the websites. I'm trying to trace my long-lost cousins," said Angel.

"What's that to do with Dwyer?"

Jen patted me on the head, like you would a dog that looked confused.

"I suspect Angel has adopted a false name. Subterfuge is at hand."

"Too right," grinned Angel. "It's amazing how quickly you can pull something together that looks like a good backstory. Anyway, I've tried to contact a woman in Taunton who seems to be the family expert. I'm waiting to see if she fills in more detail for my made up family."

"Crafty bugger," was all I could manage.

"With luck, she'll know where he is and put us in touch. I

thought we could pay him a visit," said Angel.

"Don't forget, Frankie's at a very impressionable age. Just make sure you keep him out of trouble while I'm away."

"Of course — your big walk. When do you go?"

"At the weekend. This young man is driving us to Cumbria, so he's banned from playing at detectives for the duration. After that, you've got him for most of the next fortnight. Treat him well."

"I will. Have you done much training for the walk?"

"Not so as you'd notice, to be honest. How hard can it be?"

Angel and I both looked at Jen. Did she appreciate what she'd signed up for?

"Bloody hell, that's huge," I said.

"I do my best," said Jen.

I looked again at the rucksack propped against the wall of the kitchen.

"Are you sure you can walk with that thing on?"

"It's a bit on the heavy side, but I'm sure I'll get used to it."

"Come on, let's try."

Jen took up her position, like an Olympic swimmer about to dive into the pool. I hauled the rucksack off the floor and helped get her arms through the straps. After lots of grunting and swearing, the mighty pack was in place. Jen was still in diving pose, like a number seven if it was wearing a huge rucksack.

"I'm not sure that's the ideal walking position."

"Hang on smart-arse. I'm just preparing myself."

The accompanying noise was like a serve on centre court. Upright at last, Jen tried a smile and a thumbs up, before teetering, then collapsing backwards onto the floor. She lay like a wounded ninja turtle, legs kicking. I had visions of calling for an ambulance before realising she was helpless with laughter.

"Don't just stand there looking gormless. Get me up."

I went to grab the straps, then realised I should do something first.

"No," she warned. "No photos. My retribution will be swift and sorrowful."

"Big talk for somebody who can't move."

I took several shots before putting my phone in my pocket and leaning over the prone ninja. I was off balance when she grabbed me around the neck and pulled. Helpless, I ended up lying on top of her. This was getting weird. Jen planted a huge kiss before pushing me off.

"Right. Stop messing about and get me up," she laughed. "I think I've broken my hairdryer."

"Tell me you haven't got a hairdryer in there."

"How else am I going to dry my hair?"

"No wonder it weighs a ton. I suggest you may need to rethink."

"Maybe you have a point."

Somehow we both stood up, and I wrestled the rucksack off her shoulders. She opened it and removed various items, including the cracked hairdryer.

"Most of that lot should go in the pile of stuff for me to bring when we meet up. You only need the essentials, and no, that does not include a hairdryer."

"Suppose the foot spa comes under that heading?"

"Tell me —"

"Of course not, dopey. But I'm booking a foot rub as soon as you get there."

"That's fine, but your dad is on his own. How's he doing, by the way?"

"He says he's all right, but I think he's a lot more tired than he's making out."

"I suppose this means a lot to him."

"It does, and I'll keep my beady eye on him."

"Just remember, first sign of trouble, call me."

"What would I do without you?"

"I'm not planning on giving you a chance to find out. You are stuck with me," I said.

For a second, I wondered if this was the moment. Then the doorbell rang.

"Pizza! You answer the door, I'll get plates."

Much as I love the man from our local takeaway, on this occasion, his timing was rubbish. Then again, we had dough balls, so life wasn't all bad. By the time I got to the kitchen, plates were on the table, together with two cans of Diet Coke.

"I'm not sure I'm allowed to eat pizza without wine," I said.

"Big day tomorrow. The last thing I need is to get pissed and start the walk with a massive hangover."

I was about to point out that I wasn't walking anywhere, but showed solidarity and stuck to soft drinks.

"So, are you confident you've got your new boots broken in?"

Jen shook her head, her mouth being busy with the meatball supreme. She took a drink.

"Not really. They seem comfy enough. What's the worst that could happen? Hang on, don't answer that. To be honest, it's not me I'm worried about. What if he can't cope?"

"He's very sensible. I'm sure he'll shout if it gets too much. This is huge for him. Not just the walk, but spending time with you. Two weeks of having you all to himself."

"Poor old bugger."

"I'm a little jealous, if I'm honest."

"It's not too late to come with us."

I must've looked horrified.

"Not the walk, thank you very much. I meant having you to myself," I said.

"You've got me to yourself this evening, don't forget."

"This is true. Was madam okay spending the night with her grandparents?"

"What do you think? She couldn't wait. Two weeks of being spoilt rotten by grandma. There'll be so many e-numbers I'll come back to something feral."

"She'll be fine."

"I directed the last bit at you! Eat something other than pizza and penguin biscuits while I'm gone."

"Chicken masala and KitKats it is, then."

Luckily, I was out of elbow digging reach. Instead of attacking me, Jen pulled something from her pocket and slid it across the table. It was a key. Was Jen asking me to move in? I went to stand so I could go for a hug. I rescued it just in time.

"Would you mind checking in sometimes? Water the plants, check for mail, that kind of thing?"

"Sure, no problem," I said, masking the disappointment.

"And stay out of trouble while I'm away. I don't want Angel leading you into dangerous adventures. Finding our mystery man would be great, but not if it puts you in danger."

"Yes, Mum."

A dough ball hit me on the end of the nose. Somehow, I caught it and dipped it in the garlic butter.

"Good catch," said Jen. "But you get my point. It's easy to forget that these people didn't mess about. They murdered Jason's dad and the security guard."

"I promise I'll stay out of trouble."

26

It had been a ridiculously early start. By eight o'clock, we were bumping over the level crossing.

"Welcome to St Bees," I said, with a flourish.

My previous impression of the Lake District was rain coming in sideways, the result of two school camping trips which featured zero sightings of the sun, a waterlogged tent and a visit to A&E. This morning was different. Brilliant, warm sunshine, a gentle breeze and the prospect of idleness in the air.

"What's your plan when you drop us off?"

Jen's slimmed down rucksack was on the back seat next to Ben. His own, more modest pack was in the tiny boot.

"I'm on an ice cream hunt."

"Typical."

I paid for the parking while Jen and Ben donned boots and readied themselves. Another car full of bobble hats pulled in beside us.

"You sure you don't want to come with us?" I suspected Jen's question was rhetorical.

"I'd love to. But I only had enough change to pay until lunchtime. Otherwise…"

Ben made a show of sorting through his change.

"I'm sure I've got something here."

"You're a funny man."

"I try."

"Right, there's an ice cream with my name on it."

"Nice try," said Jen. "You can at least do the first bit with us."

"How long is the first bit?"

"Don't panic. It's a few hundred yards down to the beach."

"You don't fool me that easy. I know geography. Robin Hood's Bay is in the opposite direction altogether."

"Tradition. You dip your boots in the sea to mark the start. Come on. We want a picture to prove it."

We set off down the small path that led to the beach. I felt a bit out of place — neither bobble hat nor rucksack. I glanced at Ben. He'd fallen asleep in the car long before we got out of Yorkshire. He'd looked pale and drawn. Now, with the sun on his face, he just looked excited.

"Shame Charley's not here," said Ben.

"She was looking forward to ballet all week," said Jen. "I feel guilty for not mentioning there was a beach, but we'd have needed to bring two cars. It was getting complicated."

"This playground looks good. We should bring her one day," I said.

Seconds later, we were on the beach. The two walkers stood with their boots in the water and posed for photographs. I flicked my phone into video mode.

"Would you like to say a few words?"

I expected Jen to tell me to bugger off, but Ben spoke up.

"Yes, I would." He composed himself for a second and then looked straight at the lens. "Geraldine and Charley, sorry you couldn't be with us today, but don't worry. Jen'll look after me. I'm feeling good and looking forward to us all having fish and chips on the east coast. This is one small step for man, but a giant leap for me. In fact, it seems like a bloody long way, but at least the sun's shining. Look after your gran while I'm away. Love you both."

He gave a dramatic wave and blew a kiss. I stopped the video. Then he spoke again.

"Actually, can I borrow your phone Frankie and just have a minute?"

"Of course. Here you go."

"I want to record something."

After a crash course on how to operate the camera, he strode further down the beach.

I put my arm around Jen. She was doing her best to choke back tears.

"What is it?"

"I think he's recording a message for Charley for when he…" said Jen.

Now it was my turn to shed a tear.

"The last time it was just the two of us walking in the Lake District, I must've been about ten. I was so pleased with myself for managing Helvellyn and I still remember every detail," she said.

"That's what this walk is all about. You'll make some glorious memories."

"We set off that day from Grasmere. Funny to think we'll be there in a couple of days. Not long after that, you join us in Kirkby Stephen."

"I shall be there with a smile and a ready supply of clean undies."

"That's good to know."

"How far do you need to cover?"

"It's about eighty miles to Kirkby Stephen. Fourteen today."

"You'll be fine."

"Will he?" I nodded and squeezed her shoulder. Jen took a deep breath as Ben turned towards us. "Come on Spielberg. If you've finished, there's a pint with your name on it at The Shepherd's Arms."

We all rubbed our eyes and set off back up the beach. After a brief but wise pause at the public toilets, I waved them off. I was still waving when they disappeared from view.

"Shit. He's still got my phone," I said aloud.

How much would I miss it? I was the emergency contact if anything went wrong. I set off at a sprint, downgrading to a jog, when my lungs threatened to burst after about a hundred yards. It was then that I saw Jen heading back towards me. She handed over the phone.

"I can't believe we just had our first row."

"Ah well, only two weeks to go. I'll see you in Kirkby Stephen."

After a quick hug, she was gone — again. I smiled at the unexpected chance to see Jen so soon after she'd set off. I made my way back to the village for the ice cream I'd promised myself. It was still only nine o'clock. There was plenty of time for ice cream later.

"Breakfast time."

I hunted down a window seat at the cafe for a bacon butty and coffee. I looked at my phone. I wanted to make sure that I backed up Ben's video to my Dropbox. Then the phone rang. Had something gone wrong already? I was relieved to see it was Angel.

"Hi Angel, you're up and about early."

"I'm busking in Leeds all day. Thought you'd like to know I tracked down, Dwyer. Turns out he's in Blackpool."

"That's almost on my way home."

"Just what I was thinking. Would you like the address so you can pay him a visit?"

"That sounds like a plan."

"Great, I'll email you. Got to go. Bye."

"Hang on. What do I say —"

The line was dead. Did I want to see Dougie Dwyer alone? I saw Angel as my protector, a sort of guardian angel. Nice one. I should use that. My breakfast arrived. This was now a planning session for meeting up with our new prime suspect. Tommy sauce was required.

Two bites into my sandwich, the email arrived. Angel had been busy.

Dwyer's cousin came good. Dougie was a naughty boy when he was younger - ostracised by family. He's at a nightclub / bar in Blackpool - The Double D.

Double D -Dougie Dwyer. Gangsters owning nightclubs was a cliche for a good reason. Was it a front for a criminal empire?

The stifled yawn suggested the early start was kicking in, so I ordered a second coffee. Would a nightclub be open so early? Should I find a hotel somewhere, sneak back to bed for a couple of hours, then go tonight? Then it hit me: it was Blackpool. No way would a bar miss out on the daytime drinking profits. It would be open. I needed to focus.

A text arrived from Jen. The first photo of the intrepid pair squinting into the sunshine. The Isle of Man shimmering behind them.

"No more arguments. Boots fine, and looking forward to finding a tea shop."

I smiled and accepted my second coffee from the young waitress.

Pushing my plate away revealed a tiny piece of bacon that had escaped. Glancing over my shoulder to check nobody was watching, I picked it up and chewed it. There was nothing quite like bonus bacon when you thought it was all gone. Another glance at my phone confirmed that the recent note I'd opened was still blank. It was supposed to contain my plan, a script of what I was about to say when I came face to face with Dougie Dwyer. Was I over-thinking this? There were only two questions?

"Are you Dougie Dwyer? Are you a criminal mastermind responsible for at least two murders?"

This plan assumed a positive response to question one. If the answer to question one was anything but positive, number two was a long shot.

Then again, who was I kidding? The thought that a card carrying lifetime coward was just going to march up to a nightclub owner and ask if he was a murderer was far-fetched. Why not on another day with Angel? She'd done the research, after all. Then again, Blackpool wasn't far away. Before I could bottle out altogether, I paid my bill and strode off towards the car. The ice cream would have to wait. I was on a mission.

27

Over thirty years after my first visit, I still got a thrill when I spotted Blackpool tower on the horizon. As a kid, this was a magical place, part of the annual cycle that included Santa's grotto and gorging on chocolate at Easter. Obviously I still did the chocolate thing, but I'd long since seen the seamier side of Blackpool (and Santa's grotto after that incident that I don't talk about).

It was the seamier side that I was pondering in the vast car park near the football ground. Had I left it much later, I suspect I wouldn't have found a spot. The sun was shining and northerners were trekking to the seaside.

Thanks to the map on my phone, I had a fair idea where I was heading. I negotiated the pavements, still bearing evidence of last night's kebabs, and took my life in my hands to cross a busy road. I was just about to check the map again when I spotted the gigantic neon sign fifty yards away.

Summoning a confidence I didn't feel, I pushed at the heavy door. Either it was a lot heavier than I thought or locked. A shrill voice suggested I might like to come back after twelve o'clock. I ignored the other piece of advice and looked at my watch. It was ten to twelve. It didn't look like the place to be first through the door. I headed towards the sea, dodged a couple of trams, and found a bench on the prom.

It was strange that I could just about see the Lake District in the distance, knowing that Jen and her dad were striding out on their epic trip. The Isle of Man had disappeared in a blur of mist. Maybe the weather was changing? Hopefully, they were enjoying being together. It made me think about my parents on the opposite coast. I felt guilty. After the health scares last year, I'd promised to spend more time with them, but I'd slipped back into old habits. Maybe, once we'd finished the research, I could spend a few days with them.

A couple pushing a double buggy walked towards the steps down to the beach. I assumed the kids were twins — identical shorts, shirt, and hat. One was immaculate but miserable. The other grinned from ear to ice cream covered ear. I had to remember my date with an ice cream before I set off home.

To kill time, I opened the phone app for Angel's security system. It looked impressive. I selected the main office from the home page. The system had already logged nine photos. I flicked through them. No surprises. Besides Jen and me, I recognised Flic, Jason, Melanie, Angel and Tom from the office and Demus from his visit. I didn't recognise the last shot, but the mop bucket and hoover suggested the new cleaner. Against each photo was a list of times the cameras had picked them up. It was all very impressive.

A quick check of the entries for the cottage was fine. I should get an extra camera to install at home. You never knew.

After scrolling through Facebook and Twitter, I sat back, enjoying the warm sunshine. It felt good to stretch and do nothing. Then I realised I was in danger of falling asleep. I forced myself upright and set off back to the Double D.

This time, the door was open. The first of the stag nights

had arrived and were entertaining themselves by singing along to Transvision Vamp's *Baby I Don't Care*. I made my way to the bar. The middle-aged blonde woman folded her *Daily Mirror* before coming to meet me.

"Yes, love, what can I get you?"

"I'm looking for somebody."

"You and me both, love. I reckon I've got fuck all chance of finding George Clooney in here, though. Might do better with a drink in our hands."

I was about to launch into my speech but realised she expected me to buy drinks if I wanted any help.

"Peroni, please. And one for yourself."

"Cheers. I'll have the same." She turned to the glass cabinets and splashed two drinks into plastic glasses. "Nine quid, please."

Ouch. I handed over a tenner. Maybe I needed to claim expenses for this. The music cranked up as the DJ switched to The Jam's *Beat Surrender*. The crowd cheered. An older man in his sixties, carrying a mop and bucket, pushed his way through the group. The barmaid glared at the DJ and the music reduced by a smidgen.

"He does my bleedin' 'ead in havin' it so loud this early."

At least now I felt I could ask my questions.

"I'm looking for the owner of this place," I said.

"So are a lot of people. What makes you so special?"

"I'm a researcher for a TV company. I have a few questions about a programme we're making."

"And what makes you think she can help?"

"I have reason… hang on. She? You said she?"

"Yes, she. Is that a problem? Women incapable of answering your poxy questions?"

"No, it's just… I thought… the name I have is Dougie Dwyer."

"Never heard of him."

This was a blow. I was wondering what to do next when the older bloke emerged and headed behind the bar.

"Everything all right Sid?"

"Yeah. Keep an eye on the big dopey bugger in the red shirt. He be spudling already."

Sid pushed through a door, reemerging seconds later without his bucket.

"Help yourself to a drink, Sid." Without hesitating, he grabbed a plastic glass and poured a pint. The blonde turned and smiled for the first time. "That's Sid, odd-job man and sometime bouncer. He does his best work early in the day before he gets too pissed."

"Always the same drink, by any chance?"

"Yeah, never changes." The man came to join us. "That's why we call him Sid — short for cider."

"Hello Dougie, pleased to meet you. I'm Frankie."

The man looked startled. The woman left to serve new customers.

"Ain't no Dougie here. Sid's the name."

"Sid what?"

"Just Sid."

"Okay, Sid. No need to panic," I said. "I'm not the police or a tax inspector. Whoever it is, you're busy not being. I'm not out to get him. I just want to ask him some questions. Shame you're not Dougie. I was just about to put £20 behind the bar. That would buy a few ciders, even at these prices. I'll just finish my drink, then I'll be off."

"You could leave the money anyway, just in case he comes in, like. I'll see he gets it."

"So maybe you could answer my questions, just on Dougie's behalf, sort of thing. I'm sure he'd share the drinks with you."

He thought it over, then nodded.

"I reckon that could work, aye. See what I can do, like."

I pointed to a corner by the door, away from the biggest speakers. We settled at a sticky table. At least it matched the sticky floor.

"Does Dougie own this place?"

Sid laughed so hard his whole body convulsed in the coughing fit that followed.

"What makes you think old Dougie owns this place?"

"It's his initials. Double D — Dougie Dwyer."

This time he avoided full scale cough meltdown. A grubby hand wiped the tears away. He blew his nose, checking the hankie for contents. Satisfied, he wiped his eyes again and took a drink.

"T'aint initials. It's a size. Tiffany, behind the bar. She owns it. Named it after her prize assets, if you get my drift."

"So where does Dougie fit in?"

"Dougie does odd jobs, keeps his head down until he's had enough cider for the day, then falls asleep. Rinse and repeat, as they say. Not exactly eat, pray fuckin' love, but it works for me. I mean Dougie. Works for Dougie."

"All right Dougie, sorry — Sid. What does the name Peter Parker mean to you?"

"Spiderman?"

"No, the other one. The one that Dougie used to drink with in Bradford."

"Not seen him for years." Sid let out a sigh. "Okay, we used to drink together, and I did a bit of work for him."

"What kind of work?"

"This and that. A lot of removals, cash in hand if you get me. He'd drive the van and a couple of us would do the graft, lugging sofas and sideboards in and out of grotty flats."

"Nothing more exotic than that?"

"Exotic? You mean illegal?" I shrugged and took a sip of lager. "Not that I know of. Sometimes the jobs were boxes rather than domestic moves. Never asked what was in 'em.

None of my business. So long as I got paid and could buy a pint, I was happy."

"Always been cider?" Dougie just looked at me, eyes questioning. "Your tipple, always cider? Most drinkers go for bitter or lager in Bradford."

"Never touched the stuff. It's always been cider. Suppose it's in the blood."

"So, you are a member of the Dwyer Cider family?"

"You've been busy, I see. Yes, I was the black sheep of the family. Got into bother when I was a lad. A fight in a pub on a Saturday night after too much cider. Just my luck. He was the local magistrate's son. I got six months. The old man said it was bad for the company image. Slung me out on my arse the day they released me from the nick. Cut me out of the will and everything. Not that there was anything to inherit by the time the old bastard died. Went bust in the so called financial crisis. Business closed, he lost the house and everything. The shock of it all killed Ma as well. All because of one punch. It was a good one, mind you, and the git deserved it."

Dougie took another drink. He didn't come over as the master criminal I was looking for. I even felt sorry for him.

"How did you end up in Blackpool?"

"How does anybody end up in Blackpool? One crappy job after another. Lots of cider, always cider. Sorted out a fight in here one night. Tiffany offered me a job, fixed me up with a bedsit. That was five years ago. Not planning to go anywhere soon."

"What did you know of Parker's business?"

"Fancied himself as a bit of a businessman, but it was just a couple of vans shifting stuff."

"Did he work for anybody else in particular? Did he do any driving jobs for anybody?"

"You mean the getaway driver stuff? Plenty of rumours, but that sort of stuff scared the shit out of me. I've been inside once and don't fancy going back. I made sure I was busy elsewhere if he suggested a bit of overtime."

"Why leave Bradford?"

"Saved me killing some little shit-bag at work. Arrogant little prick. Told him what I thought of him one day. He took a swing at me with the hammer he was carrying. It's a good job I was quick on my feet in those days. I gave him the slip. Set off running and never looked back."

Cheering erupted from the other side of the room. We couldn't see the fight, but Dougie proved he was still no slouch as he disappeared into the crowd, on a mission to restore order.

I caught Tiffany's eye and pushed a twenty-pound note into her hand.

"Give the old guy a bonus. I think he's earned it. Cheers."

With Big Country's *In A Big Country* ringing in my ears, I turned and headed out of the door, glad to be in the open air again. A chilly drizzle had replaced the warm sunshine of earlier.

"Sod it."

The ice cream could wait for another day. I headed for the car and was on the motorway five minutes later. It was only then that I realised I'd forgotten to ask about Parker's son and why he'd disappeared.

I was back at home, feeling better for a crafty hour's kip in my armchair. With Jen away, the whole of Saturday evening stretched out before me. Infinite social possibilities. None of them included Jen in any meaningful way, which made me restless. The obvious thing to do was have an evening at the club with Joe, Rupert, and Ambrose. Then again, the hangover from last time was still fresh in the memory, tarnishing the appeal.

I could visit my parents, deal with some of the guilt of not seeing them often enough. That seemed daft, even to me. Having driven to the west coast and back this morning, was I now considering a drive to the east coast. Maybe not. Besides, I would meet Jen at Robin Hood's Bay in a couple of weeks, just a few miles from Mum and Dad. That would seem a more sensible time to visit.

I was trying to decide what to watch on TV when a text arrived. It was from Angel.

Pint? Crown in ten?

Saved. She needed some company, so it was more or less a mercy mission. Both me and the T-shirt passed the sniff test, so I grabbed my keys and locked the door.

My local, The Crown, was forty-seven steps from my front door. I'd counted. You never knew when this information would come in handy. As I walked in the front door, Angel was at the bar. We took our drinks outside. The drizzle from earlier had not made it this far. It was one of those warm evenings when most of the world was in the beer garden. By complete fluke, a couple of seats were going spare at the end of a long table.

"I thought you'd have your guitar with you," I said.

"It's stashed in my mate's storage unit in town. He lets me use it to save carting stuff around with me. I'm back busking again tomorrow."

"You must be raking it in."

"Yeah, what with the pittance you guys pay me and the coppers from the good citizens of Leeds, I'm looking at yachts on Monday."

"Pittance?"

"All right, I'm not complaining. The work is very welcome. I did bloody great today. Even getting a few regulars now. How did it go in Blackpool?"

"Mixed, to be fair. I think we can say Dougie isn't our man. Doesn't strike me as the planning and organising type. That's not to say he doesn't have the odd skeleton in the cupboard."

I told Angel all about his back story and prison sentence. By the time I'd finished, it was my round, and I went off to the bar, returning with two pints and two bags of crisps.

"So, the two names from the photograph were both dead ends," said Angel

"It looks like it. The one thing I forgot to do was ask Dwyer about the son that disappeared."

"Shame."

"So, I'm assuming you've been trying to track down Pete?"

"I have, with bugger all success. Either he doesn't exist anymore or he so doesn't want to be found."

"Not exist as in dead?"

"It's a possibility," said Angel.

"It's also a possibility that he escaped with loads of cash and reinvented himself, new name, plastic surgery, that sort of thing," I said.

"You'd think these days he'd leave some trace. I'll keep trying. There is one thing that could help us."

"What's that?"

"You've said nothing, but I'm assuming Robbie made you an offer."

It hadn't occurred to me that Angel would know about the files.

"So, you know about that?"

"We shared a cell for months. Very little I don't know. If the files are as good as she reckons, there should be some kind of lead in there. Have you got your hands on them yet?"

"No. She was going to speak to Rupert and set something up with her lawyer. I suppose it's taking a while to get things moving."

"Might be worth giving him a nudge. Try to speed things up a bit. Anyway, much as I hate to break up the party, I've got a hot date waiting for me. I'll see you on Monday."

Without further comment, she downed the rest of her drink, patted me on the head, and left me sitting there. I was considering my next move when my phone lit up.

Feet hurt, knackered but buzzing from day 1. Can I call you at 10? xx

At once, everything seemed better. It was just after nine. Just time to pick up a takeaway and be home for the call. After texting a thumbs up emoji, I finished my pint and headed for my lamb curry.

28

Against all the odds, I'd slept like a log. That had always struck me as a stupid phrase. What did trees know about sleeping? The call with Jen lasted about half an hour. I could have talked all night, but she sounded exhausted. Everything was going well. Ben was tired but loving every minute. With the promise of another call on Sunday, I'd gone to bed early. It felt like a real treat having downloaded Caimh McDonnell's *Last Orders* on my Kindle. Reading in bed had been a big thing for me when I was younger. The discovery of alcohol, amongst other things, almost killed my reading habit. Was it contentedness or age that meant I was spending the occasional evening like that?

I was just starting my second coffee. I Am Kloot provided the Sunday soundtrack, and I was halfway through *Last Orders*. It crossed my mind that there may just be a pub lunch involved later. The loud knock ended that particular fantasy.

"Why was the door locked? What were you up to?"

"Morning Rupert, come in. I wasn't up to anything. I just haven't been out today."

"Well, good news. You're going out now." Rupert looked at his watch. "Okay, maybe not now. Half an hour, just time for you to make me a coffee."

"It's already made. Grab yourself a cup."

There were few people I would allow to interrupt such a good Sunday morning, and Rupert was one of them. He was a regular visitor and knew where to find cups.

"So, what makes you so cheerful on Sunday morning? Not like you at all."

"I resent that," said Rupert, flopping onto the sofa without spilling his drink. "I think I'm still buzzing from last night."

"Don't you ever sleep?"

"Plenty of time for that when I'm your age."

"Cheeky sod. Although, I had an early night and I feel great for it."

"Good for you. It also means you can drive," said Rupert.

"Where are we going?"

"We're meeting the family's solicitor, Mr William Roberts."

"On Sunday?"

"I don't think he's too keen on his partners noticing what he's up to. He figures Sunday is the time to get this done. He's got some kind of contract for you to sign, then you get the files."

"Contract?"

"Don't worry. It's just some kind of legal mumbo jumbo designed to keep him and Robbie out of trouble if this all goes tits up."

"Why would it go tits up?" I was alarmed now.

"He just wants to impress upon you how important it is to be careful. I suspect there's some quite explosive stuff in there. Be wise, oh great one!"

"Where's this office?"

"It's just off Park Square in Leeds. Put some jeans on while I enjoy my coffee. I'm not sure the tatty dressing gown gives the right impression."

Rupert rang the doorbell of a very grand-looking office block.

A distant electronic voice answered.

"Come on up, Dominic."

I still did a double take when anybody used Rupert's real name. Some people just looked like a Rupert. The door buzzed, and we trooped inside. The wood-panelled walls let you know this was old school. No open plan, pastel colours and giant pot plants here. The stairs were steep, and I was out of breath when we reached the first floor landing. A door to our left opened and a large, red-faced man in his late sixties emerged.

"Dominic, come through."

"Thanks Uncle William. This is Frankie."

We shook hands.

"Ah, Mr Dale. I've heard a lot about you."

"Nothing good, I hope."

"Mmm."

My attempt at levity seemed to have fallen on its arse. The solicitor waved us into two chairs next to his immense desk. There was no offer of drinks.

"I have to tell you, I have advised Roberta that she should not go ahead with this transaction. The contents of the files have stayed between father and daughter so far, and I believe that is how they should stay. However, she is adamant that I release the files to you."

It was early days, but I suspected this man was a pompous old git. Just a hunch. He continued.

"To safeguard the family, I have drawn up a simple contract, which you will sign before you leave this office today. Otherwise, you will leave empty-handed."

He reached into a desk drawer and thumped a folder on the desk. Simple? It must've been at least fifty pages.

"How do I know the contract is in my best interests?"

"It's not. In simple terms, my responsibility is to look after the family. The decision you must make is whether to take the files and live with certain conditions or walk away."

I reached out and slid the folder towards me. I'd always been an excellent reader, way ahead of other kids at my first school, but now I understood dyslexia. The words on the page appeared to swim around and lose all meaning. Maybe that was the idea that solicitors relied on. I flicked through a few pages.

"Perhaps you'd be good enough to summarise for me, Mr Roberts?"

"Of course. Once you've signed, I hand over a storage device containing a digital copy of certain files. In return, you undertake not to share these files with any third party, including, but not limited to, the police, the press or business partners. In short, you keep it secret, for your eyes only. The penalty for non-compliance will be two million pounds."

"Where would I get two million quid from?"

"That, as my grandchildren may say, is your problem. I suggest you do not trigger the clause. Dominic's father still retains the services of a professional enforcement agency. Let's just say it would be best all-round if you comply."

My first reaction was to walk away. This was scary stuff. It was clear that leg-breaking would be at the lower end of the enforcement scale. I looked at Rupert. He nodded and handed me a pen. Should I sign? The alternative was not having access to the information that could reveal our Fifth Man. The entire TV series could rest on this. Besides, it would be a complete waste of a Sunday morning if I left empty-handed. With a shaking hand, I signed and slid the folder across the desk. The old lawyer returned the file to the desk drawer and locked it away. In return, he slid across a small USB stick.

"My secretary has encrypted the contents. I will deliver a password for the encryption in two stages. You will receive the first six characters as a text message on your mobile phone. I will send the second part to you at your office tomorrow morning at nine o'clock sharp. You will need to sign a receipt. Do you have questions?"

I could ask how much he would charge for drawing up a will, but I wanted to be gone. I pushed the USB drive into the small pocket just below the waistband of my jeans. Rupert answered brief questions about how his mother was and, seconds later, we were outside and heading for the car. My legs shook as we walked. What had I just done? To make matters worse, I couldn't even access it until I got the password on Monday.

"I need a sit down," I said, sounding feeble even for me.

"Normally, I would suggest that you buy me a pint."

"How do you mean — normally?"

"Joe has plans for me this afternoon. I need to get back."

"You mean you're abandoning me to a boring Sunday afternoon by myself?"

"Unless you want to join us, but I'm not sure it's your kind of thing."

"Why what —? Oh, I get it. Maybe not. Boring afternoon it is."

Twenty minutes later, I dropped Rupert at his place and drove another two minutes to home. I wondered what to do with the day — my *To Do* list! It was about time I attacked it. As I got out of the car, I reached for my phone. It wasn't there. Tell me I hadn't lost it. Had I left it in the solicitor's office in Leeds? Come to think of it, I didn't use it there. The panic subsided as I reached the living room. My phone was on the arm of the chair. I must've forgotten to pick it up when Rupert arrived. Two voicemails. Maybe they would save me from the admin tasks that were beckoning.

The first message turned out to be a silent call. So much for providing a distraction.

The second message was from Angel. There was lots of

background noise. I could just about make out the message. Something about tracing Pete Parker and she'd fill me in tomorrow. Again, my hopes of distraction had come to nothing. At least it looked like progress in finding the middle Parker.

Another texted photo from Jen saved me from the bank statement checking. They looked happy, sitting on a bench and laughing at the camera.

Outside a bothy!

The background looked spectacular. There was a second text about a minute later.

Horrible feeling that I left the iron on. Would you check? Hardly ever getting a signal. Will call 5ish. xx

I replied, telling her not to worry. The day had a purpose again. No bank statements for me. What could be more important than a walk in the sunshine to Jen's house to check that all was well? There was no way she would have left the iron on, but I could put her mind at rest.

Another message arrived. Crikey, she's keen, I thought. It wasn't from Jen. It comprised six characters with no explanation — the first part of the password.

29

I let myself in to Jen's house. It felt symbolic somehow. She'd entrusted the key to me. I felt quite grown up. As expected, the iron was in the kitchen cupboard where I knew it lived. No need to panic. The small watering can was on the shelf below. I watered the plants while I remembered. The house was quiet without Jen and Charley. The silence was creeping me out a bit. I grabbed the first CD I came to on the shelf. It was Air Supply, so I pushed it back into place. Next was All About Eve — that would do.

By the time I'd watered the plants, it was almost time to speak to Jen. Rather than being halfway home when she called, I hung around at the house. I made a cup of tea and found the biscuits. Jen called bang on time.

"Hello you. You've just caught me sitting on your sofa having a cup of tea."

"While the cat's away…"

"Full on rock and roll lifestyle, me. Iron checked, plants watered and biscuit barrel raided."

"I expected nothing less. Sounds lovely."

"How did today go?"

"It felt like a long way, but we arrived in one piece. You'd have loved this B&B. I'm promised a huge portion of steak pie later. Dad wants to eat at six then take himself off to bed early. I think he wants some respite from me, asking if he's okay all the time."

"And is he?"

"He's fine. It's nice being able to talk for hours on end. I'll miss him when…"

"Now, don't go down that route. Live for today and all that guff."

"You're right. I wish you were here. Could do with a foot rub."

"Think how good it will be when you get one."

"How's the search for our criminal going?"

I told her all about the visit to Leeds and the wait for the password. I also mentioned that Angel thought she may have more on the son who'd disappeared.

"Just you be careful. You never know whose toes you're stepping on. Don't put yourselves in any danger. If this series doesn't happen, we can do other things. I've already started kicking a few ideas around as we walk."

"Sounds good. Anything you want to share yet?"

"Not yet. Need to let things percolate a bit."

"And don't worry about me. Do I strike you as the person to get into any danger?"

I was a bit put out when she agreed. Was I so unadventurous? We chatted away for more than an hour. I felt like a teenager, not wanting the call to end. It was Jen that drew things to a close.

"Sorry. Early start in the morning. I'll call again tomorrow."

She must've triggered thoughts of sleep in my mind. I yawned and felt very content on the sofa. The sun through the window felt warm, and the music had finished. Somehow, sitting there in silence felt comfortable. Within minutes, I was asleep.

The breaking glass changed all that. My heart rate raced,

and I leapt to my feet. The noise had come from the kitchen. I burst through the door to be met by a black-clad figure halfway through the window. With a roar, or maybe more of a scream, I made a grab for the man's leg. Like a dog chasing a car, I had no idea what I would do if I caught it.

"Come here you bas—"

The threat ended as a size ten boot met my chin.

"Oof." This was all I could manage for now.

Had I scared him off with my warrior-like performance? Either way, he appeared to have legged it. I sat on the kitchen floor in the now silent house and checked for broken bones. When I decided everything hurt but there were no breaks, I stood up. My legs shook, but I forced myself to do a quick tour of the house, confirming my theory that I'd repelled the intruder. I went back and sat on the sofa, trying to control the shaking. What should I do now? After a minute to think, I called the police.

Twenty minutes later, there was a familiar knock at the door. I was so relieved to see Smirky and Tinkle on the doorstep. They would know what to do. On duty, they were PCs Newhouse and Smith.

"I'm so glad it's you two. Come in."

I explained what had happened. Tinkle went to check the garden and the rest of the house. Smirky stayed and made notes.

"That's a nasty bruise on your face. You should get that checked out at A&E."

"No, I'll be all right. Besides, I can't leave Jen's house with a big hole in the window. What if they come back?"

This hadn't occurred to me before. The heart rate soared again.

"I'll give you a number for an emergency joiner. He'll come and board it up for the night. I'll give you a crime number too, for the insurance. So, you say Jen isn't here?"

I explained about the walk, the iron, the plants and the phone call. Smirky nodded. He could see I was getting agitated.

"Don't worry, this'll all get sorted. We'll do a sweep of the usual suspects, but to be honest, there's little chance of nicking anybody." I could hear the toilet flush upstairs. "They're unlikely to come back. Chances are, it was just somebody trying their luck. I shouldn't say this, but they'll just move on and try somewhere else."

Smirky continued with his notes until Tinkle came back with a tray containing three mugs of tea.

"Tell you what. You drink your tea, I'll give the joiner a call. He's a mate of mine, so he might do you a deal."

"Thanks, Paul."

Tinkle kept me occupied.

"What a lovely house Jen has," she said.

She'd put sugar in my tea, which I hate, but she insisted I drink it. Good for shock, she reckoned. Smirky had finished on the phone.

"He'll be here in half an hour. He'll board it tonight, then order the glass for you in the morning and he's waiving the callout fee."

"Cheers, mate. I don't know what I'd have done without you both."

"It's why we're here. And don't worry about it, he's not coming back."

There was a loud, unintelligible squawk from Tinkle's radio. They sprang to their feet.

"Duty calls," said Smirky.

"You can't have understood what that said?"

"Not a word, but it's hardly ever telling us to sit with a cuppa. You take care."

I locked the door after they'd gone, before touring the house, turning on every light I could find. I'd just about stopped shaking an hour later.

The joiner had boarded the window, and I'd swept the glass away. It was after midnight. I felt more tired than I had in my entire life. It was a warm night. With every light in the house still blazing, I lay on the sofa and slept.

Was it a noise that woke me at around 3am, wondering where the hell I was? Then the memory hit me. Not moving a muscle, I'd listened for ages before convincing myself it was all quiet. The sweat made my shirt cling, but there was no way I was opening a window. I considered moving upstairs. It seemed wrong, somehow. I would stay on the sofa, cricked neck and all, guarding the house from further invasion. At some point, I must've drifted off to sleep again.

By seven o'clock I was at the kitchen table drinking coffee. Should I contact Jen and tell her what had happened? I decided there was no point worrying her. As Smirky said, somebody had been trying their luck. Chances were, they wouldn't come back. To be on the safe side, I'd speak to Angel to get some cameras installed. On further reflection, Jen could see that as creepy. They weren't coming back. Everything would be okay.

The BBC weather forecast assured me it was going to be another beautiful sunny day for Jen and Ben's third day. They were walking from Rosthwaite to Grasmere today, only nine miles. What was I thinking? There was nothing '*only*' about nine miles. I was full of admiration for what they were both achieving.

After rinsing my cup and checking once more the house was secure, I set off to walk home. I planned a quick change and then go straight to the cottage. The delivery of the encryption password was due at nine. I'd have to get a wriggle on. I wondered what Angel had found out. Could Pete Parker be our man? It would explain why he disappeared. Was he living somewhere under a new identity, spending the fortune he'd amassed from a life of crime? If Angel had new information, maybe we'd find him soon.

The walk home was all downhill, and I was soon pushing open the front door. As I stepped inside, I felt something crack under my foot. Dad's drawing of the *Aladdin Sane* cover from just inside the door was lying face down. I cursed my DIY skills. Hanging a picture on the wall without it falling down was beyond me. I rescued the drawing and picked up the broken glass, putting everything on the small table to be dealt with later. Buying a new frame needed to go on my famous *To Do* list. At least there was no post. No lawsuit today.

I took the stairs two at a time. Well, the first six anyway, then I slowed down to a speed more befitting my current fitness levels. Out of breath, I could see my black jeans thrown on the floor of the bedroom. Nothing too unusual about that. Everything else being strewn around the floor was unusual. My first thought, oddly, was a poltergeist had struck. As I took in more of the devastation, it became obvious. The burglars had been here as well. Someone had tipped every drawer onto the bed. My wardrobe ransacked; the contents scattered on the floor. The bedside lamp lay smashed in pieces on the floor next to a framed picture of Jen. I picked up the picture and set it on the bedside table.

If I thought the bedroom was bad, the sight that greeted me downstairs was worse. The kitchen floor was a sea of smashed plates and glasses. Again, the contents of every drawer lay scattered. The kitchen window was open. Through the fog of adrenaline, I tried to think about valuables. My laptop. Sure enough, it was gone, along with my iPad from the chair arm. The expensive speakers and TV were still there, untouched. A couple of record cases smashed, the contents joining everything else on the floor. Little did the petty thugs realise that some were worth way more than the laptop.

I moved a couple of books out of my chair and flopped down. Feeling sick and shaking, I wondered what to do next. Would Smirky be back on shift? We'd exchanged mobile numbers when he worked with us on the film, but maybe it was best to go through the official route. For the second time in twelve hours, I called the police to report a break-in. A calm voice took the details and promised to get somebody out to me as soon as possible.

"Have you been having a party?" It was Angel. "The front door was open so I... Jesus, you look like crap."

"Good to see you, too. I think it was burglars."

"No shit, Sherlock. Either that or you need to have a word with your cleaner. Have you called the police?"

"Just done it. They're sending somebody round."

Angel sat on the edge of the coffee table.

"What did they take?"

"As far as I can see, just laptop and iPad," I said.

"Easy to flog."

"But there's other, more valuable stuff they just left."

Angel considered this for a moment.

"Maybe this wasn't about how much stuff's worth."

"How do you mean?"

"What if somebody doesn't like the questions we're asking? Maybe we're getting a bit too close for comfort and somebody's trying to find out what we know, or put the frighteners on us."

"They managed that."

I told Angel about the attempted break-in at Jen's.

"That's too much of a coincidence, if you ask me. Shit. The offices. I take it you haven't been this morning?"

"No, but Melanie will be in by now. We'd have heard something. Oh bugger — the cottage. That's the obvious target, if you're right."

"Okay. You stay here and wait for the police. I'll check."

"Here, take the keys." As I pulled the keyring from my pocket, I felt the USB stick. Was that what the burglars were looking for? This was getting scarier by the minute. "What time is it?"

"Just after nine, why?"

"No reason."

"I'll call you from the cottage. Once the police have been, I'll come back and help you clear up."

Angel squeezed my hand as she stood up. When she'd left, I reflected on how good a friend she was becoming. Then again, she was one of a tiny number who knew about the USB stick that was in my pocket. Was she too good to be true?

There was the familiar knock.

"Morning Frankie."

PC Newhouse stepped inside. His colleague followed, making a beeline for the downstairs loo.

"Sorry, do you mind if I just…"

She knew the way already. Smirky followed me down the hall.

"Sorry to bother you, Frankie. Looks like there's been an admin cock up at our end. We had a reported break-in here. I told 'em we'd already been out to you last night. Holy shit. What a mess."

I spread my arms as if displaying a speedboat on a quiz show.

"Two break-ins in two days?"

"Two in one night," I said. "I stayed at Jen's and got back to this."

"Bit of a coincidence," said Smirky.

"They happen," I said, clinging to that hope.

"Any idea if somebody has a grudge against you?"

"No. You've met Jen. She's the nicest person in the world."

Smirky nodded. Tinkle joined us.

"You need to be more careful when you fl — bloody hell, what a mess," she said, taking in the scene.

"Careful when I what?"

"Never mind. You don't want to know."

We cleared a space at the kitchen table. The two officers went through their standard routine. They logged the missing laptop and iPad. They seemed interested that nothing else appeared to have gone.

"This could connect to you being assaulted last night. I'll try to get somebody out to look for fingerprints. Leave the clearing up for now. I'll get them here as soon as possible."

It was the first time I'd been told not to clear up a mess. I looked around again at the destruction. Even Charley's painting was ripped from the fridge and trampled. That was the final straw. I couldn't hold the emotion and shivered despite the warmth in the kitchen. Deep inside, I knew this was not coincidence or a chance break-in. Asking questions was upsetting somebody. Should I tell Smirky and Tinkle? Should we just take the hint and abandon the project?

Before I could say anything, Angel was back. I introduced her to the police force's finest.

"Angel's joined us as a researcher," I added.

"Sounds interesting. What are you working on?" Smirky asked.

Angel hesitated and looked at me. Before I could answer, Tinkle interrupted.

"Whatever it is, could it have something to do with the break-ins?"

"What makes you say that?"

"Not got poker faces, you two. It's obvious you weren't telling us everything."

I was ashamed to say I'd underestimated Twinkle's powers

of detection. Was there any point denying it? Would telling them help? Besides, I was shit-scared that we hadn't seen the last of this.

"We're investigating a gang of jewel thieves that murdered at least two people," I blurted.

Smirky turned to a fresh page in his notebook and gave me a look. I cracked under this interrogation and told him what we'd done so far. When I'd finished, Smirky put away his pen.

"I think I need to get the experts in. At least tell DI Cagney."

Great. That's all we needed. Smirky moved outside to call Cagney. Tinkle got busy with the kettle. Angel confirmed that the cottage was secure and passed over a white card.

"The courier is very sorry he missed you and will call again tomorrow."

Shit. The encryption password. Not much I could do now. The files were something I wasn't telling the police about. Two million quid was two million quid. I pushed the card into my pocket. Angel picked up on the slight shake of my head and changed the subject.

"Have you phoned Jen yet?"

"No. I'll speak to her tonight, but I'm tempted not to tell her. I don't want to spoil the walk. It's a big thing for them."

Smirky rejoined us, confirming that the fingerprint expert was on his way. Cagney would be in touch, whatever that meant. We drank our tea and chatted about everything but criminal gangs.

The fingerprint man confirmed there was nothing useful. His work added to making the house look like a crime scene. I suppose it was a crime scene, so that was all right. Tinkle offered to come back after her shift to help with the clean-up. I thanked her but told her not to worry. She did her usual little dance and went off to the bathroom. Her colleague wrapped things up.

"If you think of anything, call me. I'll try to have a talk with Cagney, see if that spares you the bother."

"Thanks. I've got enough to do trying to put my house back together."

Closing the door, I took a deep breath before returning to the kitchen.

"We should get pissed," I said.

"With respect." Any sentence that starts like that was not about to show respect. "We haven't got time for you to feel sorry for yourself. I'll make a start in here. You go put loud music on, then sort your bedroom out. If nothing else, you can make a meal and get a decent night's sleep if we do that. Then I'll visit the courier, see if I can speed up your delivery."

I obeyed. Angel got busy with bin bags and rubber gloves. I wondered where she'd got the rubber gloves from, but decided not to worry about it. To a loud soundtrack provided by Dizzee Rascal, I got busy in the bedroom, so to speak.

An hour later, the bedroom was more or less back to normal. Jen's bedside picture now looked out at a restful place once again. It needed a new frame, but that could wait. Downstairs, Angel had performed miracles in the kitchen and was already clearing the living room.

"By the way, how are you going to speed up the delivery?"

"Look at the card again," said Angel.

I did. Penelope's Parcels were sorry they'd missed me.

30

"What if this is what the burglars were after?"

I held up the memory stick.

"I definitely think that's more likely than just a random break in," said Angel.

We were sitting in the large, open-plan office.

"I suppose it's no use to anybody without the password."

"It shouldn't be long now. I called round to see our neighbour, and he offered to get it delivered here today," said Angel.

"How did you get him to agree to that?"

"He seems reasonable once you get to know him. Quite charming."

"I don't trust him."

"Why's that?"

"Where do I start? Trying to charge us a grand to give us names of his grandad's associates for a start."

"He explained. He just wants to treat the old guy using the money."

"Okay, but then he changed his mind but kept my cash."

"I suppose that's not great."

"And what about the white van?"

"What about it?"

"Why is it always parked outside here? Why isn't he out delivering stuff?"

"Maybe he spends most of his time managing the business and only helps with deliveries when they're busy?"

"I still don't like him."

"That's it then. He's a bad-un." Angel was mocking me now. I pushed my seat back from the desk and shoved my hands deep in my pockets. "There is one thing that's been bothering me, though. The couple of afternoons I spent with the old man, I didn't think he was suffering from dementia. Okay, he struggles to speak after the stroke. He seemed quite sharp to me. Lonely, wanting somebody to talk to. Then Al steps in and comes up with the dementia story. I just worry it was deliberate, to stop me from asking awkward questions."

"It's a shame you can't see him again, now that we know a bit more."

"Maybe I can."

"How? Parker's put you on the care home's bad lads list. They won't let you in. His message to stay away was clear enough."

"Leave it with me. I might have a plan."

Tom was walking towards us.

"Special delivery," he said, handing over the slim envelope.

"Thanks Tom. And thanks for organising the new laptop."

"We bought a batch of them for the new starters. Is it okay?"

"It's great, thanks. Did you open this?"

"No. You mean the torn corner? I asked Ray about that."

"Ray?"

"The driver. Sorry, I thought you knew. I used to work there, so I know all the drivers. He just said it must've got damaged in transit."

I glanced at Angel. Could somebody have tried to open the

envelope, or was I just paranoid? Could I trust Angel? If I opened the envelope now, she would have access to the password. Was I just being stupid? The thought of trying to do this without her convinced me. I opened the package. For a moment, I thought the envelope was empty. Had somebody stolen the password? I held it over the desk and shook it. A tiny scrap of paper fell out, containing a complex, ten character password.

My paranoia stepped up a level, and I insisted we transfer everything we had at the moment to a meeting room on the first floor. I'd checked earlier. The door was lockable. I just needed to get the key from Melanie. If somebody trashed my house to get their hands on this, the least I could do was keep stuff locked away.

On the third attempt, I plugged the stick into my laptop. I entered both parts of the password — we were in. At first glance, the work Robbie had put into this was impressive. There appeared to be a search function and the ability to view by location, year, and family.

I took a deep breath, typed Peter Parker and clicked the search icon.

No results.

"What! How do you mean, no results?"

"Have you spelt it right?"

"How many ways are there to spell Parker for f —"

"Okay, I'm sure there's an explanation," said Angel, trying to calm me down.

"Maybe we just invested too much hope in this. Robbie's dad couldn't know every criminal in the north of England, could he?"

"How about you stay and play with this and I'll go off and speak to my new best friend?"

"Oh yeah, who's that?"

"I don't know her name yet, but give me a couple of hours.

There's a bus in ten minutes. I'm off to charm my way into the care home. If the database won't tell us about Parker, maybe we should try the man himself again."

I was still staring at the screen as Angel left the room to answer her phone. Was I missing something? The short answer was yes, I was missing something. That became obvious when I called Spud for IT advice.

"Did you read the manual?"

"Of course not. Why would I do that?"

"Because, I suspect it will tell you that for the search to work, you need to install the database on your laptop, not just run it from the memory stick," said Spud. He sounded smug. "Your IT skills are getting rusty."

"To be fair, even when I was full time, I never read manuals."

We chatted for a while about how the business was running. It turned out things were going well, despite his partner getting more and more silent as the months passed. I promised to call in soon and hung up. I had some software to set up.

It was a universal law of anything IT related. People who most need to read manuals are the ones least likely to read them. Whether it's somebody with no knowledge at all who expects to just do stuff, to those like me who should know better. Anyway, twenty minutes later, I could see a comforting message.

Building index. Estimated time 6 minutes.

This was looking more promising. I just had to wait.

"Does swearing at the screen make it go faster?" said Angel. She was leaning against the door frame, jacket in hand.

"Scientific fact," I said.

"Right. I'm off. I'll call you later."

Ten minutes after, with an estimated completion time of 7

minutes, patience was running out. There was only one solution. I went in search of caffeine.

Flic was spooning coffee into a fresh filter.

"Morning stranger. Not seen you for a few days," she said with a smile. "You keeping out of mischief."

"Always. You know me."

"I'm glad you're here. Are you free for lunch on Wednesday? Demus is coming over. The BBC has commissioned us, technically, you to write eight more children's stories. Demus has signed up and wants to kick things around a bit."

"Sounds great. Always up for lunch with the stars."

"He was asking how the research was going for *Burning Down The House*."

I updated Flic on progress, skipping the bit about the database.

"Keep going. If we can land that, you are going to be busy all year."

"I don't suppose you've heard from your friend Guthrie about what he intends to do?"

"Nothing yet. That's got to be good news. Maybe he's calming down and he'll forget the lawsuit. Try not to worry."

Flic poured coffee into two mugs and handed one over.

"Got to go. Got a call in two minutes. Will let you know about Wednesday."

Once she'd gone, I raided the biscuit tin and took my haul back to the meeting room. The index build had finished. It announced that there were two hundred and four entries. That seemed low, given the size of the database. Risking my credibility in the IT community, I went back to the manual. After half an hour, I worked out what was going on. The tool that Robbie had used was basic. She'd been adding keywords and hadn't got all the way through. A large part of the database was uncategorised and invisible to the sort program. I needed to call Rupert to see if he could do something clever to automate a full index.

It was a long shot but, once again, I keyed in the name Peter Parker. The crossed fingers paid off, and a single entry appeared.

Five minutes later, I wondered if Peter Parker's son was dead.

I printed the article from the database and headed off to see Joe. He was the only fluent Spanish speaker I knew, and the piece needed a better translation than the online tools could provide.

The locked door to the club stopped me, so I headed for the record shop entrance. Ambrose had an eclectic taste in music, but his choice today was surprising. Jose Carreras boomed across the deserted shop. Even at this volume, I could hear Joe singing along. Then the relevance of the song hit me.

I crossed the shop floor as the Spanish tenor reached a crescendo. It was quite something that Joe didn't injure himself. My applause triggered a theatrical bow with kisses blown to all four corners of the shop.

"You're here to rescue me. Thank you," said Ambrose, hitting the stop button on the music.

"I take it the surprise is out of the bag?"

"Yes. I've never seen him so excited. Bloody Granada on repeat all morning."

Joe burst into song again as he moved towards us. He was actually very good.

"Granada tierra sonada por mi… Hello lovely. Nice to see a smiley face after being with this grumpy bugger all morning."

"I'm not grumpy," insisted Ambrose. "It was very entertaining for the first ten minutes. After that, not so much.

Besides, not all of us are off to Spain for the week. Some of us are working sixteen hours a day for that week."

"And you shall get your reward in heaven. However, I will get my reward in GRANADA."

Again he belted out the word in true Carreras style. At least Ambrose was grinning as he shook his head.

"Can I pick out some music that might not frighten our customers away?"

"You may, but there's every chance they shall force me to reprise my performance later," said Joe with another bow.

Ambrose replaced Jose with *Aretha Live At Fillmore West*. I couldn't help but notice he started at *Don't Play That Song*, a nice subtle dig. Either Joe didn't notice or ignored it.

"So, Frankie, to what do we owe this pleasure?"

"Would you believe me if I said I just wanted to share your joy at the prospect of a few days in Granada?"

"No. What are you after?"

"Fair cop. I want you to translate this for me." I handed over the printed sheet. "It looks like it's a story from a Spanish newspaper."

Joe took the paper and began reading.

"It's from a local paper for Las Alpujarras. A tourist discovered a body in Lanjaron. It's believed to be an English ex-pat, Peter Smith, 56, heroin overdose. Police believe accidental death of a junkie. They aren't looking for anybody else in connection with the death. His widow, Pat Smith, 47 of Orgiva, is adamant that he never took drugs and believes her husband died in a tragic accident." Joe handed back the sheet. "Strange that Spanish newspapers are just as age obsessed as they are here. So who's this Pat Smith, and why are you interested?"

"To be honest, I'm not sure. I need to do more digging. Thanks, you've been very helpful."

The name had thrown me. Why was this story indexed

under Peter Parker? The obvious thing to check was whether Peter Smith and Peter Parker were the same person. I felt my phone vibrate in my pocket. A text from Angel.

I need you to be my boyfriend this afternoon. Meet me at the office at 2.30.

Today had just taken a strange turn. I checked the time. Better get going.

"Sorry, need to dash. Have a great time in Spain, Joe. And Ambrose — I'll see you later, love to Stella."

With that, I was gone. I had a hot date with Angel.

31

Angel had spotted the car pulling up outside the office and headed out to meet me.

"What are you up to now?" I asked.

"Well, for one afternoon only, you get to be my boyfriend."

"I'm flattered, obviously. But also worried."

"No need. My new mate, Corinne, has given us the thumbs up to visit the old guy in the care home. She was reluctant at first. The grandson laid the law down good and proper. We need to go now."

I set the satnav and slipped the car into gear.

"So why did she agree?"

"Parker, the youngest, gets up the nose of all the staff. She reckons the picture of the devoted grandson is bollocks. He turns up two or three times a year and buggers off early after upsetting somebody. Corinne's quite worried about the old guy. She says there's nothing wrong with his memory, but they're worried about him having another stroke. I assured her we just wanted to cheer him up. What could be more cheery than a visit from his new chum and her wet boyfriend?"

"Charming. But seriously, why do you need me there?"

"I thought you would come in handy on the off chance that

the grandson turns up."

"You mean I'm there for protection? A bit of muscle to intimidate him?"

"No. I meant you could keep the old man company while I beat the crap out of his worthless grandson."

I wasn't sure if she was joking. We were stuck behind a bus that was waiting to turn right. I told Angel about the newspaper article that Joe had translated.

"And you think Peter Smith is, or was, Parker? What would that do to the old man if it's true? Not a word of it today, do you hear me? We have to be certain before we do anything," said Angel.

"So, why are we going today?"

"We're going to cheer up an old man. If he identifies the brains behind a gang of murderous jewel thieves, so much the better."

"And what happens if his grandson turns up?"

"As I said, I'll protect you," said Angel, patting my arm. "He won't turn up. Best park around the back. You never know."

"I thought you said —"

"Just playing safe. Corinne confirmed something that I'd been wondering about. Do you remember Elgin lying about going to see the Bulls on Sunday afternoon?"

"Yes. Do you know what he was up to?"

"Corinne mentioned Parker'd had a visitor. He was wearing a dog collar. So much for them having no contact these days. She reckons he's been before, too."

"Should we quiz Parker about it?"

"I'm not sure. Let's play it by ear. I don't want to risk antagonising him."

We drove on in silence. Traffic was light, and we soon entered the grounds of the care home.

"There, look, plenty of spaces."

Not feeling reassured, I reversed into a slot. You never knew when you'd need a quick getaway. As we got out of the car, I couldn't help noticing that we were being watched from a ground-floor window.

"We're being watched from that ground-floor window," I said aloud.

Angel followed my gaze.

"Good. That's Corinne. She said she'd look out for us."

The figure in the window pointed to her right. We made our way to the end of the building. A door swung open and Corinne ushered us inside, checking that we hadn't attracted attention. For people who said they were confident that Parker wouldn't turn up, there was a lot of nervous checking going on. After Angel introduced me to Corinne, we followed her down a narrow corridor.

"Everybody is in the garden or the conservatory. I thought we could use the snug, more private. You wait in here. I'll bring Peter through," said Corinne.

"What about signing in? I could come around to reception with you."

"No. I think we keep this as unofficial as possible. The fewer people know you're here, the better."

This was all very cloak and dagger, and I was getting anxious. My mind flashed back to standing in the headmaster's office, a bollocking imminent, and the fear that was attached to it. This was ridiculous. We were here to chat with an old man. Fair enough, the old man had been a getaway driver, but he was now in his eighties.

"Here he is," said Angel, all smiles and hugs for the tiny figure in the wheelchair. Parker held on to her hand.

"This is such a pleasant surprise, dear." He spoke slowly, trying hard to annunciate. The stroke had affected his speech, but he got there in the end. "They told me you wouldn't come back. Something to do with causing trouble. I said it didn't sound like you. And who's this shifty looking young man?"

"Now, behave you old goat. He's not shifty. Gormless but not shifty. This is Frankie. He's the writer I told you about. Remember?"

Corinne was back, with a tray containing a teapot, mugs and chocolate biscuits. She poured the tea before she whispered.

"Need to keep it short today, okay? I'll be back."

As she closed the door behind her, I reached out and took a drink. Peter spoke slowly, but loud and with a slight slurring.

"So you two are bumping bits, then?" A stream of tea hurtled down my nose and through my eye sockets. "That's a nasty cough you've got there, son." Parker chuckled and set himself off on a wild coughing spree.

"That serves you right, you cheeky old codger," laughed Angel. "Never you mind what we're doing. How are you?"

"Sorry dear, I couldn't resist it. No offence, son. Here, have a tissue."

I looked at the tatty ball of tissue he was offering and quickly retrieved my own from my pocket. With normal breathing restored to both of us, the old man continued.

"I'm not so good, to be honest, love. Dodgy ticker is what they say. I just know I'm always buggered. Sleep most of the day, then get up to pee most of the night. There's no fun getting old."

"Better than the alternative," I said, then realised that was insensitive, to say the least. Parker looked at me. I was just about to apologise when he erupted in laughter again.

"You're not wrong there, son. We lost another one this week. One minute we're playing dominoes and having a laugh. Next minute he's slumped across the table and there's staff charging round all over the place. Such a shame."

"Was he a good friend of yours?"

"Couldn't stand the bloke. It was a shame cos I only

needed to win that game to take a tenner off him. I'll miss him."

"Even though you couldn't stand him?" asked Angel.

"Only one round here that could play fives and threes, course I'll miss him. Miss a lot of stuff in here."

"You must miss cars," I said, trying to steer him towards tales of being a getaway driver.

"Had some nice motors in my time. Can't beat a powerful engine at full throttle."

"You liked to drive fast?"

"Had to do in my line of work. I'm sure Angel's told you what I did for a living?"

"She might've mentioned something. Do you miss those days?"

"I miss a lot of things, son. A lot of things…" He drifted off into memories for a moment. I finished my tea and put the cup back on the tray. "I miss the wife, even after twenty years, but I miss my boy most of all. The way he just upped and left. I always thought he'd come back, put things right. No chance of that now: not even sure how many games of dominoes I've got left. I always thought Pat would calm him down, talk him into coming back."

"Pat?"

"His wife. Lovely girl. Didn't approve of my work, but Pete thought the world of her. We all did — most of us anyway"

"Really?" I almost held my breath.

"My grandson never got on with her. I suppose being a stepmum is tough. Mind you, he fell out with his dad big-style."

"Why was that?"

"He thought he'd walked out on him and his mum. Left them both behind so that he could swan off to a better life. Then his mum died in a car accident. Al came to live with us.

Never forgave his dad, even though he seemed happy enough with me and his gran."

"But last time I was here, you told me Pete came back. How long was he away?"

"Eight years in all. Eight years in prison for something he didn't do."

"And his son didn't know he'd been to prison?"

"No. Maybe we should've told him. It was difficult. He was difficult… troubled. He was only 15 when his dad got out, but he'd been through…"

Parker appeared to drift off again, a single tear rolling down his cheek. Angel moved across and hugged him. Corinne reappeared at the door.

"Time somebody was having a nap." she said.

"Come again soon, love," wheezed Parker.

"Maybe we could have a video call?"

Corinne stepped in.

"We tried him with a tablet once, but he struggled to make out details. Best in person, I suspect."

"We'll come back soon. You look after yourself," said Angel, giving him one last squeeze.

It was difficult to see this little old man as a career criminal. I had to admit, I quite liked him.

"You're quiet," I said to Angel as we drove back to the office.

"Sorry. It's sad. I know he was a bad lad when he was younger, but he wouldn't hurt a fly now. He's desperate to make things up with his son."

"Trouble is, if we're right and his son died in Spain…"

"I think the news would finish him. Then again, Corinne thinks a surprise fart could finish him."

We completed the rest of the drive in silence. It was only when we were back in the meeting room, with all the flip charts, that Angel came alive again.

"I've been thinking about Parker's son going to prison for something he didn't do," she said.

"Shame we didn't get to ask him more about that. What if he was guilty, and it was something violent?"

"So, it's not just me thinking that he could be capable of killing somebody?"

"I still don't buy it that the security guard was shot by Thompson. Nothing about how the older guys worked suggested any sort of violent streak. Let's do some digging, see if Pete Parker was out of prison at the time of the shooting," I said.

"Must admit, I hadn't thought of that. Is it more likely that he killed Jason's dad?"

"I'm not sure we'll ever know that," I said. "If the American police found nothing…"

"There must be something we can do." Angel thought for a moment. "We need to confirm whether Peter Smith is Pete Parker."

"And how do we do that?"

"We track down the widow. To be fair, I think it would be an enormous coincidence if the Pat in the paper is not his wife. If they wanted to disappear, it would make sense to change surnames but keep first names. Less chance of a calling each other the wrong name."

"Spain's a big place. How do we go about tracing her?"

"Show me the article."

I tapped away on my laptop and shared it on the big screen.

"Do you understand Spanish?"

"A little. We did it at school but, you know… Hang on, she's based in Orgiva? Where have I heard that name before?"

Before I could search online for information about the village, Angel cut in.

"*Driving Over Lemons*!"

"What?"

"*Driving Over Lemons*. Google it. Chris Stewart wrote a book about buying a farm in Spain. I'm pretty sure —"

"Orgiva. There it is. How come you knew that?"

"Like I said, reading was the one thing that kept me sane when I was inside. Robbie recommended it. The house they were planning to settle in was just down the road from there."

I was scanning the entries thrown up by Google.

"It's near Granada," I said. "We know somebody who is heading there tomorrow."

I picked up my phone.

"Joe, how do you fancy an adventure?"

By the time I'd finished on the phone, Angel was back with two mugs of tea.

"Well, is Joe up for it?"

"He sees himself in an episode of Scooby Doo, of course, he's up for it. He needs to work his magic on Rupert, but I can't see that being a problem."

"If she's still there, it shouldn't be too difficult to find her. Orgiva's not a big place."

32

The room was dark but my phone was ringing. That was never good. I answered it before I was fully awake.

"Hello?"

"Mr Dale?"

Sounded formal — another bad sign.

"Yes."

"Shit. I forgot the time difference. I'm dreadfully sorry. What time is it there."

I looked at my watch.

"Just after three in the morning. Who is this?"

"Sorry. I can call back later. I didn't think."

"Hang on. Is that Mrs Wilkinson?"

I was now wide awake and eager to speak to the widow of the man guilty of the security guard murder.

"Liz. Yes it is. So sorry to wake you."

"Don't worry. I'm glad you called."

I was fully awake now and heading for my desk.

"Your letter arrived a few days ago. I wasn't sure I wanted to drag all this up again."

"I appreciate it must be painful for you. Thank you for calling."

"You wanted to know why Gabriel changed his plea. It

was quite simple really. He wanted to provide for me and our daughter. At the point where he was arrested, he was having tests. He'd always been a heavy smoker. The doctors had an easy job and he was diagnosed with lung cancer just before the trial. He was approached by a solicitor who offered him a large sum of money to change his plea."

"Who was behind the money?"

"We never knew, not officially. My belief is that his trial would've uncovered illegal activities by some very senior officials connected to organised crime."

"Officials? You mean government?"

"Maybe, but more likely the police. Some very strange things happened around that time. Gary Stevens getting witness protection for a start. Danny O'Neill getting shot, our payoff. Lots of stuff seemed to just melt away. Gabriel paid a heavy price for it."

"So, you took the payoff because you believed Gabriel was terminally ill?"

"That's right. By doing that the trial was cancelled and the investigation was tied up in a nice red ribbon. Case closed. Of course, what they didn't factor in was Gabriel's health. Once he was in prison they began treatment. Turned out the diagnosis was wrong. The tumour was benign. After it was removed, we looked into withdrawing the confession and appealing the conviction. We just ran into a brick wall. Every move we made, we just got the same answer. The conviction was valid. Whoever was blocking it knew what they were doing. My poor husband spent the next twenty years of his life in prison for a murder he didn't commit. We were talking to the lawyers about the chances of getting parole when he fell ill again. This time it was cancer. Once he knew, he made me promise to move on. Tony had been his best friend. When Tony's wife died, Gabriel suggested that we get together. He died six months later. Me and Tony got married and moved out here to make a fresh start."

"That's quite a story. It must've been hard on you. Are you sure you don't know who's behind the payoff or who organised the robberies."

"Not a clue. I don't think Gabriel knew anything about who he worked for. He'd get instructions of where to be and when, do the job and get paid. As for whoever paid us off, I'd say don't poke a stick at them. They're very powerful and extremely ruthless."

I thanked Liz for calling and hung up. It was only then I realised I was shaking. This was serious stuff we were getting into. Was it worth it for a TV series?

The early morning call had made it a strange day. I'd sneaked back to bed until this afternoon, then given myself a stiff talking to. My doubts about it all being worth it were gone. I was more determined than ever to work out what had happened.

After reviewing what we knew so far, my money was on Pete Parker. I had no proof, but I suspected that he had committed at least one murder. They released him from prison just before the security guard was shot. Could it have been him? Somebody killed Stevens a year before Pete died. Had Parker been the killer, then succumbed to remorse and killed himself? It would be interesting to see if Parker had crossed the Atlantic just before the murder. If he'd been at home, there was no way he could've killed Stevens. It was then I'd realised I may have a contact who could help. Eugene Chandler would be the ideal person to check the immigration records.

I checked my watch. It was lunchtime in New York. The chances of getting Darlene on the phone were slim, given her workload, so I sent her an email. An hour later, I had a reply.

* * *

Frankie

Good to hear you're staying out of trouble. Your email came as a surprise. Few clients keep in touch once I save their ass! If you end up needing to defend the lawsuit, I'd be happy to put you in touch with somebody.

As for your other suggestion, without police involvement and a warrant, there is no way that this is possible. You would need to find another way to confirm that this Parker guy entered the States in the time span you suggest. Eugene only has a few months to go to retirement. He'd never countenance providing this information illegally. Sorry.

On the upside, we are planning to visit Europe next year. It would help if I could phone you and get some advice.

Keep taking the pills (maybe not)

Best regards

Darlene

The email to Darlene had been worth a shout. At least she'd got back to me straight away. I would have to think of something else.

I was still in the office when Jen called for our evening video chat. She seemed a bit more sombre than usual.

"Are you okay? You sound a bit…"

"Don't worry about me. I'm fine. I suppose a bit bruised."

"The feet?"

"A bit, but I was thinking more emotionally." Jen reached for a tissue. I wanted to reach out and hold her.

"Seems like you could do with a hug. Do you need me to come? I could be there in just over an hour."

"That's sweet but, no, there's no need. I'm not saying it wouldn't be nice, but you've got loads to do. To be honest, I need to meet Dad in the bar soon. I'll be fine after some food and an early night. It's just the conversation today got deep. He was telling me what he wants to happen, when — you know — the time comes. I agreed to help him set up a living will. That way, we decide everything up front and we can concentrate on being together rather than weighing up what to do. His main stipulation is not to resuscitate if…" Jen blew her nose. "Says the last thing he needs is for his final memory to be somebody bashing on his chest or putting a million volts through him. He just wants to slip away holding our hands."

"If you've got to go, that sounds like a nice way. At least you'll all be together. I hope you know — whatever you need from me — you've got it. If there is absolutely anything…"

"Ta. I don't think I could get through this without you being there." Jen took a deep breath. "Anyway, enough of me. Tell me about your day. Any news of murderers?"

"Well, funny you should ask."

I went over the day's events, trying not to get too long winded.

"So, you're thinking that the son was the killer and the fifth man?"

"It's pointing that way. Hopefully, Joe can track down the widow and she'll speak to us."

"You're certainly making progress. Who would've thought that my man was such a good detective?"

"I wouldn't go that far."

"Admit it, you're loving this."

"Course I am."

"Right, on that note, I need to get some food."

"Are you sure you're okay?"

"I feel a lot better just for chatting. I'll be fine after a night's sleep. Speak soon. Night-night."

"Night love, speak soon."

I put the phone in my pocket and packed up. It was time I was at home. Before I could switch off my monitor, the phone rang again. Had Jen forgotten something? Better still, had she changed her mind about me driving to be with her?

"Hello gorgeous. You just can't keep your hands off me, can you?"

"Damn, you Brits get real friendly real soon. What happened to the English reserve?"

"Darlene! Sorry. I thought you…"

"Hell, don't you go letting a girl down now." Her laugh was infectious. "Shall we start again? Good evening, Frankie. This is Darlene."

"Good afternoon to you, Darlene. Good to hear from you. How are you?"

"I'm real good. Busy as usual. Just on my way to see another dumbass client at the airport, and it reminded me to call you."

"I'm touched."

"Look, this conversation never happened — understood?"

"What conversation?"

"Good boy. Now, your boy Parker entered the US four days before they found Gary Stevens. The coroners's estimate at time of death puts your boy in the frame. Hope that's useful, even though you can't quote me. Eugene's pension is at stake."

"I understand Darlene. This is just between you and me. To be honest, it looks as if Parker is dead. We found a newspaper report from 2012 of a 56-year-old who died of an overdose. We think it was him. Thanks for this Darlene. And thanks to Eugene. Hoping to meet up when he retires."

So, Parker almost certainly murdered Gary Stevens then ended up dead of a drugs overdose.

33

"Ola. Salut!"

I was on a video call with two grins that would've graced a toothpaste ad. Rupert's beer looked inviting. Joe's drink looked unnatural, but had an umbrella.

"I take it you're having a good time?"

The two of them looked at each other and collapsed in a fit of giggles. I gathered they were having a good time. It had been a long day. After a struggle, Joe controlled himself enough to speak.

"We can't stay on long. The car's picking us up soon to take us to the Alhambra for our moonlit tour."

"Sounds very romantic," I said. Again, the giggles. What had they been up to?

"I can't wait," said Joe. "Listen, we found Pat through the editor of the paper. She refused to speak to us at first."

"At first? Does that mean she relented?"

"Yes. This one here…" Joe patted Rupert's leg, "turned on the charm."

"Did she confirm she used to be Pat Parker?"

"She did. Like you thought, they changed their names to help them disappear. She clammed up a bit when we tried to get more from her. I think she wanted to tell us more, but needed to think about it first. We told her to check you out online to prove you weren't one of the bad guys. I gave her your contact details, and she promised to get in touch tonight."

"Do you think she will?"

"I do. She just wants to get her thoughts straight."

Rupert waved like a kid that wanted to make a point in class.

"Before I forget, I automated the index build on the database. Angel had the idea of integrating the facial recognition software to generate keywords based on the photographs. You should find the search facility a lot more useful now. Listen, we've got to go, the car's here."

"Where does the facial recognition get its data from?"

"Angel has a contact. She told me not to push it. I suggest you do the same."

"Worrying. Okay, thanks, guys. Enjoy your tour."

The screen went blank. Were we any further forward? The index fix was good news. I needed to have another look. At least we knew that Pat Smith was Pat Parker, but what was she so scared of? An hour later, I was on my way to finding out.

The tanned features of a woman appeared on my computer screen. She was sitting at a wooden table. Orange trees and a barbecue were visible in the background. Draped over her shoulders, I could see a black hoodie. She sat in silence, deep in thought. For a horrible moment, I thought she'd had second thoughts and would end the call. Instead, she took a drink from the glass of white wine.

"Mrs Smith, thank you for calling," I said.

"Please, call me Pat. And we both know my name isn't Smith."

"Pat, I want to assure you I have no interest in exposing where you're living. I am, however, interested in why? Why change your name? Why have no contact with your late husband's family?"

She took the wine bottle from its cooler and poured another glass. Having a drink seemed to give her more thinking time. It was tempting to jabber on and ask more questions, but I knew patience was crucial. Finally, she appeared ready to talk.

"Let's just say some people in the UK are dangerous and are best avoided."

"You mean his father?"

"Not really. Yes, he had a temper and a chequered past, but he was a good father, good company. I couldn't say that for all his work colleagues. My husband…"

She faltered, close to tears, and took another sip of wine. It was then that a hand came into the shot, resting on Pat's shoulder. She reached up and grasped the comforting hand. Then a new voice spoke.

"Let me take this, love."

A man slid into the seat beside her. The camera moved with a jerk. When it stopped, I was looking at a younger, bearded version of Parker.

"Pete?"

"You sound surprised," said the unfamiliar voice.

"Well, maybe because I read a report that you were dead."

"A necessary deception. Nothing more. It's amazing what can appear in print when you are on good terms with the editor of the local free newspaper. We needed to disappear, make sure nobody was looking for us. The report was a way of ensuring that. My friend even tipped off the papers in Yorkshire that I was really a Parker. He also phoned me earlier today, as soon as your friends started asking questions."

"But the report gives away that Pat was living in Orgiva. What was to stop them coming after her there?"

"The day before the report appeared, we upped sticks. A quick drive to Tariffa. A boat to Morocco and a new, anonymous life."

"But you're in Orgiva now?"

"We missed this place, to be honest. We let the dust settle. Two years later, we slipped back into the country and resumed our lives here, reverting to our old passports. We were Parkers again. It felt safe, at least until your friends arrived this morning."

"We have no interest in exposing your whereabouts. Five minutes ago, I didn't even know you were alive."

"So, what are you after?"

"I just want to tell your story. What harm could it do if the world believes you're dead? We already have most of the details, the robberies, two murders, gang members dying in prison. What we don't have is your role as the mastermind behind it all."

"What? Mastermind? Me?" Parker laughed for the first time since he'd appeared. He poured himself a glass of wine. "You think I organised the whole thing?"

"Do you deny it?"

"Of course I do. I was no mastermind. I was the idiot that went to prison for eight years, even though I was nothing to do with the bloody gang."

"Why would you do that?"

"To protect my father. He wasn't your criminal mastermind either, by the way. The police suspected him of robbing a post office. He was up to his eyes as the driver. He'd just started a legitimate business, something to support the entire family. Without him, the whole thing would've fallen apart. Dad talked me into a deal. If I took the conviction, he'd set me up in business when I got out. He'd throw in a house and car. I'd have it made. His lawyer reckoned I'd get two years. Out in 18 months. It seemed a price worth paying. It went wrong when I ended up doing eight years."

Pat leaned across and said something to her husband I couldn't make out. Parker nodded and squeezed her hand.

"Look, Mr Dale. It's getting late. It's been a long day. Pat and I have a lot to discuss. If you would excuse us…"

"Of course, but just before you go. Do you know who fenced the stolen goods? They made a lot of money over the years."

"Honestly, I don't have a clue. The old man kept secrets."

"I see. Look, could we talk again? Maybe in person? My company would pay your travel expenses."

"No. Not in person. Returning is far too dangerous."

"Maybe another video call?"

"Maybe. Let me think about it. Now, we must —"

"Just one more thing before you go. Your dad is ill. I hate to break it to you, but he may not have long. He's desperate to meet up with you and put things right."

"But doesn't he already think I'm dead?"

"Apparently not. It would bring him peace."

"No. As I say, travelling is impossible. The old rogue will have to take his conscience to his maker. Goodnight Mr Dale."

The screen went blank. There was a lot to take in. I needed a drink. It was almost time for Jen to call and I could do with a chat with Angel. My heart was racing. Parker was alive. Even though he'd denied it, had we found our gang leader? From what Darlene had said, he looked like our murderer, too. I should celebrate, but there was still so much to unravel. I grabbed a beer from the kitchen, then settled in for another video call.

"How are the feet holding up?"

Not the most romantic line I'd ever used on a phone call, I

admit.

"Sore. The thought of putting my boots on again tomorrow is horrible," said Jen.

"Is it that bad?"

"Maybe not as bad as I'm making out. I'm developing some lovely callouses. They seem to alternate with the blisters. I won't be wearing open-toed sandals anytime soon. Put it that way. Not a pretty sight. Looking forward to a foot rub."

"What, with your manky feet?"

Jen laughed.

"Steady on. We're still supposed to be at the romantic stage. I thought you worshipped the ground I hobble on?"

"Of course, I do. I'll make sure I pack the massage oil when I come to meet you. How's Ben?"

"I think he's okay. Not that he would say if he was struggling. We're taking plenty of rests, but the time just flies. We have so much to talk about. What about you? Any progress with the research?"

"Funny you should ask. I'm not sure we're any closer to finding the boss of the gang. However, we *have* tracked down the son."

"And you let me go on about feet? Spill the beans. Tell me everything."

I ran through the day's events, how Joe and Rupert had convinced the exiled Parker to call. How they'd faked his death and had no contact with the family. Then there was the call from Darlene.

"So what happens now?" Jen asked.

"I'm hoping he'll get in touch again tomorrow. There's still a lot he hasn't told us."

"Shouldn't we get the police involved?"

"Maybe later. There are a few things I want to know first. Who is Parker so terrified of? He ruled out coming to

England to see his own dad before he dies, not because he hated him, but because he fears somebody else. Besides, even though his dad was a villain, I have to admit I quite like him."

"But all the crimes he committed. He was part of the gang that killed Jason's dad. Jason deserves some sort of justice, surely?"

"Agreed, but Parker won't live long enough to be dealt with by the courts. I think our best hope is for him to confess, make his peace with his son and tell us the truth. I can also think of one person who benefitted from the crimes. It just occurred to me. When I was on the call with the middle Parker, he never once referred to missing his son. I wonder why?"

"Maybe it's too painful?"

"Or maybe he's the one he fears?"

34

Angel was hard at work when I got in on Wednesday morning. The Stickies had extended to a second screen. She was making progress.

"You've been busy," I said as I unpacked my laptop bag.

"As soon as I saw your email, I had to come in. So Pete Parker called you last night? Do you think we could get him here in person?"

"He seemed adamant that he wasn't coming back. He seems terrified of something — or somebody."

"What's he scared of?"

"It could be the police. If Darlene's right and Parker was in the States, it would suggest he's the killer."

"But why would he show himself if he was the killer? Why wouldn't he just stay dead?"

"I've got no idea. Nothing concrete anyway. We need to check it out. Hypothetically, could it be the grandson, our warm-hearted neighbour?"

"Al? You serious?" Angel paused and stared at the Stickies. "Wasn't he too young? He'd only just be a teenager when the robberies were happening."

"Maybe two young to be involved then, but later... He would be around 18 when his dad disappeared after a big row. We know from Elgin that Al was in the family removal business by the time he was 16."

"You think it was a fight between father and son the caused a man to exile himself away from the rest of his family?"

"It's not that unusual for teenagers to fall out with parents. Plus, he's a powerful build with a temper."

"True. Our best chance of revealing the truth has to be getting the old guy and his son in a room together. Get them to talk about what happened," said Angel.

"I just can't see it happening. Let's give it a day or two, see if Pete comes back to us. If not, I'll chase him, persuade him to come home."

Angel's phone rang. She pointed at the handset before leaving the room to answer it. My laptop was desperate for a power cable. I obliged and settled in to catch up on emails. The most urgent one was from Flic. She was asking about progress on the batch of fresh stories for the BBC. My reply assured her that the list of ideas was coming together. I opened a folder I'd created for new ideas. It was empty. Somehow, creating stories for children and investigating hardened criminals didn't sit well together. I should take a couple of weeks away from the grown up stuff and immerse myself with Jen and Charley to get creative. But with the investigation and Jen being away, there was no chance of that.

As usual, I was missing Jen. Four days apart seemed like a lifetime, even with the nightly video calls. Right on cue, a text arrived with another photograph.

Just leaving Patterdale. Somebody demanded an extra hour in bed.

The picture was of the pair outside the Patterdale village shop, grinning at the camera. The caption read: *Dad, doing his best Wainwright impression.* I'd never noticed it before, but with his greying hair and glasses, he looked a bit like the legendary walker. He just needed a pipe.

After sending a reply, I knuckled down to listing a few ideas for stories. One involved a character taking on distinct personalities when wearing different costumes. I scrubbed it when I remembered Mr Benn. Then again, it was amazing what you could achieve in a couple of hours. I'd had a few half-written stories from ages ago and soon added another four outlines to the new folder. It wasn't as if anybody was expecting finished stories at the moment. Today's lunch with Demus was a more casual exchange of ideas. I could do this. I'd don my writer's costume and take on a make-believe personality. The germ of an idea was forming.

It was only then that I realised Angel hadn't come back. I found her downstairs at a desk in the main office.

"So this is where you're hiding," I said, taking a seat opposite.

"I came back, but you looked busy. You never registered that I was there, so I thought I'd leave you to it."

"Sorry, I was being creative. While I'm here, I've got a mad idea I want to bounce off you."

"Sounds worrying, but go ahead."

I ran through my big idea. At the end, Angel sat back.

"That's one of the maddest ideas I've ever heard!" I felt deflated and was about to object until she continued. "It's so mad it might just work. Can you make it happen?"

"I'll give it a go. Right, in the interests of paying some more bills, I'm off to lunch with a film star. Tough job, but somebody has to do it."

Flic, Jason and Demus were waiting in the restaurant bar as I arrived. I accepted the glass of champagne and decided I might just enjoy this. It felt good to see Jason on one of his excursions north. The entire meal was relaxed, and the conversation flowed. Here I was, chatting away with a genuine megastar like he was an old mate. Flic tapped her glass with her fork to get attention.

"I just need to make an announcement, if that's okay," she said. "When we set up the new company, I mentioned a fifth investor. I couldn't talk about it at the time, but I'm now pleased to confirm that Demus has agreed to take up his share. As of today, he is a full partner."

That had never occurred to me as being a possibility.

"Excellent news," I said.

We all agreed and toasted our new teammate. Demus ordered more champagne and the meeting continued.

The work element seemed minimal. I ran through the ideas for the stories and was told to get my finger out and get them written. Demus contributed an outline of a story that he wanted me to consider. There were holes in the plot, but the idea was sound. I could work with it.

Eventually, Flic steered the conversation to progress on *Burning Down The House*. I laid out what we knew so far. Jason leaned forward.

"Does that mean you have enough to write the script?"

"Not quite. Yes, Peter Parker was the getaway driver, but I find it hard to equate the man I've met with the violent thug that murdered your dad. It just doesn't add up. Then there's the question of who pulled everything together and fenced the diamonds. We're only guessing at the moment that this is one person."

"And you're sure it wasn't this Peter Parker."

"Yes. Believe me, I've given this a lot of thought. I think the relationship between the three Parkers is the key to this. What made the son, Pete, cut himself off from his father and his son? Especially after going to prison to protect the head of the family?"

"If this was a film, we'd extract a deathbed confession from Parker. The odds improve if the son were to come back to be with him," said Demus.

"I think you're right, but he's said there's no way he's coming back to this country."

"What about a video call? Would that work?"

"I suggested that to Angel, but Parker struggles to make out details on a screen. I'm worried that he wouldn't engage and we'd miss our chance."

The three of them sat back. It looked like they'd resigned themselves to not sorting this out. Time to gamble.

"I have an idea. It may sound crazy, but hear me out. What if Parker thought his son was in the room with him?"

"I don't follow," said Flic.

"I think I do," said Demus.

"You were the one that told us when we first met. It's all about the illusion. Manipulate the audience to see what you want. The two haven't met for years. We have access to the best makeup people in the country and the best actor of his generation. You could become Pete Parker," I said.

"That's crazy. Too risky." Flic seemed adamant.

"I disagree," said Demus. "I'd need to chat to him online to get the voice and mannerisms. A script shouldn't prove beyond us and, you're right Frankie, the makeup people can transform me into anybody. I think we should try it."

"We'd have to be quick. We're not sure how long the old guy has left."

"Best get on with it, then. We need a couple of days to prepare."

"Do you think we can be ready so soon?" Demus shrugged and nodded. "Okay. Let's set it up for Monday afternoon at the care home."

"I'll clear my schedule. We need to eat, then we have work to do."

A wave of adrenaline had taken hold for the afternoon. We

now had a document that, whilst not a script, summed up everything that we wanted to know from Parker, together with all the salient facts we knew already. I was still reviewing the document on the big screen when Angel arrived.

"How did lunch go?"

"Demus is up for it. Flic took some convincing, but she's on board. Could you speak to Corinne and set up a meeting for Monday afternoon?"

"Blimey. You don't hang about, do you? Leave it with me. I'll do it now."

"Before you go… I just remembered that Rupert tweaked the search facility on the database. I thought we could have a play with it."

Angel sat opposite me and stared at the screen. I loaded up the database and entered Parker's name. Old me would've complained that only one extra document appeared on the list. New me got excited that we now had twice as many. The new entry was a picture from the local newspaper, *The Telegraph & Argus* from 1992. It featured a grinning Parker handing over one of those outsized cheques at some charity function. It was hard to hide my disappointment, so I didn't.

"I'm not sure that offers us much. We already knew Parker was some kind of saint when it came to supporting charities. Why include the photograph in a database that was set up to blackmail people?"

"There must be something we're missing." Angel stood up and walked closer to the big screen. "I can't make out the caption on the photo."

"Hang on, there's a note attached to it." I read the note out loud before I remembered it was now on the big screen. "Twenty grand to the *Better Days Centre*, Lord Mayor, Councillor blah de blah and charity leader blah blah," I said.

"Have you always got bored easily?"

"It's not a smoking gun, is it?"

"I suspect it proves that Elgin lied to us at least twice."

"How on earth do you work that out?"

Angel pointed at the top corner of the screen. Even out of focus, the face was unmistakable. Just over Parker's shoulder was the only figure not wearing a bow tie. The dog collar confirmed the face was that of Eddie Elgin. Angel jabbed a finger at the screen.

"Elgin reckoned they fell out during the World Cup in Italy. That was 1990. So how come, two years later, he's standing next to him and grinning at a camera for the local paper?" Angel looked again at the screen. "Who's Nigel Nettley?"

"No idea. Where did you get that from?"

"It's the name on the cheque, not Parker."

"Interesting. Let's see if Nettley is in the database."

I tapped at the keyboard. There was one entry. It was the same photograph. At least we knew the search worked now.

"Okay. I'll add Nettley to the boards. We need to do a bit of digging, see if we can find any dirt. Have you noticed that everybody on our board has the same two initials?"

"How do you mean?"

"PP for Peter Parker, DD for Dougie Dwyer, EE and now NN."

"Do you think that's significant?"

"Not at all. Just weird," she said.

"Fancy a pint?"

"Sorry, got a hot date tonight. See you tomorrow."

I'd been rejected. Still, this lot could wait until tomorrow. Not that I had much to dash home for. Jen had already arranged not to call tonight as she'd been warned the signal would be unreliable. Sad meal for one and a night in front of the telly coming up. Wait — I could do better than that. Sad Chinese takeaway for one and a night in front of the telly.

There you go, imagination.

As usual, I ordered way more than a sensible individual could ever eat. Various containers balanced on a tray, beer on the chair arm, and an old T-shirt that could cope with stuff being spilt on it. I flicked through the TV menu.

The *Countdown* situation hadn't improved. At least I could make a start and watch one while I ate. All went well until I decided the contestants were idiots for not getting the word RELATIONAL. Dictionary corner outraged me by ignoring it as well. It was only then that I spotted it had ten letters rather than the traditional maximum of nine. I'd used the 'A' twice.

Bollocks.

I switched from the chopsticks to a fork and scraped the sweet and sour sauce from my shirt. By the time I'd done that and mopped up the beer spillage, I'd missed a couple of rounds. This was not proving to be the relaxing hour I'd envisaged. My mood improved with the eight letter word BASSINET and I got the conundrum at the end. I was back to being the *Countdown* master. That would do for the night. I switched off the TV and selected my favourite Motown playlist as my soundtrack.

Before long, I picked up my laptop and logged onto the office network. As I opened the database, *Heaven Must Have Sent You* by The Elgins was playing. Odd — as if the playlist was trying to tell me something. I typed Eddie Elgin's name into the search field again and opened the photograph. Something was bugging me about it, but I couldn't put my finger on what. Angel had asked about the name on the cheque. Maybe I'd watched too much *Countdown* and was seeing anagrams everywhere. Nigel Nettley. Nigel was an anagram of Elgin. Woopy-doo. What does that prove? Nothing. Then I saw it. Now that could be interesting. I tried to phone Angel but it went to voicemail. Leaving a message was pointless, she never listened to them. She'd see the missed call and get back to me.

I thought back to the conversation in Liverpool with Bernie O'Neill. She was convinced that somebody senior in the police had tampered with evidence and rigged the enquiry into the shooting. Would Crookipaedia be able to shed some light? I tried typing Danny O'Neill. A window popped up.

You do not have access to these files. Enter password to continue or Cancel.

I copied in the password for the database.

You do not have access to these files. Enter password to continue or Cancel. 1 of 3 attempts unsuccessful.

What had Robbie said? For her eyes only. What would happen if I tried again. Too risky. Losing access to the database would be a blow. Plus Robbie would find out. At least I'd made some progress.

I texted Angel about Nigel Nettley, and twenty minutes later, she confirmed my theory.

35

It had been an exhausting but fascinating day. We'd used the boardroom at our office for a three-hour video call to Pete and Pat in Orgiva. Demus had absorbed every speech pattern, facial tic, and mannerism. We'd had a thorough run through Parker's life with his family. I'd been making notes and prompting with questions where needed. By mid-afternoon, Demus called a halt for the day. He needed to lock himself away and commit what we'd learned to memory, ready to go again tomorrow.

After disconnecting the call, I stretched in my seat and rubbed my eyes. Angel picked that moment to slip into the room. I brought her up to speed with the outcome of the meeting.

"That's great, but you're not the only one who's been busy. Well done on the detective work last night by the way. It all stacks up." I grabbed a biscuit from the plate in front of me. Angel continued. "You were right. I've checked various sources online. Lyn is short for Lynette. As you spotted, the signature on the cheque says Nigel Nettley. This is an anagram of Lynette Elgin."

"I told you *Countdown* was good for the brain. You should watch it."

"I will, when I get to your age."

Rude.

I let it go.

"What I don't get is why? Why use a false name on a charity donation?"

"From what I can see, it's not a false name." Now I'd gone from confused to very confused. "It's a trading name. Would you care to guess what trade Nigel Nettley is in?"

Angel arched an eyebrow and waited for me to make the leap. The pressure to come up with something clever was palpable. I failed.

"I give in."

Angel hid her disappointment in my deduction skills.

"Nigel Nettley creates bespoke, high-end jewellery."

"How come I've never heard of him?"

"The likes of you and me never would. When I say high end, I mean royalty, film stars, rappers. The company does all its business online and access to the site is by invitation only. There are some incredibly expensive examples of what they do on there."

"Hang on. If it's invitation only, how come you've seen… Oh, you invited yourself?"

"Got it in one. Do you want to know something else?"

"Yes, please."

"I drove up to the Elgin household today."

"Drove? But you haven't got a car."

"I figured you weren't using yours this afternoon, so I borrowed it. Don't look like that. I kind of borrowed your spare keys when I wrote that note for you, the night I had to put you to bed." I was about to protest, but Angel continued. "It was worth it, I reckon."

"Did they speak to you?"

"I didn't try. I just wanted a peek at the back of the house. Now, why would they extend a rural vicarage and fit bars at the windows?"

"She mentioned a workshop when we were there."

"Bingo! I suspect she is a very skilled jeweller but also our fence. The reason nobody recovered this stuff is she's been using it as raw materials for a thriving business flogging jewellery to the stars."

"But the robberies stopped years ago."

"The ones we knew about did. What's stopping her from operating further afield?"

"So you think Lyn Elgin is our fifth man?"

"It's the perfect cover. Who would suspect the disabled, charity supporting wife of a rural vicar? We never considered her for a second until you spotted the cheque," she said.

"So, what about Pete Parker? Where does he fit in?"

"Your guess is as good as mine. Hired killer?"

"Jen's going to insist that we go to the police with this," I said.

"I'd say hang fire. Just to be safe, don't tell anybody what we've found, even Jen. We need proof. I can do more digging, but even if this gives us the makeup of the original gang, it doesn't explain the two murders. I'll buy Elgin as a mastermind. She doesn't strike me as a killer. Give me longer, see what I can find."

That evening, I was at home — showered, fed and relaxing with a beer. I was watching the clock tick off the seconds until Jen was due to call. It was pathetic, I knew, but we'd had to cancel yesterday's call because of poor wi-fi and no mobile signal. That meant almost 48 hours with only the odd text message. This was getting serious. Right on time, Jen's smiling face filled the screen.

"Hello stranger," I offered.

"Hello you. It's been a while, hasn't it?"

We both laughed. It sounded like Jen was missing me as

much as I was missing her.

"So, where are you this evening?"

"We're in a lovely pub called The George, and this is my four-poster bed."

Jen rotated her phone, giving me a quick tour of the room.

"What's Ben's room like?"

"Who cares? I've got a four-poster!"

"That's very caring of you."

"Don't worry, he's fine. Full of pie and probably fast asleep by now."

"Is he coping okay?"

"He is. I think we're both feeling fitter than when we set off. I'd still kill for a new pair of feet, but big news." She did a fanfare on her imaginary trumpet. Or was it a bugle? Difficult to tell. "We're out of the Lake District. We are officially east of the M6. And tomorrow I will get to see Charley and my mum." I coughed theatrically. "And you, of course. I can't wait. Are you all set?"

"We are. Your mum's arranged for Charley to leave school early and we will be there by around 4 o'clock. She's very excited. So am I, if it comes to it."

"Are you sure you don't mind a single room?"

"No. It makes sense for you to share with Charley. I'm hoping we can persuade her to take her grandparents for an ice cream at some point, give us half an hour to ourselves."

"And what do you have in mind for the other twenty minutes?"

"You've got an unpleasant streak in you. I've always thought that."

"Don't worry. Book me in for the full half hour experience. I can't wait. Foot massages take time. Anyway, enough smutty talk. How did it go today?"

"It was hard work, but Demus is an absolute genius. Peter talked us through so much of his background so I could make loads of notes. Now and then, Demus would summarise the stories in character. It's quite a transformation. Flic's calling in favours from a makeup artist and organising a fake beard. It's all very exciting."

"Just you be careful. These could be dangerous people you're setting up. I'd hate it if anything happened to you."

"It's nice that you care so much," I said, genuinely touched.

"Of course I care, silly. How on earth would we get back from the east coast if you couldn't drive?"

I'd walked into that one.

36

After an early start on another video call, Demus announced he had enough to help him prepare. He would take the weekend to make sure everything became automatic. In his words, he would become Parker.

With a couple of hours free, I took the opportunity of a quick shopping trip to Leeds. There were a couple of things I wanted before going to meet Jen. I even remembered to call at her house to water the plants and pick up the holdall of fresh clothes that she'd left on the bed. The house was secure, with no signs of further attempts to break in.

The next stop was to pick up Geraldine before going on to Charley's school. We were a good ten minutes early, so we sat in the car, chatting about the walk.

"You must be looking forward to seeing Ben," I said.

"I just want to make sure the silly beggar's taking care of himself."

"I suspect Jen's watching him like a hawk."

"She is, but I've got my spies out there as well."

"Spies?"

"On Facebook. Look."

She produced an old iPhone from her bag, opened Facebook and passed it across. The latest picture was from this morning, Ben grinning at the camera, an impressive-looking viaduct in the background. I didn't recognise the name of the person who'd posted the picture.

"So, your friends are doing the walk as well? Jen never mentioned that."

"She doesn't know. I see Jen every day. We don't need to be friends on Facebook. Why would I want my daughter seeing everything I get up to?"

"I'm confused. How can she not know your friends are walking with them?"

Geraldine looked at me like I was thick.

"Lots of people are in the area. I found a group on Facebook for people doing the walk. I asked them to keep an eye out for an old codger with cancer to make sure he was behaving. Loads of people are helping."

"And you've accepted them as friends?"

"Of course. It would be rude to ask total strangers to keep an eye on him. I only had ten friends on it before."

"How many now?"

She tapped away at the screen again.

"Nine hundred and sixty-three."

"All of them are doing the coast to coast walk?"

"Well, not all of them, obviously." Somehow, I was becoming even thicker. "Friends of theirs got in touch, then friends of the friends. It's marvellous. People from Romania, India, Russia. All of them are so friendly. One or two were too friendly. I ignored them."

Before I could broach the subject of online safety, Charley appeared in the schoolyard accompanied by one of her teachers. She knew Geraldine by name, who introduced me as Jen's partner. Charley handed over the painting she was carrying and busied herself settling into the back seat. We thanked the teacher for allowing Charley to leave early and set off northwards.

After a toilet and ice cream stop, we arrived at the car park of The Black Bull just after four o'clock. A very excited Jen was bouncing on the spot as we pulled up. She explained Ben was protecting a picnic bench in the beer garden. We decided the check-in could wait and headed for the garden.

I couldn't get over how tanned and healthy the pair of them looked. We were all soon chattering away, getting all the latest news. It was only when Ben headed to the toilet that he looked tired, a slight limp from a stiff knee, causing discomfort.

It was a perfect, warm, early summer evening. We ate outside and Charley played while we chatted. When the sun headed for the horizon, Jen persuaded Charley that it was bedtime. Ben agreed, now looking tired and drawn. Geraldine volunteered to sit with Charley and read the bedtime story. I smiled, enjoying the late sunshine and a more than acceptable pint of bitter. It gave me a moment or two to plot my next move with nothing but birdsong for company.

Twenty minutes later, Jen returned, wearing the cashmere sweater I'd brought in the holdall. She looked amazing and settled in close on the bench.

"All sorted?"

"Yes," said Jen. "Charley decided she wanted to sleep in Grandma and Grandad's room."

"Does that mean there's a vacancy in your room?"

"If you play your cards right."

She laughed as I put an arm around her. Was it too late to cancel my room? Ninety quid is ninety quid when all's said and done. I realised it was a nonstarter and should just enjoy that we got to spend the night together. A waiter appeared with a bottle of red and two glasses.

"Thought we should have this rather than you having too much beer," said Jen.

Could she get any better? I couldn't believe what I said

next but, luckily, I got away with it.

"Are you sure this is altogether wise?"

"Maybe not, but tomorrow's only eleven miles."

"Did you just say *only* eleven miles?"

She laughed and looked pleased with herself.

"Eleven's just a stroll nowadays. To be honest, there's a few much longer days coming up."

"How're the feet?"

"As you so delicately put it, manky, but I'll cope. Especially if I were to get a foot rub later."

"I suppose it's the least I could do if it means I don't have to sleep in a single bed."

"Romantic bugger."

"Hey, I'll have you know — I'm capable of romantic gestures."

"Like what?"

"Like this."

I slid the first of my purchases from this morning across the table. The flimsy gift wrapping was gone in seconds.

"Foot balm! You do care," laughed Jen, planting an exaggerated kiss on my cheek. "My hero."

"Not just any old foot balm. It's got beeswax, peppermint, and lemon essential oils."

"Is that good?"

"Good? Course it is. It says so in the blurb. Just wait till I get you upstairs. Your feet will be in paradise."

"I'll drink to that."

"Hang on. There's something else I want us to toast."

"Oh yeah. What's that?"

This was the bit I'd been plotting. I took the second package from my pocket and eased myself off the picnic bench. My legs had gone stiff from inactivity and I almost didn't make it. A touch inelegantly, I dropped to one knee. Jen shrieked.

"Jen, you mean the world to me. When we first met, I was a bit of a mess. Now in the morning when I awake, there's a smile upon my face. You've touched my heart with gladness, wiped away all my sadness."

"That's lovely. Did you just come up with that?"

"No, it's Holland Dozier Holland, the greatest songwriting team of all time, but that's not the point. Make me the happiest man in the world. Will you marry me?"

There was a pause. Oh shit, had I misread things? Messed up? Then I realised Jen was holding back tears.

"Of course I will, you idiot. Now get up. I think you just knelt in pigeon poo."

"I don't care. Come here."

We hugged as tightly as anybody hugged before.

"Oi, aren't you gonna put a ring on it?"

In the excitement, I'd forgotten about the ring. I took it from the box and slipped it onto Jen's proffered finger.

"There, it's official. No going back now," I said.

"Why don't we take the wine upstairs and seal the deal?"

"You mean…"

"Yep. I want a foot rub from my new fiancé. Come on."

37

The others had already started breakfast when we got downstairs. As we crossed to their table, Charley dashed to her mum's arms, earning a spin around, a mouthful of cocoa pops threatening the rest of the dining room.

"These sausages are the dogs danglies," said Ben. He was a man of few words, but always to the point.

"Not literally, I hope. Honestly, I don't know where he puts it. I've never seen him eat so much," said Geraldine, offering a cheek for a kiss from Jen.

"Healthy outdoor lifestyle. We're burning about a million calories a day at the moment. I recommend the black pudding too," said Ben.

"That sounds good to me," I said and ordered a full English. To my surprise, Jen ordered the same.

"What? Today's not a day for muesli. I need my calories and I intend to enjoy every single one."

We settled in at the table. Jen reached across for a slice of toast. Geraldine's fork stopped midway to her mouth.

"Excuse me, young lady. Is there something you want to share?"

Jen giggled like a schoolgirl.

"Do you mean this sparkling thing? How did you notice

that?"

Jen waved her hand like Beyonce.

"I couldn't miss it, the way you waved it around. Does that mean? Let's have a closer look."

The two huddled closer. Charley's chocolate smudged face looked puzzled.

"What is it?"

"That, oh scruffy one, is an engagement ring. It means that Frankie and I are getting married."

"Today?"

"Well, no, not today."

"Why not?"

"Because. Actually, why not?"

Jen grinned at me. I felt a response was required.

"Because," I said, "we need to plan everything and get you a bridesmaid's dress. How does that sound?"

"I could wear my Olaf costume."

"And you would look lovely, but your mum might have a few ideas about what you should wear."

That gave Charley something to think about. Jen whispered to me.

"Any other five-year-old would pick Elsa, you know, the whole princess thing. She goes for the bloody snowman. She's spending too much time with you!"

Then Charley floored me.

"Does that mean you're going to be my new daddy?"

I looked to Jen for help.

"Would you like that?"

Charley considered for a second, her head on one side.

"Sounds like a plan," she said. She held her palm up for a high five.

"It's amazing what she picks up from him, so I reckon it's a good idea to make it official," said Jen, shaking her head.

I looked around at my new family. To make things perfect,

my breakfast arrived and there was brown sauce. Jen was dipping toast into her egg.

"So, what are you lot planning while we stride into the distance?"

"Ice cream," said Charley without missing a beat.

"Oh, you think? I can see I'll have to have words with Gran and new dad."

"I've got wedding magazines to buy. So much to do," said Geraldine.

"I'm assuming you're joking. Plenty of time for that kind of thing."

Nothing suggested she was joking.

"Ooh, let's have a photo to record the moment," said Geraldine, grabbing her phone. "I want to tell all my Facebook friends, if that's okay."

"That's fine, but can I at least eat my breakfast first?"

"No. Picture first, then breakfast."

We all grinned at the camera. Then I realised that Geraldine's level of excitement would seem calm once compared to what would happen when I told *my* mum. I amused myself for a moment, imagining a world where I kept it a secret. No, I would have to tell her. The hat was getting an outing after all.

It was Sunday morning and, according to my phone, we were just entering the third minute of my call to tell my mum about the wedding. I was yet to speak. I didn't like to interrupt.

"Anyway, we're trying to get more fibre into his diet. See if that helps. You're quiet, son. Is everything okay?"

"Everything's fine. It's more than fine." Deep breath. "I've asked Jen to marry me and she said yes."

"Bugger it."

I admit to shock and a touch of annoyance at this response.

She'd been on at me for months to do this.

"What do you mean, bugger it? I thought you'd be pleased."

"Oh, I am son, very pleased. It's just that I gave the hat to the charity shop last weekend."

"What did you do that for?"

"Decluttering. There was a thing in the paper about how good it made you feel."

"Did it work?"

"No. I've got to buy another bloody hat now."

"Why not go to the charity shop? Chances are they won't have sold it yet. You could buy it back."

"I'm not going to my only child's wedding in a hat I bought at the charity shop. Honestly. Sometimes I wonder what Jen sees in you. I really do."

I wished I'd let them know by text, or maybe not at all.

"So, how's Dad? How's he getting on with the dementia support group?"

"He forgot to go this week." Was she winding me up? "Anyway, it's been lovely to hear your news, but I have to go. There's so much to organise."

"We haven't even set a date yet."

"That's my point. So much to do. Don't leave it so long before you ring again. Speak soon. Love to Jen and Charley."

Then she was gone. I felt like I'd done five minutes in the tumble drier and it was only ten o'clock. Sunday mornings should be relaxing. Right on cue, there was hammering on the front door.

"Angel, how nice to see you! Come in."

"How come the door's locked?"

"Why indeed? I often wonder why I bother."

"Who peed on your cornflakes?"

"Sorry. Ignore me. To what do I owe the pleasure?"

"I thought you'd like to make me a coffee and I'll tell you

what I found."

"Fair enough. Have a seat."

Five minutes later, I was back with two mugs and a plate of fig rolls. Angel looked as if I'd offered her a plate of kitten heads.

"What the hell are they?"

"You're kidding? Even with no chocolate, fig rolls are in the top five all time biscuits."

"Work of the devil. Why haven't you got hob-nobs?"

"Because I like fig rolls."

"Weirdo."

Before I could take the plate back, Angel grabbed two.

"I thought you didn't like them?"

"I never said that. Anyway. Can't have coffee without a biscuit. I don't make the rules. That's just the way it is."

"Now you have coffee — what have you found?"

"We were right about the Robin Hood angle. We knew that Jason's dad, Parker and the Elgins all supported charities in a big way. I've been checking on Thompson and O'Neill and they were the same. Each of them made significant donations within a month of each of the big robberies. If we believe the papers, they donated around half of the proceeds for each job."

"So, if they were such saints, how come they killed the security guard, then went after Jason's family?"

"I don't know. Something freaked somebody, but I don't know what."

"Another thing — how come Jason's dad didn't tell the police about the Elgins?"

Angel had just sneaked another fig roll.

"Ah, I've got a theory there. I suspect he didn't know. Lyn Elgin seems to have gone to extraordinary lengths to keep herself clear of the rest of them. The only connection I can find is the daycare centre. I think Parker was the only one that had contact with Elgin. It was during the time they spent at the centre. It's the only way it makes sense. Oh, and another thing. I checked the files for the security camera aimed at the office car park. You'll never guess which vicar spent half an hour with the proprietor of Penelope's Parcels on the Sunday afternoon that he was supposed to be watching rugby?"

"So he was with both Peter and Al on the same day? He's up to his poxy dog collar in this, isn't he?"

38

"Did you speak to Corinne?"

Angel nodded.

"Yeah. All set. We can use the same room as last time. I've set the new cameras up and planted two microphones. Everything that's said will upload in high definition to the cloud."

"Is this going to work?"

"I don't see why not. We've seen how good Demus is. It won't take him long to get the voice perfect."

"I'm still amazed Pete agreed to help. It must be weird for him, knowing that we could end up with his dad confessing to who knows what."

"It also proves that he's got nothing to hide, doesn't it? He'd hardly be trying to get the old man to open up if it incriminates him, too."

"But I still don't buy that," I said. "Everything points to him being guilty. What's he up to? And what about the shock of being reunited? We don't want to kill off the old man."

"Thought of that. Corinne's preparing the ground before we get there. She'll take him to the room and tell him what's happening. Hopefully, that will reduce the risk."

My phone rang.

"Pat, hi. Everything okay?"

Angel gestured she would meet me downstairs.

"Everything's fine. Just thought I'd let you know how things are going. Demus got busy over the weekend. We had another session this morning, and it made my hair stand on end. If I closed my eyes, I couldn't tell the difference. I understand he's in with your makeup artist right now."

"He is. We're picking him up in about half an hour. An hour after that…"

"Don't worry, I think it'll work. Call us afterwards. Good luck."

"Thanks Pat."

If Demus could convince Pat, we were halfway there. I locked the meeting room and made my way downstairs. Tom was standing, more like wobbling, on a swivel chair.

"I'm pretty sure you're not meant to use a chair like that," I said, visions of a compensation claim filling my head. "Imagine what our health and safety rep would say."

"He says it's okay," said Tom with a grin. "It's me."

I wagged a finger at him.

"Bad health and safety rep. Don't do it again, but well done for checking. What were you up to, anyway?"

He pointed at the multi-coloured banner he'd pinned above reception.

"It's Melanie's birthday. She's just nipped out to get sandwiches, and I wanted to surprise her."

"She kept that quiet. I have to go out now. Tell you what, get her to close up the office early. I'll clear it with Flic. Get everybody to my local, The Crown, and we'll be buying. With a bit of luck, we'll have a double celebration."

"Like she's going to believe me when I tell her that."

"You're very trustworthy — she'll believe you. Actually, I'll drop her a message just to make sure."

Angel arrived at reception, and we headed off to meet

Demus.

We were using a makeup studio on Kirkstall Road, close to the old Yorkshire TV studios. When we walked in, what I saw took my breath away. Okay, I'd only seen Pete Parker on a video call, but here he was. Then he spoke.

"Frankie, Angel — how do I look?"

"You look fantastic. And the voice is spot on," I said, somewhat in awe. I handed over a sheaf of papers. "Just a few more notes on what we need to achieve."

"Great, although I think I've got this. Shall we go?"

I was more than a little nervous as I edged the car into the early afternoon traffic. This was one of those roads that didn't experience a rush hour—just nose to tail cars all day long. None of the other drivers could recognise my famous passenger. With luck, he was about to give his best performance. Assuming the technology worked, we would capture it in high definition and top class audio.

Half an hour later, we pulled up outside the care home. Once again, Corinne was waiting by the window and ushered us inside. In the corridor she greeted me and Angel like old friends but was cooler towards Demus, a sure sign that she disapproved of the son deserting his father. She left no doubt that there'd be hell to pay if he upset Parker again.

"Right, you wait here. I'll get him settled, then call you through," said Corinne.

I glanced at Angel. She looked as nervous as I felt. It was Demus who took control.

"Relax, you two. Just do as we said and everything will be fine."

The door opened and Corinne waved us through. Demus stayed behind me. Angel went first and made a fuss of hugging Parker.

"Oi. Behave yourself, you old goat," she admonished. I

wasn't sure what Parker had done, but he was roaring with laughter. "I think Corinne told you we've brought somebody to see you."

She stepped back and Demus moved forward.

"Hello, Dad. You look well."

"Lying bugger. I look like shit," said Parker, with only a slight slur.

As rehearsed, Demus took the seat next to Parker. Pete had warned him that the family weren't huggers. It was a surprise when the old man grasped his hand, pulling Demus into an embrace.

"Good to see you, son. It's been too long."

Parker's shoulders gave away that he was sobbing. Demus said something into the old man's ear. As the sobs subsided, he sat back in the armchair. Angel was cross-legged on the floor at Parker's feet. I pulled a hard backed dining chair across to the group. It was then that I could see that the unscheduled embrace had dislodged part of the fake beard Demus was wearing. I nudged Angel with my foot and pointed to Demus. She must've noticed straight away as she sprang to her feet. She got herself between the two of them, blocking Parker's view.

"Don't you be upsetting yourself. This is a nice thing. Here…" She produced a tissue and Parker blew his nose. She turned to Demus and took his face in her hands. "Same goes for you. Any more crying and I'll have to go out and fix my face." She must've applied pressure to his right cheek because Demus got the message and massaged the beard into place. "That's better."

We were a minute in. Could my nerves stand another half hour of this? Parker was back to gripping the hand of his long-lost son. Demus went into his script and started asking questions about the care home and how his dad had been. The conversation settled into a rhythm. It seemed natural. I relaxed a little. Demus was a genius. This could work. I tuned back to the conversation just in time to hear the old man's question.

"What was the name of that scruffy dog you had? Yappy little bugger."

Demus hesitated. I wracked my brains. In all the hours setting this up, nobody mentioned a dog. This could blow us out of the water. What child doesn't remember the name of his dog? Then again, the old man couldn't remember. My heart rate shot up. Did Parker suspect something and was setting a trap? Angel was panicking as well. She looked at Parker.

"What kind of dog was it?"

She was trying to buy time, but I felt powerless.

"It was a mongrel. About sixteen different breeds in one."

Demus appeared unruffled.

"Are you sure that was me, Dad?"

Parker looked deep into his son's eyes for what seemed like ages.

"You're right. It was young Al that had the dog, not you. You were…" His sentence trailed off as he realised where his son had been. Angel's shoulders relaxed. "I still blame myself every day. Eight years. I should never've suggested that you took the blame."

We were back on the script.

"You weren't to know the judge would give me such a harsh sentence. The solicitor thought I'd get eighteen months at most. I still think it was the right thing to do. You shouldn't fret over it. It's in the past. You were too valuable to the family to be stuck away in prison. "

Parker looked across at me. Demus knew what he was thinking.

"Don't worry about Frankie and Angel. They know everything already. Besides, even if they wanted to go to the police, what could they do to you now?"

"I suppose you're right, son. They say you should try to make amends before you die. That's why I'm so glad you came today. Al should be here, too. You two should bury the hatchet."

"That's just what he threatened to do if he ever got hold of me."

The two of them managed a short laugh. The old man blew his nose again before continuing.

"That might've been my fault. I thought it was the right thing to do. Let him think you'd just disappeared. It was years before he found out you'd been in prison. Then you got out, reinvented yourself. I was pleased that you didn't want to follow in my footsteps. I was so proud of you, rebuilding your life. Carpentry's a proper profession, making furniture from scratch. You were a gifted craftsman. Meeting Pat was one of the best things that ever happened to you. Then, just as everything is looking up, the idiot goes and shoots that security guard."

Hang on. That was news. Demus didn't miss a beat.

"You mean it was Al that shot the guard? But Gabriel went down for that. How —"

"A few words in the right ears. Gabriel was thick as two short planks, plus he had previous. Al was 15. The police never even considered him as a suspect."

"What was Al even doing on the job?"

"That was my fault. We were short of a body. Al was big for his age, keen to learn the business. I said he could come along just to watch. Somehow, he got hold of a shotgun. Silly little sod got excited. We got him out of there so quick his feet didn't touch the ground. I think that's what tipped him over the edge. He was never the same after that. We'd just set up the removals company. That was my attempt to go straight. No more robberies. I tried to keep him on a short leash, but within a year, he was using the trucks to move drugs around. I thought we planned our jobs well, but he was in another league. By the time he was twenty, he had fingers in every business you could think of."

Angel again moved towards Parker, offering him her water bottle and replacing the used tissue. Such a long speech was exhausting for him. He took a deep breath and started again.

"He was violent. Obviously, he had a temper. We'd all seen that, but this was different. He seemed to enjoy it. I can't believe how badly I played it. I wanted to shock him out of it. Get him to see sense."

"What did you do?"

"I'm so sorry, son." Tears engulfed Parker, who now looked all of his eighty-odd years.

"What did you do?" Demus raised his voice a little.

"I'm so sorry…"

"Dad, I get that you're sorry. What the hell did you do?"

Through the tears, I could just make out the reply,

"I told him you were going to shop him to the police, and that you had all the evidence in a big folder and you were going to turn him in unless he stopped the violence. I'm so sorry."

"So that's why he attacked me? In my workshop. That psycho came at me with an axe because you told him a pack of lies? I had to defend myself, take a lump hammer to my son's knee. I left him there in a pool of his own blood, got in the car with Pat and left everything. All because you came up with some stupid scheme to get him to mend his ways. Fucking brilliant."

I'd forgotten that this was Demus, not Parker's son. It was absorbing. Then it hit me. This was dynamite. We had to go to the police. Al Parker was a murderer with a vast empire of criminal activities under his control. I no longer felt bad about taking an instant dislike to him. We still needed the names of the boss and the fence, the ultimate beneficiaries of the robberies. Come on Demus, get him to tell you who was in charge.

A sudden coughing fit almost overwhelmed Parker. He clutched at his chest. It froze me to the spot. Angel jumped up to do what she could. She screamed at me to get help. Corinne was there in seconds. She produced an inhaler and a portable oxygen mask.

"I think you need to go," she said. "He'll be fine, but I think that's enough for today."

The three of us looked around, feeling useless. We trooped towards the door as Corinne got busy. Demus spoke first.

"I feel like I should insist on an ambulance. Go with him to the hospital."

"I don't see how you can," whispered Angel. "Corinne knows best what to do. If the worst happens and he dies, the police will get involved. It's one thing convincing an old man that you're Pete Parker, but the police?"

"You're right. Too much of a risk. So what do we do now?"

"I think we need to go to the police eventually," said Angel.

"Eventually? Why not now?" I asked.

"I think we should sleep on it. Review the footage. We also need to bring the real Mr Parker up to speed."

"You're right. I for one need a drink. Pub?"

"I'd love to, but I need to get back to Manchester tonight," said Demus.

"I could give you a lift, no problem."

"No, you go to the pub with Angel. Drop me at the train station. At least nobody will recognise me. It's been quite a day. I can't wait to do it all again when we make the TV series."

Demus crossed the room to where Parker was breathing through the oxygen mask. He moved in close, said a few words. The old man grabbed his hand but couldn't speak. Corinne intervened, and the three of us headed back to the car.

I was just about to get in when my phone vibrated. It was Darlene. I pointed at the handset and walked a few feet away as Angel and Demus climbed into the car. There was no small talk. Darlene was in a hurry.

"Listen. I was thinking about the conversation the other night. You said the dead guy was in his mid-fifties so around forty when he came over. It can't be him. I checked the entry card. This guy was only eighteen. Sorry to be the bearer of bad news. Got to go. Bye."

39

"This is not the way home," said Angel. "Where are we going now?"

I'd ignored the turning to the M62 and was heading towards Halifax.

"I thought we'd have a trip to Skipton. Given what we now know, I think it's time we had a quiet word with the Elgins."

"Good idea. This could be fun."

It didn't take long to skirt around Halifax and Keighley, and we pulled up outside Elgin's house at around four o'clock. Normally, I would be nervous in this kind of situation and look to Angel for help. This time, confidence and adrenaline flowed through me. I was ringing the doorbell before Angel had closed the garden gate. It threw me when Eddie Elgin appeared around the corner of the house carrying a sledgehammer. I must've looked worried.

"Demolishing an old coal store in the garden. Lyn wants some raised vegetable beds. What can I do for you, Mr Dale?"

"We were hoping to speak to you about your relationship with Peter Parker."

"I told you last time. I don't have a relationship with Peter Parker. Not seen him for years."

"But we know that's not quite true, is it Mr Elgin? We believe you visited him at the care home."

Just then, Elgin's phone rang. His ringtone was The Charlie Daniels Band's *The Devil Went Down To Georgia*. This struck me as odd for a vicar. I was still thinking about this when Elgin sighed, ending the call.

"Lyn says you'd better come in."

Elgin propped the sledgehammer against the wall, kicked his boots off and told us to follow him into the familiar living room. Lyn Elgin was waiting for us. There was no offer of tea. Instead, she poured a large measure of gin into a crystal glass, added ice and tonic and took a deep drink.

"Eddie, would you get drinks for our guests?"

"I don't think they're staying long enough for a drink." Elgin looked at me. I held up a hand.

"I'm fine, thanks Mrs Elgin."

"Nonsense. Eddie, please."

"But —"

"No!" Lyn Elgin was quite sharp with her husband. "It's over, Eddie. At least we can be hospitable while we talk. Gin okay with you both?"

Angel and I both nodded and sat down as Lyn Elgin gestured to the leather Chesterfield. Eddie Elgin busied himself with glasses. His wife showed her need for a refill. Before I could speak, she asked me a question.

"What would you like to know?"

"We believe you were involved with Peter Parker in a series of robberies going back several years and have built an extensive business selling stolen jewellery online."

"What gives you the right to —"

Eddie Elgin was once more silenced by a look from his wife.

"Eddie, relax. We knew this day would come. It will be a relief for both of us to get this out in the open."

Elgin crumpled, tears in his eyes. He sat on the floor beside his wife's wheelchair and held her hand. Lyn Elgin took another drink and sighed.

"It's going to be okay, love, don't worry." I felt awkward, witnessing Eddie Elgin's life unravelling, but his wife remained calm. She continued. "It all started when I stepped off that kerb by the off-licence. It was all my fault. I never looked. The car swerved but hit me, anyway. It left me in this chair. The driver wasn't so lucky. She collided head on with a truck coming the other way, killed instantly. I suspect you've worked out who the driver was."

I was about to admit that I didn't have a clue, but Angel answered.

"Elaine Parker."

Who the chuff was Elaine Parker? I didn't have to wait long.

"Peter Parker's daughter-in-law," said Lyn Elgin, nodding. "Peter recognised Eddie at the inquest. He got in touch. Against all the odds, we became friends. When I started visiting the daycare centre as part of my rehab, he got involved, started raising funds, that sort of thing."

"It's a bit of a leap to go from that to robbing jewellers," said Angel.

"It all seemed quite logical. Peter had just organised a sponsored walk for the centre. It raised a few hundred pounds, but it frustrated him it was a drop in the ocean. After a long night in the pub, I suggested a way to raise big money for the centre."

Lyn Elgin sipped her gin before continuing.

"Understand, I'd spent a lot of time in the hospital staring at the ceiling, thinking about the future. It almost drove me mad. When I wasn't staring at the ceiling, I was reading crime novels or doing puzzles. I sort of combined the two and amused myself by treating the robberies as a puzzle to be solved. I loved the planning and wanted to put it into action. Peter was a big Sinatra fan and loved the idea of doing a real life *Ocean's Eleven*. We invented Nigel Nettley as a front. My only stipulation was that I didn't meet anybody else from the gang. Peter and I only ever met at the day centre. He recruited them and was the only contact."

"When did they all agree to donate so much to charity?"

I was glad that Angel was asking questions. I was too absorbed to think straight.

"It was part of the recruitment. Peter had a lot of contacts. We worked out which of them had personal reasons for wanting to help. In my mind, we were doing a good thing. They signed up to donate at least half of everything they made."

"Proper little Robin Hoods," said Angel.

"Funnily enough, I proposed the idea over drinks in the Robin Hood. That was the last time I went. After that, Eddie and Peter met there once a week to play dominoes and discuss the work. I stayed home, made plans, and turned my hobby into a business."

"The jewellery?"

"I'd always loved making rings and necklaces. Now, I had the raw materials to go upmarket. It was all pre-internet, so it relied on word of mouth. A friend recommended a friend and so on. Nigel Nettley became the business. Prices went from £20 when we started to thousands within a couple of years. When the internet came along, we went global. All by invitation only. No advertising, no shops, no raw material costs, no questions asked."

"Sounds idyllic. Then you killed a man. What changed?"

It was almost as if Angel had slapped Elgin. Her demeanour changed — a burst of anger.

"Peter's grandson worked out who I was, that I was the one that killed his mother. He'd have killed me as well if it wasn't for the fight with his father."

"This was after it came out that young Parker had killed the security guard?"

"The idiot changed everything. I wanted nothing to do with the gang anymore. Peter tried to shock him out of the thuggery but it backfired. Al attacked his father. Pete defended himself with a hammer. Smashed the lad's knee to pieces. He was in the hospital for weeks. Pete upped and left. We came to live here. Peter talked sense into his grandson. It looked like things had calmed down."

"Then Parker tracked you down?"

"He turned up at the house one night. We both assumed we were going to die."

Angel passed the box of tissues from the coffee table. Lyn Elgin took a moment to compose herself. Eddie took up the story.

"Al Parker was a violent, angry young man. We were terrified. Then it was like somebody flicked a switch. He was calm, icy cold. If anything, he was even more terrifying. He told us he would spare us on one condition. Parker wanted us to work for him."

"He just took everything," said Lyn, calm once again. "It was simple: we now worked for him. If I continued to plan jobs and make the jewellery, we would be safe. He knew where our daughters lived, where they worked, everything. The threat was genuine. So, for the best part of twenty years, we've run the Nigel Nettley business from here. Neither of us have seen a penny in all that time. Same goes for the charities."

I piped up at last.

"But how has he got away with it for so long? Wouldn't the tax people or somebody investigate?"

"Parker is thorough. Over the years, he's built a vast organisation to deal with his various business interests. To the public, he drives a van and delivers parcels. That deception has served him well and his team is very skilled at maintaining that illusion. They're also skilled killers. They got to Gary Stevens even though he was in the States and living under a new identity." Lyn Elgin stroked her husband's hair. He was still sitting on the floor. He looked distraught. "So, what happens now? I take it you'll go to the police?"

"I think we have to," I said.

"Can I ask a favour?" I paused and waited for Lyn to continue. "Get the police to come to us before Parker. I need to make sure they protect my daughters before we take Parker apart. Could you also wait until tomorrow?"

"What difference does that make?" I asked.

"It's our wedding anniversary today. The whole family is due for a meal. It may be the last time we'll all be together. Give me that, at least."

"Of course," said Angel, rising to her feet. "I'm sorry we had to do this."

"Don't be. I suspect we'll sleep well tonight for the first time in twenty years. I'm relieved it's over."

We were back in the car before either of us spoke.

"Poor woman," said Angel.

"Don't forget, she's been a criminal for a quarter of a century."

"But both her and old man Parker are so nice."

"By the sound of it, they all were. Apart from the psychotic grandson. There's one thing: this will make a damned good TV series."

Angel snorted.

"Trust you. I want my name on the credits when it gets made. Special researcher, something like that. So, boss, what do we do now?"

"Tomorrow, we go to Cagney and let him take the glory

again. That gives Lyn her last family night and we get to celebrate. Pub?"

"Lead on."

By the time we got to the pub, Melanie's birthday party was in full swing. The raucous cheer as we entered was more to do with my credit card going behind the bar than anything else.

The new team was bonding if the laughter was anything to go by. Melanie was popular with her team. I needed to get to know the new starters. In my defence, I'd been very busy. With today's revelations that workload could go through the roof. I needed to tell Jason that the grandson was behind the murder. We still needed to prove it, but maybe we should leave that to the police. It was then that I realised Jason was here. I went over to join him and brought him up to speed with our afternoon's work.

"Are you saying that Dad's murderer works right now in the office next door to ours?"

"It looks that way."

Jason got to his feet.

"What are we doing sitting here? Let's sort this out."

"Easy, Rambo. Don't forget, if we're right, the bloke is a vicious thug. What chance would we stand? We need to be clever about this. Angel's right. We should make sure we've got our footage as proof, then go to the police. I'll start the download as soon as I get home and call Cagney first thing in the morning."

"Maybe you're right, but I'm not sure how I feel, laughing and joking in the circumstances."

"I know it's difficult, but this could be the start of getting justice after all this time. Besides, as a partner, the team is looking to you for leadership. Sup up and get a round in."

Jason went to the bar. Flic arrived, greeted by more cheers just ten minutes later. It was strange that Jen was the only team member to be missing. I got a text from her to say she would call me at nine o'clock. That should ensure I left before things got out of hand.

I needn't have worried. By around 7.30, the numbers dwindled. All, in particular Melanie, had had a good time.

"I'll share a cab with Melanie, make sure she gets home," said Angel. "Don't forget your card is behind the bar."

I paid up and walked home. Cooking a meal was out of the question and the Indian takeaway arrived half an hour later. By then I'd downloaded the footage from this afternoon. Watching it back was better than watching any TV drama. I couldn't believe we'd pulled this off. Not only had we made Parker happy, but we now knew his fifteen-year-old grandson had committed the murder of the security guard for which they had sent Gabriel Thompson to prison. On the stroke of nine, the phone rang.

"Somebody's had a good evening. How come you're partying without me?"

"Is it that obvious?"

"You appear to have a bit of a stagger on."

Busted. Jen could tell everything about me, even over a dodgy video call.

"Double celebration. It's Melanie's birthday and the performance this afternoon went like a dream."

I took Jen through a blow by blow account of the day. She agreed we should go to the police first thing tomorrow.

"Anyway, how are things with you guys?"

"Okay, I think." Alarm bells rang. "Don't worry, just a change of plan. Today was the furthest we've done in a day and it's taken it out of Dad. He's knackered, to be honest. I almost called for a doctor, but he wouldn't entertain the idea. The only thing he would concede was having a rest after tomorrow."

"Will that do the trick?"

"Not sure, but we can see how he is after a day off. What it has done is bugger up the accommodation for the week. I've rebooked all but the last night. They're packed out for miles around by the look of it."

"That's a shame, after all that effort. The must be something we can come up with."

"Well… here's the thing. I wondered if your parents might put us up for the night."

"I'm sure they would, but they'll be what, forty miles away? How would you get there?"

"Well…"

"I could come and drive you. See my parents, then drive you back to pick up the walk again."

"Why didn't I think of that? What a great idea! Do you think they'd mind?"

"You're joking. With that ring on your finger, it would amaze me if Mum let you leave after one night. I'll call them to arrange it. She was bad enough when I told her the news. This could tip her over the edge. Shall I call you tomorrow morning once it's organised?"

"Better to wait until evening. Once we get a way from towns, the phone signal is unreliable. I usually switch the phone off to save the battery. You never know when you'll get to recharge. I'll call you at nine again. We can have a longer chat then. I need to get some sleep. I'll check on Dad, then get an early night."

"Okay, love. Sleep well."

I added a reminder on my phone to make sure I called Mum tomorrow and went back to writing up what we'd learned this afternoon. Ten minutes later, I stretched and yawned. Jen's idea of an early night seemed like a good one. I had no idea then, but I needed my sleep. Tomorrow would be a shit show.

40

The early night had done me good, and excitement at the prospect of seeing Jen again at the weekend gave me a spring in my step as I jogged down the stairs. I even picked up the post from the mat instead of ignoring it.

My mood turned when I saw the US stamps on the envelope. Heart pounding, I sat on the bottom step and pulled the official-looking documents from the envelope. It confirmed my fears. I was being sued. I felt sick. Losing would cost me everything — all because of two small pills. I had to speak to Darlene. She was my connection to the American legal system. She would know what to do.

I grabbed my phone then realised it would be just after three in the morning in New York. No points for guessing what her reaction would be if I called now. I needed to get to work. Selling the TV series may be my only hope. I shoved the envelope into my laptop bag and headed for the car.

For once, there was no white van. I could see Melanie's car, but that was it. She would have fresh coffee on the go. I grabbed my bag, locked the car and set off towards the office.

Engines roared as a Jet 2 plane took off, skimming over the business park. Flying off to exotic climes for a honeymoon had been the plan. Then I'd got that envelope. It was all so unfair. It had been a while. It would be nice to fly again.

Then I did.

Accompanied by what I can only describe as a fucking almighty bang, I was flying backwards, several feet in the air and onto the roof of my car. The front of our office block appeared to be chasing me. In my confusion, I covered my head and slid down the back of the car, taking shelter from the rain of glass and concrete. All this in silence. Then I noticed the low rumble, deep in my ears, and a fire alarm a hundred miles away.

What the hell…? Had the plane come down? I peered around the car. The only wreckage I could see was our building. Some kind of explosion? A gas leak? No, everything was electric powered. What? Shit — Melanie and the others.

I fumbled for my phone and dialled 999, then realised I still couldn't hear anything. I kept shouting into the phone that I needed an ambulance and the fire service at the business park and hoped they'd understand. A pall of thick, black smoke was billowing from the centre of the building. Melanie was in there.

I got to my feet, stumbled back to the building, and stepped through the gap where the front door used to be. I shouted again.

"Tom, Melanie."

No sign of Tom behind reception. Maybe he hadn't arrived yet? Pushing on to the open plan office, the wave of acrid smoke hit me in the back of the throat. It pushed me backwards, coughing and retching into reception. I could see one cushion still on the sofa as if nothing had happened. It would do as a makeshift mask. I could see orange flames licking through the black smoke coming from the far corner. There was still no sign of anybody. Maybe Melanie was in the kitchen?

I picked my way through the mess of upturned chairs,

glass, and several of the letters from the *Happy Birthday* banner, floating like confetti. My hearing seemed to clear a little. The fire alarm was much nearer and hurt my ears. As if I didn't have enough to deal with, it was raining — the sprinklers. My head was spinning. Still no Melanie, as the dark closed in. I cracked my head as I fell. There was a mug on the floor. Elsa was the last thing I saw as it all went black.

"Melan…"

Then I was rising, moving through the air at speed. Was I dead? Flying again? En route to some celestial resting place?

I came to in an ambulance. An oxygen mask appeared, and I was told to take deep breaths. I was soon coughing up black nastiness and could sit upright. When the coughing passed, I could see the activity outside through the ambulance doors. Everything was flashing blue and looking busy.

Melanie! I ripped the mask off and attempted to shout, but it came out as a feeble croak.

"What about Melanie? She must've been in there. She's always first in. I have to find her. What about the others?"

I went to stand. My wobbly legs were no match for the paramedic.

"Let the experts do their job. You concentrate on breathing. Mask back on, please. My name's Russell. Can you remember where you are?"

I pointed at the mask that was strapped to my face. Russell nodded and removed the straps around my ears.

"Frankie Dale. I work here.

"Stay there, Back in a minute."

Russell jumped from the ambulance and strode across the car park to speak to the nearest firefighter. I was feeling stronger and saw my chance to escape. I got to the door before I had to sit down. At least the air was clearer now. The slight breeze seemed to blow the smoke back over the building. I couldn't believe the devastation. Then I could hear somebody shouting my name. Was I hearing things? No, there it was again. This time, I stood up and peered out.

It was Melanie. She was behind a police tape, unable to get closer. She was safe. Relief flooded through me, and I risked a few tentative steps. The policeman saw me coming and lifted the tape for Melanie to get through.

"Frankie. What happened?"

"Some kind of explosion. I thought you must be in there."

"Flic told us all to come in late — no point being in and hungover."

"But your car —"

"Too pissed to drive home last night."

"So getting plastered saved your life?"

"You could say that. And booze is supposed to be bad for you."

"Does that mean there's nobody in the building?"

"It should do. Only you, Flic, Jason, Angel, and Jen have keys. I open up for everybody else. Do you think we should tell them?"

Before I could reply, Melanie had collared one firefighter, who was getting ready to go back inside. My mate Russell spotted me and ushered me back to the ambulance. I protested but agreed to be checked out in the hospital.

Eventually, the fire service confirmed that I was the only casualty. That I'd fallen over and banged my head sounded pathetic, given the scale of the damage. Once again, I left a fire-scene in the back of an ambulance.

41

"Please, would you just lie there and rest? The doctor will be here soon."

The nurse sounded pissed off with me. I'd just failed in my third attempt to break out. I had stuff to do. Admittedly, I wasn't sure what that stuff was. I was still trying to piece together what had happened. The only thing that made sense, if you could call it that, was that Parker was behind this. Did he know we were discovering the truth about his criminal activities? It would make sense if he was behind the break-ins as well. Was he after our evidence? Was I being warned off? If he wanted to scare me, it was working.

I took another few breaths with the oxygen mask over my face. A familiar head poked through the curtains. It was Smirky.

"Paul, good to see you."

"Aye up Frankie. We seem to see quite a lot of you. Can I come in?"

"Be my guest. Kate not with you?"

"She'll be here in a minute, just in the ladies. Right. Any idea what this morning was all about? You were very lucky."

"Lucky? I don't feel very lucky at the moment."

"It could've killed you."

I had to be honest with myself — I hadn't thought of that. My leg started to twitch and shake. I shuffled around on the bed. All that did was start the other leg twitching. As I tried to speak, my jaw joined in the fun, shaking. This was weird.

"Are you okay? You look a bit… Nurse!"

Smirky called through the curtains and the nurse was back in seconds.

"How can I help?"

"He's shaking like a puppy shi— he's shaking a lot."

The nurse took my wrist and checked my pulse.

"Delayed shock. Adrenaline will do that. All the more reason to stop trying to escape and let the doctor have a proper look at you. It will wear off by itself. Play nice, or I'll go get a big needle."

She grinned at me, and I submitted. Tinkle replaced the nurse. She made herself comfortable on the end of the bed.

"Have a seat," I said, smiling at how things had changed since we'd first met.

"Thanks. Got any grapes? I'm starving."

"Aren't visitors meant to supply the grapes?"

"Technically, we're not visitors," said Smirky, trying to keep an air of professionalism. "We are police officers trying to find out the facts leading up to your arrival at A&E."

"That would be the bang," I said.

"Bang?"

"Fucking big bang."

Smirky stopped writing in his notebook.

"Well put. You're not the first person to describe it like that. The fire service is still investigating the cause of said bang. I have to ask this, were you storing anything in the office that would explain the big bang?"

"Like what? Big bangy things?"

"I know it sounds daft. Until the investigators tell us what caused the explosion, we're stuffed, unless you know something."

This was the point I should tell Smirky and Tinkle the facts. More than once, I'd promised that as soon as we knew what was going on, we'd hand it all over to the police and they could take over. I just didn't feel ready to do that yet. I needed time to think, pull the evidence together. If nothing else, I didn't want Cagney and Casey taking all the credit for my work again.

"No, nothing. I turned up for work as normal. Before I could get into the office, the whole thing exploded. I was worried that our office manager was inside and tried to get her out. I didn't realise that she'd been sleeping off a hangover instead of opening up as usual."

"Okay. We'll leave it there for now. Once we get the report, I know your mate, Cagney, will want a word. Until then, do as the nurse says and get some rest."

"And some grapes," said Tinkle as she stood up. She squeezed my hand and they both left.

I decided maybe I would benefit from a snooze, wriggling about to get comfy, I strapped the mask back on and closed my eyes. All I could see in my mind was the black smoke billowing towards me and the rain of glass and concrete.

Was all of this because of the digging we'd been doing into the Parker family? Just how far would Al Parker go to protect himself? Was the script for a TV series worth all of this? They had attacked me, ransacked my house and bombed the office. It shouldn't be this difficult. Why not stick to writing children's books? Telling daft stories about spiders from Mars or why spots can be cool. That was easier than getting blown up. It had also more or less paid for my house. This new TV series had almost destroyed that house. The irony of the chosen title hit me. *Burning Down The House*!

My mind drifted back to last year, making the film in the Dales with Roddy. We'd written a nice, feel-good script, made a nice feel-good film, and it made us all feel good. Why did I think I could solve murders and unmask master criminals? Maybe I should leave that to Vera and Lewis. I should just stick to writing nice things.

I felt sleepy, but at least the shaking had stopped. Every time I felt myself nodding off, a machine beeped, or an alarm sounded. How was anybody meant to rest in A&E? My phone vibrated. I gave up trying to sleep and sat upright again. It was Flic. I assured her I was okay, and we even managed a joke about remodelling the office.

"Look, I've got something that may just cheer you up. Have a look at what's trending on Twitter, see if you recognise anybody. Give me a minute and I'll send you a link to a Facebook group that'll give you more detail. Oh, the police are back. I'll have to go. Will call again later."

By the time Flic ended the call, I was already opening Twitter. What could be so important that Flic made time to tell me when everything else was going on? Then I saw it. The top two trending topics: #MeToo; #GuthrieArrested.

It took a moment to process what I was seeing. Dozens of women had come forward to claim that Guthrie had abused his position of power. Flic had hinted at this, but things were now accelerating. There were pictures of my almost-employer in handcuffs. I felt dreadful for the women that he'd abused, but the implication for me was clear. I was not Guthrie's top priority for the foreseeable future. Would this mean the end of the lawsuit?

Flic sent through a text that just said *Facebook*. I took a deep breath. The shock was playing silly buggers with my brain. Instead of opening the app, I cried. Just one tear, then another, then great all-engulfing sobs and uncontrollable anguish. Where the hell was this coming from? What a clusterfuck. I'd made such a mess of things, but maybe there was light at the end of the tunnel?

"What's up with you? You big soft bugger."

It was Angel, slipping through the curtains and going on the attack.

"It's all such a mess."

"Like what?"

"Everything?"

"Fair enough. Got any grapes?"

"No. What's the big, sodding obsession with grapes?"

"I don't know. I don't even like grapes. It's just what you get in the hospital, innit? Mardy arse."

"I'm not a mardy arse," I protested. Then I thought about it. "Okay, I was a bit of a mardy arse. But it's all just such a mess."

"So you said. But I beg to differ. You've just got engaged to a woman who is way too good for you. You're about to be commissioned to write a six-part thriller for TV. Yesterday couldn't have gone any better. Lyn Elgin filled in all the gaps. We got a recorded confession from Parker and he dropped his grandson in it from a great height. He confirmed the thug had shot the security guy. That alone should be enough to put him away for a long time. Blowing up the office just proved that he's desperate."

"How do we know it is him that blew it up?"

"Here." Angel took out her phone and tapped away a few times. She passed it across. "That, my mardy-arsed friend, is Parker in the office at 3.37am carrying a holdall. He goes through all the desks but finds nothing. I think the naughty boy then planted a bomb. If he couldn't steal the evidence against him, why not blow it up?"

"He can't think he'd get away with it?"

"Who knows? He's desperate, cornered like an animal. He's capable of doing desperate things."

"At least nobody got hurt."

"Except you."

"Fair point. What about Flic and Jason? Do they know what's happened?"

"Don't worry. Melanie's spoken to everybody from the office. They're all safe and well. I don't think Parker cares about them. I don't want to panic you, but this seems personal. It looks like he's got it in for you."

"Jen! I've got to call Jen," I said, scrambling to find my phone.

"Is that wise?"

"She has to know."

"Why? She's miles from nowhere, oblivious to all of this."

"Exactly. What if he goes after her?"

"How would he know where she is?"

My phone was still in my hand. I glanced at the Facebook logo and a bolt of panic shot through me. No! Please tell me… After a quick search, I tapped on her profile. I could hear that Angel was asking a question, but I had to do this. There he was. Al Parker, grinning at the camera, was on Geraldine's list of friends.

"Here," I said. "Jen's mum has been accepting friend requests on Facebook. Parker's been able to follow the itinerary. He knows where she'll be."

"Call her," said Angel.

I hit speed dial.

"Straight to voicemail. She'll be somewhere with no signal. How did you get here?"

"I sort of came in your car."

"My car? How? Of course, you still have a key."

It seemed churlish to ask for it back in the circumstances.

"Sorry."

"At least it came in handy. Come on, we need to find Jen."

I stood up a bit too quick and the entire room spun. I grabbed Angel's arm to steady myself.

"You okay?"

"I will be. Just help me get to the car."

Beyond the curtain, the whole of A&E looked chaotic. Nobody noticed us slip out. The fresh air outside helped to clear my head, and we were soon by the car.

"You drive," I said, heading for the passenger door. Angel handed me the parking ticket attached to the windscreen.

"Sorry. Was in a bit of rush."

I threw the ticket over my shoulder. Angel hit 50 before we were out of the car park, pinning me back in my seat. A whole fresh fear took over.

42

"Where are we going?"

"My house," I said, clinging onto the seat. "We need the maps."

The roads were quiet. Somehow, we reached the house in one piece, almost certainly having triggered the speed camera at the top of the road. I handed over my door key.

"In a plastic wallet on the kitchen table."

"Are you okay?"

"Dizzy, to be honest. I'll be fine. Just grab the maps."

Angel was back in no time and handed over the clear plastic wallet. My hands were shaking, but I found the right map for today's walk.

"A1 north, quick as you like," I said once I'd found the right place.

"I need left or right, not used to driving out of town."

"How are you on motorways?"

"Never been a problem."

"That's a relief. For a horrible minute, I thought you were going to say you'd never driven on one."

"I haven't."

"You said it was no problem?"

"It hasn't been, so far. How hard can it be?"

Once again, we proved how well my car accelerated as Angel turned right and set off towards Harrogate.

"How long will it take?"

"Depends on traffic," I said, "and on whether we live that long."

"I feel safe."

"I'm so pleased. Lights."

Whether Angel had spotted the red light, I would never know, but we screeched to a halt. I checked my phone.

"Geraldine posted a photo of Jen and Ben outside *The White Swan* in a place called Danby Wiske."

They didn't have a care in the world, grinning at the camera. Jen was wearing the bright orange T-shirt I'd delivered earlier in the week. It matched her raincoat, that was strapped to the top of her rucksack. I tapped at the satnav and entered the postcode for the pub, then tried to call Jen again.

"No reply. She must've sent the picture, then switched off her phone again."

"What time was it posted?"

"Just after one o'clock."

"At least we know where they were. "

"But so does Parker."

We drove on in silence for a moment. As we passed the airport, the blackened building that had been our office until this morning stood out. A lone fire engine was still spraying water at the back of the building. In sympathy, the blue skies of this morning were being replaced by grey clouds and a stiff breeze.

I went back to the map and tried to figure out where they were likely to be by the time we got into the area. Then I realised the problem with staring at a map in a speeding car so soon after having a bang on the head.

"Best pull over," I said, sweat rising.

Angel looked across.

"Jesus, you're a funny colour."

"Pull…"

By the time we stopped, my door was open, and I was leaning out, spoiling things for several people sitting outside the farm shop cafe who'd been enjoying lunch. I'd hit the "no littering and no dog fouling" sign. On another day that would've made me laugh.

"Right. That does it. I'm taking you back to the hospital," said Angel, looking worried.

"No. Jen needs me. Needs us. If some nutter is making this personal… He thinks he's already wiped out us two with his fireworks. Jen's the obvious target. Come on. I'll be okay."

Angel shrugged and the screech of rubber on the road showed that we were off again.

"Do you have any mints?"

"We don't have time for you to be eating mints."

"Not me, you tool. You. Your breath stinks like…"

She had a point. I rummaged in the centre console and struck gold with half a pack of extra strong. It looked like they'd been there for a while, but I shoved three in my mouth.

"What are we going to do when we get there?"

"I've got no actual idea. I suppose, track down Jen and her dad and keep them away from Parker. The biggest problem is the route. Although most of it is close to the road, the better walking is across fields. We may have to be on foot. "

"And just how far do you think you'll get on foot?"

Angel had a point. My record today was not good.

"I've got an idea."

I called Smirky. Over the next five minutes, I explained everything. Meeting Parker with Demus, the footage of Al Parker breaking into our office, and the theory that he was targeting Jen.

"You realise I've got no choice but to update Cagney?"

"Great, if you must, but we need help now, not next week."

"I hear you. It's outside our area but sod it. We finish our shift in five minutes. Nothing to stop us from coming as civvies. We're on our way."

We were almost at the junction with the A1. Thick, black clouds had swallowed up the last patch of blue sky. The first blobs of rain hit the windscreen.

"Are you sure you don't want me to drive?" I said.

"No. What's the worst that could happen?"

I didn't bother answering that. Today had been bad enough without speculating further. Traffic was crawling. We may have been safer, but this was far more frustrating. For a full ten minutes, we crept along in second gear. Then, for no apparent reason, the road ahead was clear, and I was once again pressed back in my seat like an astronaut on takeoff. Angel let out an excited squeal and I almost found religion. At least we were moving more quickly. I kept my eyes peeled for police patrols but, much to my surprise, we were soon pulling off the motorway and heading along very narrow, twisty lanes. After what seemed like hours, we pulled up outside the *White Swan*. The road was narrow, with parking at a premium.

"Keep the engine running. I'll nip in and see if anybody knows what time they left."

"Stay where you are," said Angel. "I'll go."

I had to admit that wasn't a bad idea. I tried Jen's phone again, but couldn't get through.

Angel was back, already soaking wet from braving the downpour.

"Here, get these down you."

She handed over a pork pie, a bag of cheese and onion crisps and a plastic glass of orange squash. I was about to point out that cheese and onion made my breath smell, but that was already beyond saving.

"Any news? I asked with a mouth full of pie."

"The landlord remembers them being here. Says they left about an hour ago. He reckons by now they'll be at a place called East Halsey."

I updated the satnav and, once again, Angel floored the accelerator.

Angel drove up the main street of East Halsey, in places under a couple of inches of water. I was scanning the pavement through the gaps between parked cars, but there was no sign of Jen and Ben. A tall, almost impenetrable hedgerow protected the fields beyond the road. Angel eased the speed up to 30mph as we reached the end of the row of parked cars. My heart leapt as my fears were confirmed.

"White van," I said, pointing up the road.

Sure enough, the distinctive lettering told the story — it was Parker's. Angel pulled over and parked in front of it. We both jumped out of the car. The van was empty.

"Engine's still warm. Not been here long," said Angel. "What now?"

"Let's drive further, see if we can spot them."

We returned to the car; me brushing raindrops and stray crisps from my shirt as I went. The impromptu lunch from the pub had served its purpose. My legs felt less wobbly. Before long, we approached the junction with the A19. Four lanes of busy traffic.

"What do you reckon?"

"I think we need to stop," I said. "If we end up on the dual carriageway, it could force us miles out of the way. Can you get turned around?"

"Watch me."

Angel executed a three-point turn with breathtaking speed. Had she seen the car, headlights blazing, bearing down on us, or did we just get lucky? The blast of an angry horn suggested it had been a close thing. The driver screeched past us and my adrenaline kicked in again.

"Pull over by the van. If I give you a boost onto the roof, you should be able to see over the fields."

We stopped. Angel was quick to climb onto the roof of the van. It can't have been the first time she'd done that.

"Anything?"

"No, I can't get a clear view." Angel kind of abseiled down the side. "Shame. I hoped that would leave a bigger dent. Do you feel up to driving?"

"I think so. Why?"

"I'm going to go across the fields, see if I can catch up with them. No offence, but I'm going to be quicker on my own. You drive to the end of this road again. See what you can see."

"What if there's no sign of them?"

"That's as far as my plan goes."

We had little choice. Angel climbed through a gap in the hedgerow and sprinted away. The rain hammered on the roof of the car as I got in.

Once again, the adrenaline was making my legs shake. I took a deep breath and waited for the world to stop spinning. I nudged the car into gear and set off up the road. Just short of the dual carriageway, I pulled over by a gate. I had a better view of the field. My heart leapt. A bright orange raincoat was just visible in the distance. Jen and Ben were around 50 yards short of the busy road. I tried the phone again, willing Jen to have it switched on. Nothing. Then I saw the burly figure limping along the path, maybe 400 yards behind Jen. There was no sign of Angel.

A proper run seemed beyond me, but I shuffled along as fast as I could. I was soon out of breath and the world was spinning again. The rain was so hard it made breathing even more difficult. Once more, I was sick. The crisps weren't a good idea, after all. I stumbled on like a like a drunk at the end of a long night. Up ahead, Jen and Ben were almost at the road. Parker was closing on them. It was then that I saw Angel. She was approaching the road but was several hundred yards further south on a different path to Parker. I had to do something.

Clearing my head again, I crashed on towards the main road, emerging through the hedgerow a good 50 yards from Jen. I tried to shout. Lack of breath and the thundering noise and spray from the trucks thrashing both ways rendered my screams pointless. I broke into a run again. As I charged towards them, Jen and Ben saw a gap in the traffic and set off, heads down, launching themselves towards the central reservation. A silver BMW hurtled along the outside lane, overtaking two trucks. I probably screamed again but could hear nothing, despite being almost level with them by now. Relieved when they reached the middle of the road, then terrified as Parker burst out of the field and headed straight for them. It was then I saw he was carrying a hammer.

I charged, praying that I was quick enough. My brief playing career, and all the years of watching rugby league flashed through my mind, not to mention how quickly the cars were heading towards me. I was across one lane, one to go. My shoulder contacted Parker's ribcage, my head tucked to the side. Driving with my legs, using every ounce of strength I had, Parker's body almost folded sideways. I heard the air go from his lungs above the roar of engines and the screech of brakes.

Then, for the third time today, I was flying. I was aware of incredible pain in my left leg, but kept a firm grip on Parker. We both hurtled through the air, spinning and out of control. Black smoke engulfed me, followed by a series of loud bangs. By some miracle, I landed on top of Parker, arms still wrapped around him after a perfect tackle. I knew he wasn't moving. Then, once again, everything went black.

There are only so many times you want to be in the back of an ambulance in one day, but I was more than pleased to be in here rather than being scraped off the outside lane of the A19. Yet again, I was wearing an oxygen mask, and a paramedic was telling me to stay still. The searing pain in my leg convinced me she was right. I rested my head and took a deep breath.

The paramedic moved aside.

"There's somebody here to see you, but don't move."

I opened my eyes and there was Jen; her face smeared with mud and tears. She carefully moved into position to hug me whilst avoiding the leg that was sticking out like a sore, well, leg.

"You've had quite a day," she said through more tears.

"And it's not even teatime yet."

Jen clutched at my hand. I assumed one kiss was enough based on the breath situation. Then she was hitting me, punctuating each word with a slap.

"What. The. Fuck. Were. You. Doing. Playing. Silly. Buggers. In. The. Road?"

"Ow." She stopped hitting me, but huge sobs engulfed her. I think I preferred the hitting. "It's a long story. Where's Parker?"

"He's in the back of a police car." Jen hit me again.

"If I promise to tell you everything, will you stop hitting me?"

"Suppose so," she said, hitting me once more.

I pushed the oxygen mask to my face for a couple of breaths, then continued.

"Lyn Elgin was the fifth man — woman — whatever. Parker killed the security guard. That's the younger one. It's so confusing that they all have the same name. The grandson was the one that planted the bomb in our office."

Jen started hitting me again.

"Bomb? What bomb?"

"Did I not mention the bomb? Yes, there was a bomb. No casualties, unless you count me, and even then, it was only a bit."

I was relieved when another head appeared at the door of the ambulance, and Jen stopped clobbering me. It was Smirky, but different. He was wearing a black hoodie, but his uniform was still visible underneath.

"Am I interrupting?" He grinned at Jen and she relaxed. At least she didn't hit me. "The guys from Northallerton have got Parker in a police van. We need to take him to the hospital to get checked out, but we'll keep him well away from you. He's clammed up and won't admit the attack on his dad."

"Attack? What attack?"

"Careful," I warned, "she'll start hitting you."

The slap this time was a lot lighter and more playful.

"They want to get you to the hospital now to get that leg checked out."

"What about the car driver that hit me?"

"He's fine, just shaken up. He was lucky that no one was on his inside when he swerved. We've given him a bollocking for being in the outside lane in the first place, but I'm just glad you appear to be okay."

"I'll be fine. The leg hurts like something that hurts a lot and Jen keeps hitting me, but otherwise all good."

Smirky waved, and our paramedic replaced her. She asked if Jen was coming to the hospital.

"I'm not letting him out of my sight," she said.

"What about Ben? What about the walk?" I asked.

"Dad's sitting in your car with Angel. They're going to follow us to the hospital. Now, put the oxygen back on and let us look after you."

The door slammed, and the convoy set off towards The Friarage Hospital in Northallerton.

43

For the second time in a week, I'd driven north up the A1. Only last Thursday, I'd returned to the scene of my close scrape with a BMW and the tackle on Parker. It felt weird, dropping Jen and Ben at the exact spot where their last attempt at completing the coast to coast walk had come to an abrupt stop. The blisters had healed, and the pair were determined to cover the final forty-seven miles over four days. The recent chemo session had hit Ben hard. Geraldine had taken some convincing that it was a good idea. It was only when the oncologist gave his blessing that we confirmed the plans.

For a while, I'd been on crutches. Jen had insisted that I stay at her place so she could look after me and she'd done a brilliant job. I'd tried to persuade them to continue with the walk, but both had insisted they wanted to be at home. It would have been a shame after getting so close to the end, but, as Jen said, we were all still alive.

Our new office, on the other hand, would be several months before it was back up and running. Flic was leading the search for temporary accommodation. My only request was that we ran a full security check on the neighbours. I would veto any premises harbouring hardened killers before we moved in. Meanwhile, most people were working from home. Jen and I had the sanctuary of the cottage. It was familiar and safe and I'd been so glad to be back.

Now, without the aid of crutches, I was heading for the coast again. It was a lovely late summer afternoon as we got our first view of the sea. I pulled into a lay-by and got out of the car. Geraldine checked on Charley, who was fast asleep in the back seat. After a luxurious stretch, I leaned back on the bonnet and, arms folded, smiled at the scene laid out in front of me. There was something special about the sea air in Yorkshire. Then again, everywhere feels special at the moment.

Work was going well. We'd written three scripts already and outlined the other three episodes of *Burning Down The House* - series one. I stressed the 'series one' bit to myself and smiled again. We had agreed to the contract for series two. The plan was to make the second batch of six episodes so they could air them to coincide with the end of Parker's trial.

Thanks to our work, the police charged him with the murders of both the security guard and Jason's dad. Even Cagney acknowledged our efforts when he did his big press conference.

Geraldine joined me.

"Funny to think they're over there somewhere, so close to finishing the walk," she said.

"You must be very proud of the way they've tackled this."

"I'm not sure proud is the right word. Sometimes I've wanted to batter him for being so stubborn. Then I want to wrap the silly old bugger in a blanket, not let him out of my sight."

"What's the latest news?"

"He's got another month before the next scan. I think that's the hardest bit for him now. Scans every three months mean you're never more that six weeks away from one. I count the days, knowing that the next one could show things getting worse," said Geraldine.

"But so far, all's good."

"You're right. Ben's trying to teach me to worry about the stuff I can affect rather than what I can't. The tests come under the heading of pointless worrying. One nurse said something very profound this week. We need to not let this narrow our lives. There's a temptation just to focus on the treatment. We have to live life to the full."

"So we should celebrate weekends like this big time?"

"True. Is it too early for a gin and tonic?"

"Never. Come on, let's find the bar."

I smiled again, and we got back in the car. Time to get to the hotel. There was a pint awaiting me. As I indicated to turn into the car park, a huge, very shouty motorbike screamed around my outside and into the first parking space. Before I could show my annoyance with the rider, she'd dismounted and removed her helmet. Angel was almost crying with laughter.

"I might have known you were the lunatic," I said.

"No point having a new toy if you can't torment the old people. Do you want a go?"

"No thanks. I'm quite happy in my car."

"Spoken like an old man. Come on, time you bought me a drink. Hi, you must be Geraldine."

"I gather you're Angel. Nice bike. I might take you up on the offer of a ride. I'm living life to the full. Then again, a large G&T is my priority."

Charley was now awake. Within seconds, she was wearing Angel's crash helmet and being piggy-backed into the hotel. I grabbed the suitcases and followed.

44

Last night had been a quiet, sober affair, compared to some Saturday nights. Sunday afternoon was warming up nicely. We were sitting in the hotel garden. Joe, Ambrose and Stella were trying their best to distract me, but my stomach was churning.

"I think I need the loo," I said.

"You've just been. Calm down," laughed Joe. "He's coming."

I turned to see Rupert taking the stone steps to the lawn two at a time.

"Action stations. Go, go, go!"

He was being dramatic, but I did as I was told. We stood facing the sea; me taking deep breaths and trying to convince my stomach to play nice. The two speakers burst into life and Billy Joel's *The Longest Time* drifted across the garden. This was it. I risked a glance over my shoulder. There she was. She looked perfect. The white silk dress off-setting the red of her hair and the roses she carried. Charley led the way, scattering more rose petals as she went. It shattered the illusion when she ran across to me and demanded a fist bump.

Angel stepped forward and got Charley back on track. Jen was gliding down the steps, her dad beside her. I couldn't help noticing Ben wasn't exactly gliding, more like a light hobble. Then I realised he didn't have any shoes on. Geraldine caught my eye and mouthed 'blisters'. I laughed and tried to relax.

As the music faded, Jen took my hand and nudged my foot with hers. I looked down and saw that she was still wearing her walking boots under the dress. I looked at her and we both got the giggles. The celebrant stepped forward to get things started. It was odd because I thought it was going to be a woman that performed the ceremony. Something must have happened. As best man, Rupert didn't seem phased at the last minute change.

The ceremony started. It was only then I noticed it. The huge red boil on the end of the man's nose. It was like nothing I'd ever seen before. It seemed to follow me if I moved my head.

"Please repeat after me."

Oops, time to concentrate. I made my solemn vows. I was trying to place the guy's accent. When he started, it was Welsh. He put my vows to me in a thick Geordie accent. Jen got Italian. This was weird. I decided it was just my imagination and tried to forget the boil and concentrate on Jen. Then we got to kiss, and the music started again. We were married. To *God Only Knows* by The Beach Boys, we walked back up the garden towards the hotel.

I was aware of confetti and rice being thrown and applause from our family and friends, but it was all a blur. The photographer took over and started getting us to pose with the sea in the background. Jen tugged on my sleeve and leaned in close.

"What was going on with that bloke's nose? I just wanted to pop it and have done with it."

"I'm quite glad you didn't, on balance."

Just as I was about to ask if she'd noticed the strange

accent, he was there, beside us, posing for a photograph. Terrific. We would record the boil for all time. The photographer wanted us on either side of the boil, looking straight at it. Odd. Then the man reached up and ripped it off. I don't mean popped it. He took his nose off. Then his hair and eyebrows. Left behind was Demus.

"Demus, how the hell did —"

"It was Flic's idea. Hope you didn't mind."

"Not at all. Does that mean it wasn't legal?"

"All legitimate, I promise. I am official and everything. It's a long story."

"Tell us over a drink later."

Right on cue, a tray of champagne flutes arrived, and the party began. I grabbed a couple of glasses and made my way over to where my parents were sitting. Dad put down his sketch book and looked at the champagne glass as if it had just farted.

"Don't suppose there's a beer anywhere?"

A waiter overheard as he passed with an empty tray.

"Pint?"

"Yes please. Tetley's if possible."

"Back in a minute."

I made a mental note to make sure Rupert had organised a big tip for the staff. Mum took both glasses.

"Saves going to the bar later," she said.

"I can't help noticing that, after all these years, you're not even wearing a hat. Couldn't you find one you liked?"

"I found a lovely hat, thank you."

"So…"

"There were comments."

Dad picked up his sketch book again.

"All I said was —"

"Never mind what you said. It didn't need saying in the first place."

I wasn't worried. This kind of bickering passed for normal. The chances of it escalating to an all out row were minimal.

"What's that you're drawing, Dad?"

He turned the pad towards me. I could see it was me, standing by the ornate rotunda in the garden. The first few strokes of an outline taking shape next to me.

"I couldn't put Jen in until I saw the dress."

"Bloody hell, Dad. It's brilliant."

"Wedding present, if I ever get it finished."

I took that as a hint and waved Charley across to show her new gran her dress. A few minutes later, Rupert put both hands to his mouth and let out the loudest whistle I'd ever heard.

"If I could just have your attention for one moment. Thank you. Now, we'll do all the usual stuff like speeches and food in about half an hour. First, though, Jen and Ben have some unfinished business, especially if he can get his boots back on. They are about a hundred yards short of completing the coast to coast walk after a couple of hundred miles and the odd visit to A&E."

This got a laugh and Joe shouted something rude from the back. Rupert pushed on.

"Okay, I'd like to ask you all to follow the adventurers down to the sea for the official dipping of the boots."

In a long snake, we all trooped down the hill to the beach. The sun was just setting. The photographer wanted the shot of me and Jen with the sun on the horizon. I persuaded him to take the same shot, but with Ben and Jen hugging. That was one for the album. The walk was done. Then, from the hotel, came the roar of an engine being revved like the start of a Grand Prix. Everybody stared as Angel's motorbike edged its way down the road. Then I realised Angel was standing beside me. As the figure got closer, I saw it was Geraldine, complete with helmet and posh frock from John Charles. The crowd parted as she approached the beach, stopping in front of Ben. Without being asked, he jumped on the back and they roared away up the hill to huge cheers.

After a quick photo with the sun disappearing, we strolled back up the path, surrounded by our friends. Most of those friends were trying hard to appear cool, yet still watch the famous actor as he posed for photos. Demus had been so generous. I'm still not sure how he'd done it, but somehow, the hotel became available to us at short notice for the wedding. I suspected that one or two pensioners were enjoying a week in the south of France rather than bracing walks on the Yorkshire coast.

"What was the deal with Geraldine and the motorbike? I didn't know she could handle a beast like that."

"I'm going to have words with her," said Jen. "There are photos of them from years ago on bikes. I think they sold them and grew up when I appeared. What the hell was she thinking?"

"She was thinking about me." Neither of us had noticed Ben appear at Jen's side. "It was this thing about not allowing cancer to narrow our lives. For the two minutes I was on the back of the bike, I never once thought about being ill."

"But it's dangerous," said Jen.

"You mean it could kill me? Well, it can bugger off and get in the queue."

Jen was about to protest, but she saw her dad was right. She hugged him, just as Charley appeared on the other side of the room. She was wearing Angel's crash helmet and using it to bounce off various hard surfaces. I earned myself a stern look by laughing.

"I'll have a word," I said. I hurried off to suggest another hobby for the afternoon. Geraldine arrived just before me and Charley surrendered the helmet without a struggle. She listened intently, then set off in a straight line towards Ben.

"I told her that Grandad needed one of her special cuddles," she explained. "I take it I'm in trouble with your new wife?"

"She wasn't best pleased, but Ben is working on her."

"Good. Because we've just agreed that we are going to tour Spain on Harleys as soon as he gets clear of the chemo."

"You're going to buy Harleys?"

"Rent. As Ben says, buying is optimistic under the circumstances." Geraldine laughed and touched my arm. "Don't look so horrified. You're family now. You should get used to our sense of humour."

I reflected on the comment later in the evening. Was it really only a couple of years since I'd sat in the pub, alone and miserable? Then Ambrose had issued the tweet challenge and everything changed. Because of that, I'd met Jen, and the rest was a rollercoaster.

Jen tugged at my hand, breaking me out of my reverie. Everybody in the room was looking towards me. What had I missed?

"Come on, they won't let us get away without a first dance," said Jen.

It was only when we got to the dance floor that I realised Angel had her guitar. Standing next to her was Toni, my songwriting partner for my one and only hit. Angel played the intro to *One More Indian Summer*. Toni and Angel sang in perfect harmony. We danced like nobody was watching and everything was fuzzy and, for once in my life, I didn't fall over.

As Toni and Angel took a bow, I saw the chance to head towards a seat. I stopped in my tracks as Joe started the disco. *The Love You Save* by the Jackson Five was the perfect start. Jen shrieked and jumped into my arms. This time I did fall over. It didn't seem to matter. Jen picked me up as everybody in the place joined us on the dance floor.

Acknowledgements

When I started out writing The Fifth Tweet I had not idea where I was going, how to get there, or what happened at any stage. I became like a five-year-old permanently asking How, Why, What, Where, and When? The internet became a patient and knowledgeable parent, providing many answers. However, I could not have done this without the skills, patience and all-round help of a number of people.

Jessica Jackson answered texted questions, reviewed ideas, provided encouragement, suggested better words and put up with my general level of incompetence.

Valuable advice on an early draft was provided by Russel McLean in the form of an editorial assessment through Jericho Writers. Check out Russel's books at www.russelmcleanbooks.com Jericho Writers provide so much information and encouragement to aspiring writers -

www.jerichowriters.com

Keith Finlinson, Martin Hetherington, Linda Bowes, Lynne Cooper, and Auggie Lopes provided valuable feedback as advanced readers.

Pulp Studio once again designed a great cover.

About the author

Roy Burgess was once an IT manager. This involved sitting in a cubicle and making stuff up. Having retired from this high octane lifestyle, he now sits in his home office and makes stuff up.

The Fifth Man is his third book in a trilogy. There may be more than three. Who knows?

West Yorkshire born and bred, Roy spends a lot of time staring out of the window at the Leeds - Liverpool canal. Music is a constant companion to his writing. If he's not writing he listens to more music and presents two shows on OverTheBridgeRadio.com A playlist of songs and artists mentioned in the book is on Spotify - just search for The Fifth Man. Roy is also the proud owner of an OEIC (whatever that is).

* * *

Keep in touch with Roy by signing up for the mailing list at royburgess.com

Twitter — @royburgess40
Facebook — @royburgess40
Instagram — royburgess40
Mixcloud — roy-burgess

Now that you've read The Fifth Man, please take a moment to leave a review and rating on Amazon / Goodreads. It doesn't have to be a huge essay, just a few words can make all the difference.

If you would like to read the short story prequel to the Fifth Trilogy, sign up for the mailing list at royburgess.com

The Fifth Tweet - The Fifth Trilogy Book 1

Would you trust the first five tweets in your timeline to rebuild your life? Frankie did. It worked. Right up to where it didn't.

Frankie's girlfriend has walked out and taken with her an original copy of Ziggy Stardust, two grand from their savings account, the charger for his electric toothbrush, and his best mate and business partner.

Because of the Twitter challenge, things improve.

A fictional character based on his new girlfriend points the way to fame and fortune, but is The Woman In The Yellow Raincoat too good to be true? Is real-life mirroring fiction? How will our hero cope with a toothbrush on borrowed time?

Available now from Amazon in paperback and Kindle.

* * *

Reviews on Amazon:

"This is one of those 'I couldn't put it down' kind of books!" - JKF ☆☆☆☆☆

"I'm in the USA, and quite a few things I didn't understand... for instance, what in the world is a "bacon butty?" - Susan VW ☆☆☆☆

"Really enjoyed this book. The writing style was easy and flowed well." - Paul ☆☆☆☆☆

The Fifth Thunderbolt - The Fifth Trilogy Book 2

Frankie is in love with Jen but is afraid to tell her. Together, they are working on a film script about a kidnapping.

Roddy Lightning was a big star in the 60s, with his band, The Thunderbolts. A teen idol, with a habit of marrying his fellow Thunderbolts, he became a punk rebel in the 70s, a Hollywood star in the 80s, and a junkie in the 90s. At 78, he's a loveable senior with a twinkle in his eye, a lust for cake, and a failing memory.

Frankie risks everything to make him the star of the film, but when Roddy disappears, all seems lost. Is real life mimicking the film?

Can Frankie get the girl, find his errant star, make a success of his film and save his OEIC (whatever that is)?

Reviews on Amazon

"I love how these books are structured. I

could read a little and potentially put it down for later. I could but I didn't as I wanted to see what happened next. Another book read in a couple of days as I couldn't put it down ....just waiting for the next one Roy. Get writing!!!" - Jeanette ☆☆☆☆☆

"I love Roy M Burgess' witty writing style, and after reading his debut book last year, I was looking forward to Book 2. It did not disappoint at all. There are several cleverly woven threads running through this book: an adventure, a kidnapping, a love story, all told with the author's deft and humorous touch. I'm still smiling at our hero's adventures!" - Nifty Girl ☆☆☆☆☆

Available now from Amazon in paperback and Kindle

Printed in Great Britain
by Amazon

29502979R00189